PENGUIN TWENTIETH·

VILE BC

Evelyn Waugh was born in Hampstead in 1903, second son of Arthur Waugh, publisher and literary critic, and brother of Alec Waugh, the popular novelist. He was educated at Lancing and Hertford College, Oxford, where he read Modern History. In 1927 he published his first work, a life of Dante Gabriel Rossetti, and in 1928 his first novel, *Decline and Fall*, which was soon followed by *Vile Bodies* (1930), *Black Mischief* (1932), *A Handful of Dust* (1934) and *Scoop* (1938). During these years he travelled extensively in most parts of Europe, the Near East, Africa and tropical America, and published a number of travel books, including *Labels* (1930), *Remote People* (1931), *Ninety-Two Days* (1934) and *Waugh in Abyssinia* (1936). In 1939 he was commissioned in the Royal Marines and later transferred to the Royal Horse Guards, serving in the Middle East and in Yugoslavia. In 1942 he published *Put Out More Flags* and then in 1945 *Brideshead Revisited*. *When the Going was Good* and *The Loved One* preceded *Men at Arms*, which came out in 1952, the first volume of 'The Sword of Honour' trilogy, and won the James Tait Black Memorial Prize. The other volumes, *Officers and Gentlemen* and *Unconditional Surrender*, followed in 1955 and 1961. In 1964 he published his last book, *A Little Learning*, the first volume of an autobiography. Evelyn Waugh was received into the Roman Catholic Church in 1930 and his biography of the Elizabethan Jesuit martyr, *Edmund Campion*, was awarded the Hawthornden Prize in 1936. In 1959 he published the official *Life of Ronald Knox*. For many years he lived with his wife and six children in the West Country. He died in 1966.

Waugh said of his work: 'I regard writing not as investigation of character but as an exercise in the use of language, and with this I am obsessed. I have no technical psychological interest. It is drama, speech and events that interest me.' Mark Amory called Evelyn Waugh 'one of the five best novelists in the English language this century', while Harold Acton described him as having 'the sharp eye of a Hogarth alternating with that of the Ancient Mariner'.

Richard Jacobs was brought up in north London and read English at Oxford University, where he gained First Class Honours and studied

Waugh's satire in postgraduate research. He has subsequently taught for many years in secondary and tertiary education. He has contributed articles and reviews to many periodicals and is the author of 'The Novel in the 1930s and 1940s' in Volume 7 of *The Penguin History of Literature: The Twentieth Century*. He is Head of English at the College of Richard Collyer in Horsham and is preparing an edition of Waugh's *The Ordeal of Gilbert Pinfold* for Penguin Twentieth-Century Classics.

EVELYN WAUGH

Vile Bodies

PENGUIN BOOKS

PENGUIN BOOKS

Published by the Penguin Group
Penguin Books Ltd, 27 Wrights Lane, London w8 5tz, England
Penguin Putnam Inc., 375 Hudson Street, New York, New York 10014, USA
Penguin Books Australia Ltd, Ringwood, Victoria, Australia
Penguin Books Canada Ltd, 10 Alcorn Avenue, Toronto, Ontario, Canada m4v 3b2
Penguin Books (NZ) Ltd, 182–190 Wairau Road, Auckland 10, New Zealand

Penguin Books Ltd, Registered Offices: Harmondsworth, Middlesex, England

First published by Chapman & Hall 1930
Published in Penguin Books 1938
This edition published in Penguin Books 1996
3 5 7 9 10 8 6 4 2

Set in 10.5/12.5 pt Monotype Baskerville
Typeset by Datix International Limited, Bungay, Suffolk
Printed in England by Clays Ltd, St Ives plc

CONTENTS

ACKNOWLEDGEMENT

The debt owed, in the preparation of this volume, to the published work of Martin Stannard will be apparent in many of its editorial pages. But a more specific sense of gratitude needs to be conveyed: for his hospitality, help and patient advice, extended in Leicester and in letters; and for the quite unexpected (and protracted) loan of his copy of the manuscript of this novel. I hope he isn't too disappointed with the result.

INTRODUCTION

At the mathematical centre of this brilliantly funny, anxious and resonant novel is this sentence, in a paragraph of its own: 'He did this with a man called Ginger.' In the manuscript, long presumed lost, used in the preparation of this edition (which follows it here as elsewhere), that one-sentence paragraph is succeeded by an empty space on the page, one of the novel's many rhythmically pointed 'white lines' (as Waugh called them). It is a signal moment.

'He' is Adam Symes, the nearest *Vile Bodies* has to a centre of consciousness, and here he's a newspaper gossip columnist short of invention. A few pages earlier in the novel he has created a glorious figment called Imogen Quest. It's not incidental that the names Adam and Imogen Quest feature in an early, rather painfully autobiographical story called 'The Balance'.[1] But Adam now invents, or rather reinvents, Ginger.

> As a last resort, on those hopeless afternoons when invention failed and that black misanthropy settled on him which waits alike on gossip writer and novelist, Adam sometimes found consolation in seizing upon some gentle and self-effacing citizen and transfiguring him with a blaze of notoriety.
>
> He did this with a man called Ginger.

The rather coy 'and novelist' may shed some sidelight on Waugh's predilection for inventing elaborate, or just trifling, fictions for citizens he routinely came across, as if they should have been in some putative novel-in-waiting, a tendency that the diaries suggest was becoming a distinctive habit at about this time. (An economical illustration might be this, the entire entry for Monday 29 August 1927: 'A Scotsman covered with blood came to dig a pond in the garden'.[2] But also suggestive is the idea-cluster (quest,

---

1. See Stannard, pp. 115–19.

invention, consolation) at the pivotal moment at which Ginger, who becomes Adam's rival for the woman, enters the story.

The two things that are more or less popularly known about *Vile Bodies* are, first, that it's Evelyn Waugh's second novel, following the dazzling success of *Decline and Fall* (1928) – following (the idea is) in its shadow, or even as something of a sequel or spin-off; and, second, that Waugh's first wife left him (for an allegedly Ginger-like young Etonian) during its composition, thus administering a psychic blow from which he never fully recovered.

Even before publication Waugh told a friend how much he dreaded his verdict, because 'when anyone says they liked *Decline & Fall* I think oh how bored they will be by *Vile Bodies*'.[3] And later he encouraged others to feel that the real damage was to the novel – to see *Vile Bodies* as scarred by the 'sharp disturbance in my private life' which upset the latter part of the book, written 'in a very different mood from that in which it was begun', and marking what he assumed would be an obvious 'transition from gaiety to bitterness'. Whatever popularity it had, Waugh suggests in the same 1965 Preface,[4] was due to mere modishness, its flavour of the month at the turn of the decade.

But *Decline and Fall* was, emphatically, not the overnight sensation which launched the brilliant career, and to which *Vile Bodies* was then a secondary instalment. The opposite was the case. *Vile Bodies* itself not only did launch the glamorous literary career but it rescued Waugh from the humiliatingly hand-to-mouth penury which characterized his life after university and through the publication of *Decline and Fall* – which sold slowly, though attracting good reviews and a coterie reputation. And though it may be the case that some new readers come to the second novel after reading the first, it is in no sense a parasitical dependant.[5] *Vile Bodies* is a very different thing. I hope to argue that it is a novel with a longer

2. *Diaries*, p. 288.
3. *Letters*, p. 41.
4. See Appendix.
5. *Decline and Fall* is rather archly referred to in one of *Vile Bodies*' few footnotes (all of which tease at the fiction–history relationship): a reasonable ploy to draw

reach, that it sounds history (and not just Waugh's personal history) in a more complex and radical way than, perhaps, has usually been allowed for – in a way, at least, that Waugh doesn't seem to have anticipated.

The other notion, that the novel is spoiled by its sudden transition from one mood to another, might surprise most readers. The early reviewers noticed nothing of the kind (though many commented on the apocalyptic last few pages); nor did I, reading it as a schoolboy, and nor do I now. There is a seamlessness and artfulness about the novel's form and development of ideas that is in loosely tensed ironic relationship with its seemingly random inconsequences. Consequence is one of the novel's subtly deployed motifs.

Waugh disparaged the novel on a number of occasions and seemed to feel a need to keep returning to the charge. One charge, that the book just happened to plug into the merely faddish and its idioms, is rudely enough contradicted by sales records. It's not as if it was a novel like Arlen's *The Green Hat* (1924) – mischievously invoked when Adam overreachingly invents the green bowler as the ultimate fashion accessory. The contemporaneity of *Vile Bodies*, its concern with faddishness as an idea (gossip columns, bright young people, parties), none the less enables it to make 1930 speak with an urgency that connects with later, continuing and very contemporary concerns.

Waugh's dislike was highly personalized; he wanted it not to be – he wanted a reason for it not being – an achieved thing; one reason to hand was the break-up of his marriage. Paradoxically, he also needed to suggest that its composition was something external to him, achieved on automatic hold. Thus the 1965 Preface's insistence that the novel was 'totally unplanncd', that its author then had the ability to throw off the requisite number of thousand words a day – and thus the rather ambivalent remark about his being on the fringes of the group the novel (partly) deals with. The phrasing suggests a difficult attitude towards an awkward addition to the family.

---

commercial attention to the earlier novel. From the start Waugh needed to be and was an astute self-advertiser.

Vile Bodies ends with an ambivalently conceived child, as does Waugh's 'Sword of Honour' Trilogy, thirty years later. (I suggest below the significance of the father as a dominant idea in the novel's substructure.) The relationship Waugh had with this novel is also curiously premonitory of that shiftily pseudo-autobiographical novella *The Ordeal of Gilbert Pinfold* (1957). In both cases there was a need to present the texts as if they were distanced case studies. With *Pinfold* it was the only way difficult personal material could be both dealt with and evaded at the same time – as if neatly framed. In the case of *Vile Bodies* the anxieties of the relationship were a means, perhaps largely unknown to its author, of releasing and opening up for unresolved scrutinies personal and socio-historical material that Waugh's later novels are never so unguarded about again.

Waugh started work on *Vile Bodies* in June 1929, the month of the formation of Ramsay MacDonald's second Labour government. He told Henry Yorke in July that he had written 25,000 words in ten days. 'It is rather like P. G. Wodehouse all about bright young people'.[6] To Harold Acton at the same time he described himself as 'chained to this novel . . . a welter of sex and snobbery written simply in the hope of selling some copies'.[7] Both those charges are surprising, but then the comparison with Wodehouse is also misleading.

He was twenty-five. The previous two years had been momentous and difficult. In April 1927, shortly after being sacked from the last of his schoolmastering interludes, he had met Evelyn Gardner, the youngest of four sisters, then living with a girlfriend who had just got engaged to the painter Henry Lamb. The second half of that year had seen some hand-to-mouth literary jobbing (for the *Daily Express*, for magazines), the writing of his *Rossetti* biography, the beginning of work on *Decline and Fall* – but also some more or less determined studying at the Central School of Arts and Crafts, because a literary career still seemed unappetizing as well as unlikely. He was attending, not very wholeheartedly, the

6. *Letters*, p. 36.
7. ibid., p. 37.

partying rounds, sexually diffident (upset at one party when a girl, who promised to kiss him, didn't), and, by the standards of most of his young contemporaries, inexperienced.

In December, after an autumn of increasing intimacies with Evelyn and her small, lively and clever circle, he proposed to her and she accepted (on the telephone). They were married in June 1928. Her mother, Lady Burghclere, was 'inexpressibly pained'. *Decline and Fall* was finished and *Rossetti* published. The couple, unable to live for more than a few days together earlier, moved into a small Canonbury house in September, as the novel, now published, began to sell, if slowly. 'She-Evelyn', as she became known, fell sick with German measles while Waugh banged out as many articles as his agent could secure for him, and as the gossip columns began (partly because he told them) to notice him.

In the new year an opportunity arose for a few months' belated honeymoon and for the gaining, at a shipping company's expense, of Mediterranean literary experience. The travel book *Labels* (1930) was the result. They set out during February and almost at once she-Evelyn fell much more dangerously sick with pneumonia, near-fatally for a time. Only the latter stages of the tour were unclouded, at least for Waugh: the couple were visited, during her sickness, by his closest friend, Alastair Graham, of whom more below. They returned to London just after Labour won the election. Waugh 'chained' himself to his new novel in the Oxfordshire countryside, leaving she-Evelyn to enjoy the London parties with her circle of friends; he visited at weekends.

Exactly how much of *Vile Bodies* Waugh managed to write before 9 July is open to question. On that day she-Evelyn wrote to say that she had fallen in love with John Heygate, one of her regular chaperons and companions; she felt confused and needed help. Waugh's reaction, apart from a reeling sense of disbelief, was to attempt two weeks of normality in London, attending parties at his wife's side and hoping that what he presumed about sense would somehow prevail. The idea that emotional, and sexual, attentiveness had been less than assiduous on his part doesn't seem to have been among his responses. After that fortnight he decided on divorce, and, when a month of failed reconciliation attempts by the two families had passed, the petition was filed in September. Waugh's friends offered solace and hospitality. Waugh wrote to Acton that 'Evelyn has been pleased to make a cuckold of me with Heygate'. He did not expect Acton's reply: 'Are you', he wrote back, 'so very male in your sense of possession?'[8]

Vile Bodies had meanwhile stalled. By the end of September Waugh had written to Henry Yorke – 'it has been infinitely difficult . . . it all seems to shrivel up & rot internally and I am relying on a sort of cumulative futility for any effect it may have. All the characters are gossip writers'[9] – and he probably wrote the last extraordinary pages just in time for the Wall Street Crash of late October. A few weeks of desperate, and more or less fruitless, seeking for magazine work followed. A restorative stay with Bryan and Diana Guinness in their house in Paris led to a Christmas resolve to move his life forward. He wrote again to Yorke: 'I am going to stop hiding away from everyone . . . one conclusion I am coming to is that I do not like Evelyn and that really Heygate is about her cup of tea'.[10]

On 14 January 1930 *Vile Bodies* was published; on 18 January *The Times* carried notice of the divorce. By mid May Waugh calculated his temporary income at 'about £2,500 a year. I feel rather elated about it'.[11] In August he published a magazine article about marriage. This, on the one hand, describes the notion that happiness in marriage hinges on a happy sex life as 'mischievous nonsense'; and, on the other, demands better sex education for the young who 'will not then marry out of curiosity or inexperience'.[12] He was received into the Catholic Church on 29 September.

What is the subject-matter of *Vile Bodies*? One answer might be that the novel puts to work two familiar narratives, both of which have at once specific and generalized cultural significance. These are the treasure hunt and the search for the father.

8. ibid., pp. 38–9.
9. ibid., p. 39.
10. ibid., p. 41.
11. *Diaries*, p. 309.
12. *Essays, Articles and Reviews*, pp. 94–6.

'Treasure hunts were one of the Bright Young Things' favourite party occupations[13] and the plot of this novel, in so far as it has one, is Adam Symes's hunt for his £1,000 (or even £35,000) treasure. The game has been taken seriously; the metaphor literalized. In the same way, another of the Young Things' favourite games, the fancy-dress hoax, is literalized when a columnist, desperate for the big story, has to resort to fancy-dress disguise – with, in his case, appallingly serious consequences. But the treasure hunt has broader significance: it is the quest for the grail, and in this context the grail is the paradoxical and unstable mix of needs – for sensation and consolation, for difference and consequence, for permanence and yet for ways of not being trapped.

It is a quest with peculiarly charged significance for the post-First World War generation, one which may be said to have obscurely needed the consolation prize for being the generation-after; and – as it is a story of desire endlessly deferred in a tissue of inadequate substitutions, reflections, shadows – it is also one made familiar through the findings of neo-Freudian psychoanalysis. In terms of literary ancestry, one might say that the novel is *Through the Looking-Glass* (quoted twice in the book's epigraph) crossed with *The Waste Land* (which furnished the title for Waugh's fourth novel – *A Handful of Dust* [1934] – where the cuckolded husband story finally gets full treatment). Waugh was currently enthusiastic about both Carroll and early modernist writers. The montage and cutting techniques of the novel, much commented on, are a response as much to Eliot as they are to cinema.

Adam's quest for his treasure is simultaneously his search for the father. His pursuit of the elusive Drunk Major ('it seemed odd that a man so bulky could be so elusive'), who may or may not have the fortune that Adam may or may not have won and that he needs to marry Nina, is a hunt both for treasure and for a father-figure. (Evelyn Gardner's uncle – her father was dead – was the definitive treasure-hunter: he discovered Tutankhamun's tomb.) Just as the grail is dispersed, contradictory and confusing, so the novel is liberally stocked with father-figures who drift in and out of focus as

13. See general note, The Bright Young Things and Their Parties.

obstacles or goals, sometimes one or the other or both or neither. Father Rothschild (the novel's first named character),[14] the Home Secretary, the two Prime Ministers, Outrage and Brown, Mr Rampole, Lord Monomark, Colonel Blount and the Drunk Major are a collective if comically ineffective stern (wrathful, phallically threatening) father, the object of both fear and a kind of exasperated derision – and of longing – for the younger generation in their bright young pursuits, of which Adam's quests are the novel's paradigm.

The relationship between the generations after the catastrophes of the first war has been much studied and discussed. One particularly suggestive idea, in this context, is Martin Green's. Quoting Waugh's friend and contemporary Cyril Connolly ('I was, without knowing it, in search of a father – or father-replacement'), he goes on to observe that the adolescence of these young men is modernism's too, and that writers like Joyce and Hemingway were ideal replacement fathers because they were 'nobody's father'.[15] Waugh attempted to grasp some of the anxieties of the relationship between the generations as early as in teenage contributions to Lancing school debates and magazine editorials ('there are now practically only two generations – the very young and the very old')[16] and, like most thinking young people at the time, he often adverted to it. Two articles written just before *Vile Bodies* take up significantly different positions on the issue.[17]

But also locked into the pressure chamber of ideas was Waugh's vexed relationship with his own father. This is explored with some candour by Waugh himself in *A Little Learning*; Martin Stannard adds considerable material, subtly discussed, including the observation that the young Waugh was particularly anxious about the sheer bodily physicalities of his very male father (and elder brother).[18] Stannard has a nice phrase for Waugh's extended

14. See Note on Names.
15. Green, p. 159.
16. *Diaries*, p. 103; see also *Essays, Articles and Reviews*, p. 11.
17. *Essays, Articles and Reviews*, pp. 45–7 and 61–3.
18. Stannard, p. 37.

male ancestry: 'a family riddled with blustering patriarchs'.[19] And it's worth adding that the young Waugh was more or less consciously under the spells of two contrasting father-replacements: the elegant schoolmaster J.F. Roxburgh and the aesthete artist Francis Crease, whose quill knife Waugh accidentally mutilated in an embarrassingly Freudian gesture.

The title of the novel is a commercial come-on (recognized recently by Penguin, who now market T-shirts emblazoned with a reproduction of the original paperback cover), a half-ironic reference to the burial service – Christ 'shall change our vile body, that it may be likened unto his glorious body' – but one might also cite two instances of 'vile' in Shakespearean tragedy, an angry demand for a genuine-article father and an uneasy recognition of patricidal impulses in the young. 'O thou vile king, give me my father' is Laertes' rather absurd opening line to Claudius on his return to Elsinore (Waugh was fascinated by the play from an early stage – he identified Hamlet as a fellow undergraduate in a student magazine article).[20] 'Our flesh and blood, my Lord, is grown so vile / That it doth hate what gets it' is Gloucester's attempt to share his predicament with King Lear's – and Lear is rather awkwardly, and thus revealingly, alluded to in the novel when Adam watches a man in a train making elaborate calculations in a notebook: ' "Has he given all to his daughters?" thought Adam'. ('He' is italicized in the manuscript.)

For it's the ambivalence of the treatment in the novel that is most telling. The novel is haunted by something never actually allowed expression: the need for the hero-father, for someone to be getting adulthood right after the appallingly costly mistakes made earlier on the battlefields. Adam's late father is revealed to have been a professor: but in the manuscript's first attempt he was going to be Admiral Sir Oliver Fenwick-Symes (with an Honorary Lady wife) – these are paradigmatically senior fathers. The 'hunger for permanence' that Father Rothschild diagnoses as 'almost fatal' in the younger generation can be very variously read in terms of

19. ibid., p. 10.
20. *Essays, Articles and Reviews*, p. 15.

seriousness. But it seems clear that this hunger can only be satisfied by other people, somewhere, taking the adult roles on, properly – which, of course, they fail to do. The two crucial fathers in *Vile Bodies*, Colonel Blount and the Drunk Major are more childish (and the book opens with a wrath-child) than adult (Colonel Blount is usually observed in motion 'trotting' like a toy animal). The novel's most stinging satire is reserved for the rich, complacent, stupidly repressive parents of Lady Ursula – the nicely named Stayles. This very painfully realized scene in Chapter 8 is closest in manner to the satire of *A Handful of Dust*. (It's also enough to rebut any charge of damaging snobbery in this novel.) The father-figures in *Vile Bodies* are individually comic, ludicrous and ineffectual, but collectively they evoke longing as well as exasperation.

Thus also the crucial ambivalences of the father-figures' motivations, their unknowability. It is never possible to be absolutely certain whether the Drunk Major is or isn't a fraudster or whether Colonel Blount is or isn't as dotty as he seems. Waugh's delicate precision of phrasing does the work. A typical adverb for the Drunk Major is 'distantly', for Colonel Blount 'dreamily'; but one keenly comic moment for each has the Drunk Major, when especially drunk, looking at Adam 'craftily', and Colonel Blount, when dottily failing to recognize Adam on their third meeting, 'giving Adam a searching glance'. There's also symptomatic instability when the Major first utters a word: the phrase used is 'shocked in spite of himself', as if there were some other kind of self somewhere else, in some green-room of characterization, to be in spite of.

Nor is Father Rothschild as readable as he might appear. The narrative has an unstable hold on this character who himself seems to hold (but doesn't) the political strings. His 'hunger for permanence' speech in Chapter 8 and his subsequent forecasting of war due to 'radical instability in our whole world-order' suggests the kind of solidity of insight to counterbalance the other two dominant father-figures, but it is undermined by its own collapse into bathos ('it's all very difficult') and the sad-comic picture of him then disappearing on his motor cycle into the night, and from the novel, to 'transact' more ineffectual business. The tone is difficult to assess. (The manuscript originally had a much fuller but also bathetically rhetorical treatment of the 'radical instability' speech.) The insights seem without depth. Waugh's ambivalence is suggested in the 1965 Preface where he almost suggests that he has to apologize for an overly satirical portrait of a Jesuit – which is presumably the opposite of most readers' response to him.

The ending of *Vile Bodies* is the meeting with the father, the goal, the treasure, the end of the quest. The Major is a General (leap-frogging over, as if to supplant, his earlier double, the Colonel); and he is sober. A kind of Old Hamlet, he has 'Chastity' in his warm nest-like motor car – and there too is Adam, a kind of baby in the parental bed. This is Hamlet's impossible and all-too-recognizable wish. But, of course, there are necessary and very different things to say about this remarkable ending.

Subject-matter? Adam and Nina (and Ginger); the Bright Young Things; their vile bodies. But so much here is paradoxical.

The title suggests titillation (albeit, more mutedly, serious matters like the burial service as well) and the impression the novel has generated since its first reception is of a welter (Waugh's word) of unconstrained hedonism. But even allowing for sexual standards obtaining then in novels (and allowing, perhaps, for some self-censorship after Waugh's experiences with editorial blue pencils over *Decline and Fall*) there is remarkably little sex in *Vile Bodies*.

Adam and Nina are lovers, engaged as the novel opens; they sleep together for the first time in a hotel (in Chapter 5) – which is divine for him, but not for her – and for the second time, on a hearthrug in the next chapter – less of a pain for her this time; and only later (in Shepheard's, before Ginger takes her away; at Doubting Hall over Christmas) by inference. The elder generation wistfully and enviously assume that sex is rampant at 'these parties of theirs' but we don't witness it. At the dirigible party two characters are observed to be 'making love to each other' but Waugh's diaries make it clear that he used this phrase in its less carnal sense. (In Chapter 2 the lesbian Mrs Panrast is 'making up to Nina'; in the manuscript it was 'making love to'.) These bodies aren't vile – indeed they seem curiously childlike, presexual. (This is explored further below.) The novel's first reference to a part of the body, its only suggestion of an even potentially erogenous part, is the generalized Bright Young People's 'tummies' – the manuscript first had 'the middle' so 'tummies' was a deliberate move towards the infantile – and to Miss Runcible wriggling.

And the parties. Waugh's diaries, recording parties he attended back visiting Oxford as well as in London, make it clear that these featured the kind of physical, sweaty unpleasantness (and, according to other evidence, violent fights, even death)[21] that is signally absent from the novel. One comparatively light moment in the diaries has John Betjeman mildly observing, after a fracas, 'Yes, I noticed a cocktail in Wanda's face'.[22] The *Vile Bodies* parties record people not really partying, or partying just out of camera-angle. Boredom or affected boredom is characteristic. The novel's first party (there are, in fact, very few) is 'repulsive' according to a gossip-columnist guest. The novel's main male character notably falls asleep during it – twice. (He then sleeps through the party's last phase, which topples the government.) Copious quantities of drink are consumed – but only one character is more or less permanently drunk and he is by definition not a bright young party-goer. The only significantly drunken speech comes from an American judge. The dialogue of the young at the motor races is hazy rather than drunken. (The manuscript deletes a reference to Miss Runcible having had 'a drop too much'.)

The presentation of the Bright Young People themselves is shot through with paradox. Who are they, even in the novel's own terms? Agatha Runcible and Miles Malpractice, certainly; Adam and Nina, less certainly; Archie Schwert, identified from the start as only half-included as a source of money and derision – and that (give or take a gossip columnist or two and the rather shadowly presiding Johnny Hoop) is about it. There's a strange, accidental pathos in the impression that this infamous 'set' seems, despite the narrative gestures towards 'all' the young things, to be so depleted in number. Broken up by the later stages of the novel ('how people

21. See Carpenter, p. 169.
22. *Diaries*, p. 315.

are *disappearing*, Adam'), they seem curiously vulnerable to dissolution from the outset (as historically appropriate).

Whether Adam, the novel's notional hero, is or isn't one of them is something to do with this; another idea might be that Waugh has, in an act of strange transference, represented his own rather uncertain and shifting relations with this set – itself a shifting and uncertain entity, at least part newspaper invention – in the way the novel's young things hover somehow between being a material and substantial body of people and a kind of fictive penumbra (more talked about than doing) on the edge of the Adam–Nina point of view. (In Waugh's early story 'The Balance' Adam is significantly not invited to a young things' party.) It certainly comes as a shock when, in Chapter 6, they are suddenly, very materially and hostilely, pictured 'popping [out] all together . . . like a litter of pigs, and . . . squealing up the steps'. It's precisely that sense of narrative distance and critical perspective that is usually absent in the way they are part realized or intimated.

And who is Adam? And what is his and Nina's relationship? Here, if anywhere, is the novel's centre of interests. The novel's opening gesture is the burning of a life (and the confiscation of a Purgatory, 'pending inquiries'): Adam has written his memoirs so he has presumably had a life worth telling. The customs officer is 'genuinely appreciative' as he reads it. But what could it have possibly contained? The scene at his publishers suggests a literary track record (Benfleet is the director 'with whom Adam always did his business') but a first-novel contract is then rather easily foisted on him. A gossip column later refers to him as 'the well-known novelist' but in context this looks like a friendly invention. No earlier books are ever referred to; a newspaper social editress has never heard of him.

More to the point, the opening of *Vile Bodies* insists that there is nothing significant or notable about Adam – precisely, nothing worth telling about. 'There was nothing particularly remarkable about his appearance. He looked exactly as young men like him do look.' And later: '. . . said Adam in no particular manner.' This is a young man identified as being not particularly identifiable. (The manuscript and the later corrected typescript both show evidence of a more sharply characterized figure in the early pages, so, again, conscious decisions to whiten the picture must have been taken.) And his place among the other young people is also a problem. At the outset he is pointedly not with the Bright Young Things. He travels separately on the boat and only joins them on disembarkation – but then he stays not with them in their 'perfectly sheepish house' (whoever it is among them who do actually live there; we later learn that Miss Runcible doesn't – a typical slippage of ideas about the Young Things) but at Shepheard's Hotel (the flickering wordplay with 'sheepish' is perhaps not accidental).

He and Nina seem, as the novel progresses, to be part of the set, even their representatives, but a counter-stress intimates that they are placed obliquely to the others, their relationship with each other marking them out as somehow attempting to become identifiable and characterized people – the goal of filling those emptinesses that hollow out the novel's other protagonists. The novel may be read as the story of this attempt, to be people who feel and love. Of the novel's many sources of pathos, this is the most structured: a wistfulness attends the very delicately delineated tracing – as if through glimpses – of this story. The fragile, almost impossibly economical dialogue carries a freight of plangent feeling.[23] Most telling of all is the painfully muted symmetries of Chapter 11: and the manuscript has additional and accidental pathos here[24] because Waugh ends one attempt at the dialogue with a confusion of speech attributions, as if in confirmation of the interchangeability of Adam and Nina's twinned, mutual predicament.

The delicacy and tenderness are brittle – and are broken – but no other relationship in Waugh is treated with this particular poignancy, the emergent vulnerabilities in such wry relation to the cool surface sophistications. And it is a disservice to suggest that feelings or culpabilities are unequally weighted: that Nina must somehow be cold or callous. Her feelings are delineated with remarkable tact. The novel, whatever the author might retrospectively have decided, is scrupulous in its sympathies. Even

23. Compare *Critical Heritage*, p. 107.
24. See Notes.

Ginger is more a figure of bathos than contempt: he is introduced, in the passage I started with, by the word 'gentle' and in their last dialogue (in Chapter 12) his barrage of evasive clichés – '. . . when you come to think of it after all well look here damn it I mean d'you see what I mean?' – is met with this: ' "Not quite," said Adam gently'.

It's worth pausing over that adverb. The other time the word is used is in preface to Rothschild's 'hunger for permanence' speech in Chapter 8, as he addresses the particularly childish Prime Minister. ' "Don't you think," said Father Rothschild gently, "that perhaps it is all in some way historical?" ' One might have expected something like 'gravely' in this instance, and 'coolly' in Adam's case. 'Gently' is, as it were, in spite of the novel's satiric vigilance – a glimpse of a tenderness quite at odds with any notion of anything shrivelling up. There is something wistful, out of reach, shadowing this story of a quest. And Waugh's sympathies perhaps have a more delicate reach in this novel than he later usually chose to deploy.

In the presentation of Adam Symes it is not difficult to see some uneasy (part wish-fulfilling, part apprehensive) self-projection.

The writer with a track record but no trace of publications (*Rossetti* and *Decline and Fall* didn't make the breakthrough into celebrity that Waugh clearly hoped for); living in an extravagantly eccentric hotel, and therefore beyond his means before he even gets there, rather than in a sheepish house (as perhaps Waugh would have described the family home in Golders Green); father a professor (or at least an admiral, rather than an exasperatingly middle-brow, cricket-loving publisher with a taste for theatricals); returning, not like the other young people from weekending but from living in Paris (with all its sexy and modernist associations: his brother Alec, according to a diary entry,[25] went there 'for fornication');[26] a light traveller with a taste for heavy reading (Dante in the original, texts on economics: neither would have been on

25. *Diaries*, p. 252.
26. In an odd premonition of Waugh's period of escape in Paris after the marriage break-up, a young thing refers to the time 'since you went away'.

the young Waugh's bedside); part of and not quite part of the bright set, as if at first near-invisible to them (Miss Runcible greets him with 'Adam, darling, I never saw you on the boat');[27] perhaps part conscious of invisibility, of being not particular or remarkable, perhaps, like Prufrock, worried lest he's more an attendant lord, or a hollow recorder, than a full-throated Hamlet (Waugh was upset to note the recorder scene with Rosencrantz and Guildenstern being cut from a production of *Hamlet*), apprehensive about being or being thought 'intense' or 'sentimental' – and in search, again perhaps part consciously, for the consolations of personhood which attachment to another can bring.

Adam Symes may not be Evelyn Waugh in 1929 but may say more interesting things about him than do any other of his creations – even *Pinfold*.

The consolations of attachment. One candidate for most startling and unguarded entry in Waugh's early diaries, given how carefully he policed their personal revelations (and excised whole sections – for instance, those relating to his undergraduate life and to his first marriage and its break-up), is this, from 24 June 1924, a few months before his twenty-first birthday, shortly after leaving Oxford. He visits Kew with Alastair Graham, with whom Waugh had formed the most intense and lasting of his homoerotic attachments. He finds the gardens 'very very beautiful' (an unusually unguarded commendation) and they go from there to Hampton Court. The maze is a disappointment. Then he writes: 'We will build a maze of brick with a really exquisite grotto inside'.[28] We will build. This is an unguarded revelation and it's also one of the rare future projections in the diaries. The surprise is in its lightness: the notion, casually recorded, of a kind of homoerotic sanctuary, bricking out the world, with an intricately beautiful interior – a future that has nobody but Alastair and Evelyn there.

Some years later, when Waugh was staying with Alastair at the

27. Four years before the novel Waugh, meeting Elizabeth Ponsonby, a model for Miss Runcible, for the first time, has this rather self-conscious, worldly reaction: 'Two years ago, or less even, I suppose I should have been rather thrilled by her' (*Diaries*, p. 226).
28. ibid., p. 162.

Graham home, Barford House, Mrs Graham, a model for Lady Circumference, is observed 'looking hard at me' while complaining about being 'left without a *man* in the house'.[29] Another expressive diary entry records Alastair and Waugh enjoying the house without the mother. 'We dined in high-necked jumpers and did much that could not have been done if Mrs Graham had been there'.[30] Those jumpers are elsewhere commended for being 'most convenient for lechery' and noted as making Waugh 'look exactly ten years old'.[31]

The two moments in the novels that come to mind here are, on the one hand, in *Brideshead Revisited* where Charles Ryder, watching Julia Flyte motor away from the house, 'felt a sense of liberation and peace' in realizing how free, alone together there, he and her brother Sebastian now were. And the other is Adam and Nina's Christmas at Doubting Hall ('later they put some crumbs of their bread and butter on the windowsill and a robin redbreast came to eat them. The whole day was like that'): another poignant revisiting of this sense of liberation and suspended time, and a womb-scene, like the novel's very last, very different moment of suspension.

In the years leading up to *Vile Bodies* Waugh's sexuality was an uncertain thing. As a schoolmaster he was erotically attracted to a number of the boys; when he had to beat his favourite Edmund at Aston Clinton he told his diary (in a rather guardedly mannered oxymoron) that he did it 'with mixed feelings and an ash plant'.[32] (Such an attachment is mutedly clear in *Decline and Fall*.) He visited a gay brothel in Paris in December 1925, though nothing came of it.[33] A nervous unease, as well as diffidence, with women emerges from the diaries. One rather nervous attempt at a joke reads 'after the second day Olivia decided to menstruate'.[34] The evidence is that he encouraged others into excesses but remained

29. ibid., p. 291.
30. ibid., p. 218.
31. ibid., pp. 188, 197.
32. ibid., p. 254.
33. ibid., p. 240.
34. ibid., p. 219.

an aloof observer himself; but the diaries also suggest a niggling anxiety about whether others were sleeping together or not.

The impression is that loving Alastair meant a kind of sexualized presexuality, a highly paradoxical but enchanted space (a grotto within a maze) and that the quest for this kind of relationship is the quest for a twin or double as much as for the other. And it is precisely this that struck contemporaries about the two Evelyns' relationship. They were like two little boys, according to Nancy Mitford, she 'un ravissant garçon, un page'[35] – the adjective is marvellously ambiguous – and the Canonbury flat was, in Harold Acton's phrase, a 'sparkling nursery'.[36] It seems clear that neither Evelyn had considered the implications of their marriage with much reflection, and that both might have had needs that the marriage wasn't likely to answer fully. She-Evelyn might have wanted a boy version of her sisters (she told Alec Waugh that married life was never as happy for her 'as I've been with my sisters').[37] Playing at being twins ('a juvenile brother and sister', according to Acton)[38] was the impression widely perceived. This may have been appropriate to the party age (according to *Vogue* 'it was a good time for twins, and there was a pair at every party'),[39] particularly as fashion also dictated that women should be as girl-like, or rather boy-like, as possible, Eton-cropped by preference and, of course, presexually slim. But appropriateness to adult marriage is another thing.

The suggestion is that this wistful presexual sexuality was also displaced on to Waugh's presentation of the Bright Young Things. If in reality (or, more likely, in Waugh's heated imaginings) they coupled together all over at parties, here in this book they're not going to; if Waugh was, in reality, a wistful or near-innocent observer and on a quest for something, which Alastair and she-Evelyn may have together represented, then, as if for consolation, the young things too will be. And that's not only true of Adam and

35. Quoted in Carpenter, p. 177.
36. Quoted in Stannard, p. 157.
37. A. Waugh, p. 191.
38. Quoted in Carpenter, p. 195.
39. *In Vogue*, p. 67.

Nina (whose names curiously resonate together and whose relationship is as much that of twins, or as nanny and child, as of adult lovers) but even of a character like Agatha Runcible.

And in this respect a remarkable piece of casual journalism returns us to Waugh's instinct to denigrate the novel. A few months after its publication, Waugh wrote a piece for the *Daily Mail* describing Miss Runcible as 'crazy', 'dissolute' and 'sordid' – and as the 'heroine' of the story.[40] Most readers will find this very odd. Miss Runcible begins and ends as a victim; the opposite of sordid, she is the most absurdly, touchingly childish of these child-people. Sexually unattached, she seems as oblivious of sex as she is of politics and history. She is an emblem of the novel's need to suspend the processes of time in a paradox of glamour and innocence – which is, perhaps, exactly why Waugh turned on her, of all of them, afterwards.

The novel is pervaded by twins and doubles – a symptom of that wistful longing suggested in the Adam–Nina and also the Waugh–Graham and he/she-Evelyn relationships.

So much comes in pairs. There are the two tipsy old ladies embarking, with, among others, two private detectives, on a Noah-like voyage presided over by the wrathful father, at least one of the ways of reading the figuratively rich opening chapter. There are two Prime Ministers. There are two old gossips in two train journeys. There are two gossip columnists. There are two shy partying *ingénues* (Miss Brown, Mary Mouse). There are Ginger and Gilmour. There are two young men called Edward (Ginger and Throbbing) and, if it comes to that, two other men (a sub-editor and a mechanic) called Edward(e)s. There are two mild and obliging old gentlemen (pseudo-fathers) with wittily complementary names: Rampole and Titchcock. There's a sheepish house and a Shepheards Hotel; the latter is run by Lottie and the old ladies in Chapter 1 have been staying at the Lotti.

Less incidentally, there is the doubling of the treasure-bearing father (Blount, Major); there is the Adam–Ginger rivalry; and

40. *Essays, Articles and Reviews*, p. 73.

there is, established early on in the scene at the publishers, the elusive and suggestive Adam–Johnny Hoop doubling.

Hoop, who seems to preside over the younger set but who the novel only actually glimpses two or three times, once as a double himself, disguised as the wife of someone who also happens to be at the same party, is important in his shadows. The last mention of him is a columnist's report of his imminent departure to live for a time in Paris, in order to paint – the novel's opening gesture (Adam's return from living for a time in Paris) in reverse. He is what Adam/Waugh both fear and are fascinated by (Waugh at this time wanted to paint rather than write). He was Johnny Hatte in the manuscript and this indicates (via a famous Young Things hoax in which Waugh was involved)[41] that Brian Howard is lurking in the recesses here. Howard was the most brilliantly unstable and manically homosexual of Waugh's contemporaries; everything that the Waugh–Graham relationship was mutedly in quest of was violently shadowed by the self-destructive, cruel impulses of this Dionysiac figure, presiding over the novel – but, in a typical paradox, he is largely absent, uncharacterized, drained of colour and danger. Hoop's autobiography (Howard's, unlike Waugh's, would indeed have had much to say), due originally a fortnight after Adam's (perhaps a revealing order of publications), 'sails a bit near the wind in places' and that hardly sounds very threatening.

Another figure who shadowly inhabits the recesses of the novel's unconscious as a double is Alec Waugh, Evelyn's elder brother. There is evidence that Waugh was troubled by Alec in the early years both of his life and of his career. The father's favoured son, cricketer, novelist, indefatigable traveller and convivial manabout-town (said to have invented the cocktail party in 1924), he was also famous for being expelled from public school for homosexuality and then writing about it in a best-selling novel (*The Loom of Youth*, 1917). Preternaturally mature (nicknamed Baldhead by Evelyn's set) and an apparently successful heterosexual adult, he was a standing source of anxiety for Evelyn, though also a source

41. The story is told by, among others, Carpenter, p. 169.

of some derision. Evelyn was often mistaken for Alec at parties and functions – which can't exactly have increased his grasp on self-confidence. He was also very anxious about the gender-ambivalence of his first name (white with fury when the *The Times Literary Supplement* reviewer of *Rossetti* wrote about 'Miss Waugh'; the manuscript betrays a flurry of uncertainty and cutting when Adam is first named, the double-barrelled surname being the point at issue). Adam's search for the partner-twin may be seen as a response to Waugh's need to find the consolation and reassurance to escape from the threat of opposites like Howard and Alec.

The doublings in *Vile Bodies*, which extend unsurprisingly to the level of language ('too too [etc]'; 'do you . . . or do you'), is part of its sense of time in suspension. The hunger for permanence, which manifests itself in the headlong impulse to 'go faster', as in the first of the Carroll epigraphs, as in Miss Runcible's nightmares, is the search for the consoling reflection – the returning look of the Looking Glass, where everything is both comfortingly there and bizarrely different (as in gossip columns about oneself), the look of Narcissus (Adam and Nina as each other), the infantile need for the nanny as extension of the self (Nina, whose name anagrammatically suggests Nanny, does in effect nanny Adam in the novel's most tender scenes. Later Waugh novels give us a number of memorably actual nannies).

This is the novel's most persistent paradox: the double articulation between a longed-for childishness and a glitteringly sophisticated but brittle knowingness. The paradox is tellingly manifested at the linguistic level. The feature that became (to Waugh's irritation) the novel's badge of especial modishness – Miss Runcible's 'too sick-making' (etc) – is itself a revealing example, suggesting that experiences somehow happen (as in a child's vision) rather than the self actively being agent. Experiences seem to bounce off the young things: to remain unaffected as children they have to bounce the experiences off them. The fear seems to be of being affected, altered, separated – a fear of allowing anything to suggest that they aren't always already there. Adam and Nina's quest for solidity of selfhood in each other is more difficult still in the light of this passive sense of self – especially as the world of the novel, as suggested earlier, exerts a process of unmaking and falling away. The scene depopulates, becomes less social, less specific.

Innocence and knowingness are both somehow encoded as a double register in the novel's language: it evokes worldly-wise experiences in a voice and manner that somehow hold those experiences in cool suspension – fastidiously glistening, enamelled, cooled of hand-wringing exasperation or of gleeful indulgence. The manuscript significantly tries on and then decides against material like 'Divine Discontent . . . who it may be mentioned was by far the prettiest of the angels'. And the reviewers were quick to pounce on the one serious lapse of tone, in a passage significantly about Adam and Nina's sexual inexperience (a very raw nerve) which Waugh silently dropped after the first edition (and the corresponding page in the manuscript is missing, perhaps torn out): 'The truth is, that, like so many people of their age and class, Adam and Nina were suffering from being sophisticated about sex before they were at all widely experienced'.[42] The humour of early Waugh is famously delicate, precise and dazzlingly timed but *Vile Bodies* has a particular charge, coming as it does out of, and dealing at the same time thematically with, such a combination of paradoxical and anxious attachments and detachments.

The brilliantly tonal use of brackets round material that floats half in, half out of narrative voice, held delicately in tonal shadow (the result can be wry shaded comedy but also, as in the end of Chapter 6, an almost shocking poignancy); the blurrings of narrative and dialogue ('so they all drank some gin together in the back parlour and they woke Mr Titchcock up and made him help with the luggage and they gave him some gin, too, and he said it was all the same to him whether he slept on the floor or in bed, and he was very pleased to be of any service to anyone and didn't mind if he did have another drop just as a night-cap, as they might say'); the marvellously long-thrown arcs of rhythmic–dramatic material (the Adam–Gilmour–Ginger exchange at the St Christopher's Social Club in Chapter 8, with its cool deployment of 'then', 'and'

42. The scene in Nina's flat, Chapter 6. See Stannard, p. 195 and *Critical Heritage*, pp. 97 and 102.

and 'so' is especially artful, and touching as well as comic) – these are examples, but a full account of characteristic features is not possible or desirable here. None the less, in those features mentioned it's the sense of the author as somehow both in and on the edges of the scene – suspended somewhere between recorder, celebrant, critic – that emerges and that resonates with the ambivalences of Waugh's position in the novel's places and meanings.

The novel's form, again, suggests one thing and is another. The impression is of a random collection of incidents in a makeshift succession of chapters. But the novel is solidly put together and artfully structured. (The manuscript betrays only one serious losing of the way – in a couple of false starts to a stretch of dialogue, one of them suggesting a sudden engagement between Nina and Archie Schwert.)[43] There are thirteen numbered chapters (13 is the number of the fateful racing-car) and a 'Happy End'. The time span for the numbered chapters can be reconstructed as between the day before Armistice Day and, six weeks later, the Friday of Christmas Day. Ginger appears exactly half way through. Adam and Nina first make love a third through and, by disobeying Monomark's father-like (thou-shalt-not) edict, lose Adam's job two-thirds through. There are three deaths, of increasingly jarring intensity (a fourth, of the young man who loses the bet with Adam, appears in the manuscript, cut as presumably being too emptily cruel); there are two kinds of pressured marriages and two kinds of honeymoon. War is a motif subtly established from the outset and rain (despite one's vague impression of an *Alice*-like garden-England) mutedly persists. (As, in rhyming consonance, does Nina's 'pain'.) Despite the fact that the financially desperate Waugh was trying to get his agent to hawk the bits of text around before book publication, the sense of an evolving, subtly shaped and controlled whole is remarkable. (Perhaps only the end of the Downing St chapter looks too like the end of a discrete short story – it did in fact appear separately.)[44]

*

43. See Notes.
44. See Stannard, p. 191.

I'd like to end by suggesting the importance of recognition and recognition-scenes as a way of holding some of the novel's concerns and anxieties in focus.

Vile Bodies starts with a father-figure (Rothschild) recognizing a son-figure (Adam); it ends with the son recognizing the father (the Major/General). Those incidents mark out an ironic meta-history: from Noah, through all that rain, to apocalypse. Framed within that larger frame is, among other local narratives in counterpoint, the story of Miss Runcible, mis-recognized at her start and at her end, at the customs (as a smuggler) and (as if a competent driver) at the motor races. Colonel Blount and the Drunk Major's failures to recognize Adam (the Oedipus story stuck in reverse) are the rhythmically patterned underpinnings of the plot.

Recognition is a doubling: a repetition, a sense of history going round in circles (like the motor race) or in mirror image (as in an unrewound film: 'there was a whirring sound, and suddenly there appeared on the screen the spectacle of four uniformed horsemen galloping backwards down the drive' – so there's one apocalypse we don't need to worry about). The ending is a recognition (that a second war is inevitable and imminent, recognizing Rothschild's earlier analysis) and/or it's a recognition of history in repetition (a re-vision of the first war). History is either rushing headlong into the one or condemned to repeat the other – which are versions of the same idea.

The evidence, not least from the manuscript, is that Waugh was at pains to drain the novel of local historical specificities (in the opening chapter Adam was to have had a bitter reflection about England as 'a million dead and a million unemployed'; references to Russian communism were removed from speeches by Mrs Ape and Rothschild); the result, intended or not, is to historicize the novel in a more anxious way. The anxiety is that of a generation calling for recognition and a sense of consequence; for acknowledgement (at least) that their tears (as in the second of the two Carroll epigraphs) are indeed genuine, and that the baffled notion that 'if a thing's not worth doing well, it's not worth doing at all' has a political message to convey. And the anxiety is also that of a man for whom the notion of recognition suggests further related and urgent needs (as son, adult, writer – and lover). Humphrey Carpenter is right to say that 'considering when it was written and by whom, it is remarkable how little of *Vile Bodies* is a roman à clef':[45] for this is a text which unlocks radical and unconscious needs and fears, both peculiarly his and not only his.

The effect suggested is of history (personal, social, political) being on the edge, in transition but in strange stasis, about to fall but not falling. Waugh much later spoke of Wodehouse's world being one where 'there has been no Fall of Man . . . The gardens of Blandings Castle are that original garden from which we are all exiled'.[46] He thought, as we saw above, that *Vile Bodies* was turning out like Wodehouse – and this is a symptomatic, understandable misassessment. But the one book he was going out of his way to commend, at the time he was writing *Vile Bodies*, was a very different text, Henry (Yorke) Green's *Living* (1929).[47] *Vile Bodies* and *Living* are signally, richly complementary novels. More than once in *Vile Bodies* England's landscape is evoked in the way that suggests the influence of *Living*.

> Nina looked down and saw inclined at an odd angle a horizon of straggling red suburb; arterial roads dotted with little cars; factories, some of them working, others empty and decaying; a disused canal . . . men and women were indiscernible except as tiny spots; they were marrying and shopping and making money and having children. The scene lurched and tilted again as the aeroplane struck a current of air.
>
> (*Vile Bodies*)

> She saw in feeling. She saw in every house was woman with her child. In all streets, in clumps, were children.
>
> Here factories were and more there, in clumps. She saw in her feeling, she saw men working there, all the men, and girls and the two were divided, men from women . . . Yes and in every house

---

45. Carpenter, p. 188.
46. *Essays, Articles and Reviews*, p. 567.
47. *Letters*, p. 35; *Essays, Articles and Reviews*, p. 80.
48. *Critical Heritage*, p. 98.

was mother with her child and that was grey and that fluttered
hands . . .

(Living)

Green's evocation of working people, but more specifically of
the couple Bert and Lily, trapped in their attempts to make a life,
as history's processes (economic, family) close in on them, is
fraught and politically charged; but Waugh, albeit less consciously
and from an apparently different set of ideological presupposi-
tions, is working with the same anxious elements. The two novels
are the difficult, edgy guide to the turn of the decade.

The sense of edginess and precariousness pervades the tone of
Vile Bodies as well as its events (described by a reviewer as 'dancing
on a volcano, carousing on the edge of a precipice'),[48] the tone of
something wistful and vulnerable beneath the glitter. And it cor-
responds to the ambivalences, traced above, in Waugh's own sense
of function and place: and the strange impression we have of the
novel's here-and-now, for all its contemporaneity, sliding out of
sight and out of history. And what seems half in sight at the edge
of the decade, for Waugh no less than for the rest of the troubled
world, is the precarious recognition of history ending, and
beginning.

SELECTED READING

This list restricts itself to material relatively easily available. Articles in academic journals are excluded. Place of publication is London unless otherwise stated.

Work by Waugh:

A Little Learning (1964). The first volume, and the only volume, of an autobiography. It takes the story as far as his schoolmastering after Oxford.

The Diaries of Evelyn Waugh, ed. Michael Davie (1976).

The Letters of Evelyn Waugh, ed. Mark Amory (1980).

The Essays, Articles and Reviews of Evelyn Waugh, ed. Donat Gallagher (1983). As well as articles mentioned in the Introduction, the short essay on Ronald Firbank (pp. 56–9) is important, though perhaps too much has been made of Firbank's influence on early Waugh.

Paris Review Interview, with Julian Jebb, in *Writers at Work*, Third Series (pp. 103–14) (1968).

Vile Bodies, a Play in Twelve Episodes, adapted by H. Dennis Bradley (n.d. 1932?).

Principal sources cited in the Introduction and notes:

Stannard: Martin Stannard, *Evelyn Waugh, The Early Years* (1986). References are to the Flamingo paperback (1993). The first volume in an indispensable and marvellously achieved two-volume biography.

Critical Heritage: *Evelyn Waugh, The Critical Heritage*, ed. Martin Stannard (1984). Valuable collection of contemporaneous reviews and articles (pp. 95–112 are on *Vile Bodies*).

Balfour: Patrick Balfour, *Society Racket* (1933). An illuminating 'critical survey of modern social life'.

Carpenter: Humphrey Carpenter, *The Brideshead Generation* (1989). A lively cultural history centred on Waugh and his friends.

Green: Martin Green, *Children of the Sun* (1977). This 'narrative of decadence in England after 1918' is often tendentious but very valuable on its two presiding figures, Brian Howard and Harold Acton.

A. Waugh: Alec Waugh, *My Brother Evelyn and Other Profiles* (1967).

In Vogue, ed. Georgina Howell (1975).

Other critical material:

Alain Blayac (ed.), *Evelyn Waugh, New Directions* (1992). A varied collection but with a diverting essay (pp. 62–84) by Donat Gallagher on the Vatican and Waugh's divorce.

Malcolm Bradbury, *Evelyn Waugh* (1964).

James F. Carens, *The Satiric Art of Evelyn Waugh* (Seattle, 1966).

A. E. Dyson, *The Crazy Fabric* (includes essay on Waugh) (1965).

Terry Eagleton, *Exiles and Emigrés* (1970).

Paul Fussell, *The Great War and Modern Memory* (1975). A superb and wide-ranging survey of the impact of the First World War on later cultural and social life.

Stephen J. Greenblatt, *Three Modern Satirists* (Yale, 1965).

Jeffrey Heath, *The Picturesque Prison* (1982).

Ian Littlewood, *The Writings of Evelyn Waugh* (Oxford, 1983). This is the best-balanced recent contribution to the criticism of Waugh's work.

David Lodge, *Evelyn Waugh* (Columbia, 1971). A stimulating pamphlet.

William Myers, *Evelyn Waugh and the Problem of Evil* (1991). Stylish and well received, but the section on *Vile Bodies* (pp. 13–20) is an extraordinarily aggressive reading.

Sean O'Faolain, *The Vanishing Hero* (1957).

Frederick J. Stopp, *Evelyn Waugh, Portrait of the Artist* (1958).

NOTE ON THE TEXT

The first edition of *Vile Bodies* was published in 1930 by Chapman and Hall. It contains one short passage later excised about Adam and Nina's sexual inexperience (see Introduction) and an Author's Note, also dropped from later editions, of which the 1938 Penguin is the standard reprint. This Note reasonably insists that the novel is 'in no sense a sequel to *Decline and Fall*' and yet directs the reader to the earlier book in order to make 'some of the minor motifs' in *Vile Bodies* 'clearer'. It also says that the novel's 'action' is 'laid in the near future, when existing social tendencies have become marked . . . I have assumed a certain speeding up of legal procedure and daily journalism'.

The text of *Vile Bodies* here printed is, substantively, that of the Revised, Uniform Edition of 1965, to which Waugh contributed a Preface.[1] (Misprints have been silently corrected; textual differences between the Uniform Edition and the earlier Penguin are minor.) But in two features the present edition departs from the 1965 text: in the restoration, from the evidence of the manuscript, and the remarkable surviving fragment of typescript, both of a number of 'white lines' and of a smaller number of instances of punctuation (and layout) which are clearly intended for special effect. A word about these departures is required before I attempt a brief account of the novel's textual history.

Layout of text and punctuation are two features where editorial intervention can be most confidently suspected in a text's evolution. The need to save space and paper, and the imposition of regularity or publisher's house style, can help to explain differences between manuscript (or typescript) readings and those in early editions. That is, they flow from non-authorial decisions made consciously, if misguidedly, and not in error.

1. See Appendix.

The evidence is that 'white lines' marked rhythmic units for Waugh and that he took considerable care to signal them clearly – and, indeed, that he was adding them to the manuscript and type-script during its complex path towards publication. The same is true of the punctuation. Waugh's typical punctuation was eccentric, uneven, often incorrect by any standards of usage. To restore seemingly nice examples here and there is to run the risk of just introducing mistakes (and to choose between examples would obviously be invidious). But whole speeches (for instance) utterly devoid of commas, or whole paragraphs in brackets, are a clear matter of dramatic and tonal pointing.

In both these cases it is easy to see the rationale behind editorial changes to normal conventions of layout and punctuation. For Waugh to have emphatically reversed these changes, insisting on his apparent oddities, would not perhaps have been commercially straightforward. (Nor would it have been easy, as he almost certainly didn't have the original and the later-added examples in front of him when correcting.) Waugh had had a bruising time over the text of *Decline and Fall* because of its presumed indecencies; it was rejected by one publishing company because of them, and the second (Waugh's father's) insisted on major surgery before going ahead. It's likely that Waugh wanted to avoid any such editorial run-ins over this novel – certainly at the particular time of its movement towards publication.

Differences in substantives are more problematic. It is very difficult to ascribe these with certainty to errors by one or another of typists, authorial errors corrected by him or by someone else, authorial second or third thoughts, editorial interference, or to the author agreeing with what were originally errors. Without complete evidence of all the documentation, the difficulty of decision with substantives makes the only safe course that of adopting the readings in the edition which has the authority of a known final correction – which is the 1965 edition. This does mean sacrificing many readings that we can be virtually certain Waugh would have preferred if the materials for a Platonically ideal text had been available to him whenever appropriate. But they never were. And they aren't now. We have, as described below, a history but there are gaps and the evidence is incomplete. And, in addition, as argued in the Introduction, Waugh had an uneasy relationship with this novel. An even-tempered and reflective approach to the task of correcting proofs was perhaps not very likely in 1930, especially given the unusual circumstances both of the novel's interrupted composition and of its textual fortunes from manuscript to printed form. An uneven and incomplete picture of evolving substantive development is suggested by the history. The words hadn't settled down together.

These circumstances and the strange history of the text have been brilliantly reconstructed by Martin Stannard.[2] Briefly, there are two unusual features about the textual history of this novel. First, the manuscript is not with (nearly) all of the others in the Texas university library which acquired all Waugh's books and papers after his death; long presumed lost, Stannard found it at the home of the Guinness family (from which he was allowed to photocopy it. That copy was kindly lent to the present writer for the preparation of this edition). It was sold at auction and is now in unknown hands. That Waugh chose to give it away (even if to its dedicatees, who were a great solace to him after the marriage break-up: the manuscript inscription has the phrase 'as it is your book') rather than have it among the rest in his library is indicative of his difficult relationship with the novel.

Secondly, there does survive at Austin, Texas, a long fragment of typescript, corrected in Waugh's hand, corresponding to the first four and a bit chapters in the present text. This is the only segment of typescript from the pre-war novels to have survived. (I have also been able, through the kindness of Martin Stannard, to study this for the present edition.) This came, not from Waugh's library, but through a series of hands, including dealers', having, presumably, been first 'lost' from the offices of Waugh's agent A. D. Peters. The problem is that the corrections inked on to this typescript do not correspond with the final printed text: it cannot have been used in the preparation for the printer.

2. See Stannard, pp. 204–6. I should add that the case made there for differences in tone between the typescript and the printed text seems to me overemphasized.

Stannard's very plausible hypothesis is that the manuscript was part-written and sent off to the typist who returned the parts of manuscript and typescript (two copies, including a carbon) for Waugh's corrections (he used these typescripts as rough drafts); the corrected segment of typescript was then sent to Peters (possibly for hawking around magazine editors) while Waugh kept the carbon copy, the uncorrected one (he had no reason to bother to transcribe his corrections). Then she-Evelyn wrote to tell Waugh about her relationship with Heygate. Stannard suggests that signs of disturbance in the manuscript indicate that this was probably when Waugh had finished Chapter 6. Much later, when Waugh was at last able to get back to the novel, he finished the manuscript – and later corrected the whole novel, using, crucially, that clean (uncorrected) carbon copy of the first segment. The composite, uniformly corrected typescript becomes the first edition (and, as would have been usual, it disappears in the printing process).

So the emendations and corrections inked on to the Texas segment of typescript are, on the one hand, a unique resource for studying Waugh at work, polishing and refining, and, on the other, a rather sad thing as, for reasons that are now clear, no stronger bibliographical case can be made for (re)introducing them into the text of the novel than for introducing other readings from the manuscript that have not survived, either through error or choice. And, of course, the typescript fragment only deals with just over a quarter of the whole.

One example of the variants will have to suffice. At the beginning of Chapter 2, after her ordeal at the hands of the Customs officers who search her, Miss Runcible, according to the printed text, says 'The way they looked'. The manuscript shows that Waugh wrote 'The places they looked in'. But that last 'in' was written in a very small squiggle so it's not surprising that the typist made this 'The places they looked'. Working on this typescript Waugh improves it radically by inking over 'The way they delved'. Later, when revising the whole novel, he has in front of him 'The places they looked' (in the uncorrected copy of the typescript), which doesn't make obvious sense. Perhaps vaguely remembering 'the way' and/or forgetting 'delved' he makes it 'The way they looked'. This is the weakest of the three variants but it stands.

The policy adopted here is to follow the 1965 text, but with thirty-eight 'white lines' and some significant dramatic/tonal punctuation (listed below) restored where the received text shows clear editorial imposition of a normalized style, inconsistent with an original conception especially when confirmed by the typescript. For the 1965 edition Waugh would presumably only have had a printed text with which to correct.

A sampling of substantive variants is discussed in the main body of notes.

'White lines' additional, and in one case alternative, to those in the 1965 text and deriving from the manuscript, confirmed by the typescript when available, are in this edition on pages:
8 (after 'faith'), 9 (after 'wriggled'), 12 (after 'they said'), 14 (after 'Auntie'), 15 (replacing the one after 'land soon'), 25 (after 'I should say'), 35, 39, 46, 54, 60, 67 (two), 68 (after 'don't you think?'), 75, 80, 89 (four), 91, 98, 104, 108, 113, 128 (after 'oysters'), 147 (four), 161 (two: after 'at all' and 'excitable'), 166, 174, 189.

Those deriving from inked instructions on the typescript (that is, Waugh adding them as he revised) are on pages:
10, 11 (after 'harbour': a gap of a kind was in the manuscript but the typist missed it), 14 (after 'cards').

There are a few examples of 'white lines' in the printed text and not in the manuscript or typescript (e.g. on pages 82, 159–60, 173 [two]), suggesting that Waugh was still adding them at the later correction stage.

Departures from the 1965 edition in punctuation, derived from the manuscript and typescript, are on pages:
23 (no commas in 'Right . . . gent'), 33 (separate paragraph for the bracketed material), 34 ('Tears . . . now' in brackets [as typescript only]), 36 (bracketed paragraph), 135–6 (two bracketed paragraphs), 146 (new paragraph at 'Then a mishap'), 164–5 (punctuation of Ginger's long speech), 186–7 (punctuation of Nina's letter:

the manuscript even scrupulously deletes a stray comma), 188–9 (punctuation of Chastity's speech).

Waugh's intentions, at any of the stages of the text's evolution, for the punctuation, and indeed the wording, of the King of Ruritania's speeches in Chapter 3 seem beyond certain reconstruction. Therefore 1965 is followed. It is also followed, against the manuscript evidence, in the very many examples of single punctuation mark variants, often rhythmically (or just grammatically) very expressive, but for which editorial interference is that bit less easy to argue for than in the larger-scale examples above.

Vile Bodies

With Love to
BRYAN MOYNE AND DIANA MOSLEY

'Well in *our* country,' said Alice, still panting a little, 'you'd generally get to somewhere else – if you ran very fast for a long time, as we've been doing.'

'A slow sort of country!' said the Queen. 'Now, *here*, you see, it takes all the running *you* can do, to keep in the same place. If you want to get somewhere else, you must run at least twice as fast as that!'

'If I wasn't real,' Alice said – half-laughing through her tears, it all seemed so ridiculous – 'I shouldn't be able to cry.'

'I hope you don't suppose those are real tears?' Tweedledum interrupted in a tone of great contempt.

–Through the Looking Glass

Chapter One

*

It was clearly going to be a bad crossing.

With Asiatic resignation Father Rothschild S.J. put down his suitcase in the corner of the bar and went on deck. (It was a small suitcase of imitation crocodile hide. The initials stamped on it in Gothic characters were not Father Rothschild's, for he had borrowed it that morning from the *valet-de-chambre* of his hotel. It contained some rudimentary underclothes, six important new books in six languages, a false beard and a school atlas and gazetteer heavily annotated.) Standing on the deck Father Rothschild leant his elbows on the rail, rested his chin in his hands and surveyed the procession of passengers coming up the gangway, each face eloquent of polite misgiving.

Very few of them were unknown to the Jesuit, for it was his happy knack to remember everything that could possibly be learned about everyone who could possibly be of any importance. His tongue protruded very slightly and, had they not all been so concerned with luggage and the weather, someone might have observed in him a peculiar resemblance to those plaster reproductions of the gargoyles of Notre Dame which may be seen in the shop windows of artists' colourmen tinted the colour of 'Old Ivory', peering intently from among stencil outfits and plasticine and tubes of water-colour paint. High above his head swung Mrs Melrose Ape's travel-worn Packard car, bearing the dust of three continents, against the darkening sky, and up the companion-way at the head of her angels strode Mrs Melrose Ape, the woman evangelist.

'Faith.'

'Here, Mrs Ape.'

'Charity.'

'Here, Mrs Ape.'

'Fortitude.'

'Here, Mrs Ape.'

'Chastity . . . Where is Chastity?'

'Chastity didn't feel well, Mrs Ape. She went below.'

'That girl's more trouble than she's worth. Whenever there's any packing to be done, Chastity doesn't feel well. Are all the rest here – Humility, Prudence, Divine Discontent, Mercy, Justice and Creative Endeavour?'

'Creative Endeavour lost her wings, Mrs Ape. She got talking to a gentleman in the train . . . Oh, there she is.'

'Got 'em?' asked Mrs Ape.

Too breathless to speak, Creative Endeavour nodded. (Each of the angels carried her wings in a little black box like a violin case.)

'Right,' said Mrs Ape, 'and just you hold on to 'em tight and not so much talking to gentlemen in trains. You're angels, not a panto, see?'

The angels crowded together disconsolately. It was awful when Mrs Ape was like this. My, how they would pinch Chastity and Creative Endeavour when they got them alone in their nightshirts. It was bad enough their going to be so sick without that they had Mrs Ape pitching into them too.

Seeing their discomfort, Mrs Ape softened and smiled. She was nothing if not 'magnetic'.

'Well, girls,' she said, 'I must be getting along. They say it's going to be rough, but don't you believe it. If you have peace in your hearts your stomach will look after itself, and remember if you *do* feel queer – *sing*. There's nothing like it.'

'Good-bye, Mrs Ape, and thank you,' said the angels; they bobbed prettily, turned about and trooped aft to the second-class part of the ship. Mrs Ape watched them benignly, then, squaring her shoulders and looking (except that she had really no beard to speak of) every inch a sailor, strode resolutely forrard to the first-class bar.

Other prominent people were embarking, all very unhappy about the weather; to avert the terrors of sea-sickness they had indulged in every kind of civilized witchcraft, but they were lacking in faith.

*

8

Miss Runcible was there, and Miles Malpractice, and all the Younger Set. They had spent a jolly morning strapping each other's tummies with sticking plaster (how Miss Runcible had wriggled).

The Right Honourable Walter Outrage, M.P., last week's Prime Minister,[1] was there. Before breakfast that morning (which had suffered in consequence) Mr Outrage had taken twice the maximum dose of a patent preparation of chloral, and losing heart later had finished the bottle in the train. He moved in an uneasy trance, closely escorted by the most public-looking detective sergeants. These men had been with Mr Outrage in Paris, and what they did not know about his goings on was not worth knowing, at least from a novelist's point of view. (When they spoke about him to each other they called him 'the Right Honourable Rape', but that was more by way of being a pun about his name than a criticism of the conduct of his love affairs, in which, if the truth were known, he displayed a notable diffidence and the liability to panic.)

Lady Throbbing and Mrs Blackwater, those twin sisters whose portrait by Millais auctioned recently at Christie's made a record in rock-bottom prices, were sitting on one of the teak benches eating apples and drinking what Lady Throbbing, with late Victorian *chic*, called 'a bottle of pop', and Mrs Blackwater, more exotically, called '*champagne*', pronouncing it as though it were French.

'Surely, Kitty, that is Mr Outrage, last week's Prime Minister.'

'Nonsense, Fanny, where?'

'Just in front of the two men with bowler hats, next to the clergyman.'

'It is certainly like his photographs. How strange he looks.'

'Just like poor Throbbing . . . all that last year.'

'. . . And none of us even suspected . . . until they found the bottles under the board in his dressing-room . . . and we all used to think it was drink . . .'

'I don't think one finds *quite* the same class as Prime Minister nowadays, do you think?'

'They say that only *one* person has any influence with Mr Outrage . . .'

'At the Japanese Embassy . . .'

'Of course, dear, not so loud. But tell me, Fanny, seriously, do you think really and truly Mr Outrage has IT?'

'He has a very nice figure for a man of his age.'

'Yes, but *his* age, and the bull-like type is so often disappointing. Another glass? You will be grateful for it when the ship begins to move.'

'I quite thought we *were* moving.'

'How absurd you are, Fanny, and yet I can't help laughing.'

So arm in arm and shaken by little giggles the two tipsy old ladies went down to their cabin.

Of the other passengers, some had filled their ears with cotton-wool, others wore smoked glasses, while several ate dry captain's biscuits from paper bags, as Red Indians are said to eat snake's flesh to make them cunning. Mrs Hoop repeated feverishly over and over again a formula she had learned from a yogi in New York City. A few 'good sailors', whose luggage bore the labels of many voyages, strode aggressively about smoking small, foul pipes and trying to get up a four of bridge.

Two minutes before the advertised time of departure, while the first admonitory whistling and shouting was going on, a young man came on board carrying his bag. There was nothing particularly remarkable about his appearance. He looked exactly as young men like him do look; he was carrying his own bag, which was disagreeably heavy, because he had no money left in francs and very little left in anything else. He had been two months in Paris writing a book and was coming home because, in the course of his correspondence, he had got engaged to be married. His name was Adam Fenwick-Symes.

Father Rothschild smiled at him in a kindly manner.

'I doubt whether you remember me,' he said. 'We met at Oxford five years ago at luncheon with the Dean of Balliol. I shall be interested to read your book when it appears – an auto-biography, I understand. And may I be one of the first to congratulate you on your engagement? I am afraid you will find your father-in-law a little eccentric – and forgetful. He had a nasty attack of bronchitis this winter. It's a draughty house – far too big for these days. Well, I must go below now. It is going to be rough and I am a bad sailor. We meet at Lady Metroland's on the twelfth, if not, as I hope, before.'

Before Adam had time to reply the Jesuit disappeared. Suddenly the head popped back.

'There is an extremely dangerous and disagreeable woman on board – a Mrs Ape.'

Then he was gone again, and almost at once the boat began to slip away from the quay towards the mouth of the harbour.

Sometimes the ship pitched and sometimes she rolled and sometimes she stood quite still and shivered all over, poised above an abyss of dark water; then she would go swooping down like a scenic railway train into a windless hollow and up again with a rush into the gale; sometimes she would burrow her path, with convulsive nosings and scramblings like a terrier in a rabbit hole; and sometimes she would drop dead like a lift. It was this last movement that caused the most havoc among the passengers.

'Oh,' said the Bright Young People. 'Oh, oh oh.'

'It's just exactly like being inside a cocktail shaker,' said Miles Malpractice. 'Darling, your face – eau de Nil.'

'Too, too sick-making,' said Miss Runcible, with one of her rare flashes of accuracy.

Kitty Blackwater and Fanny Throbbing lay one above the other in their bunks rigid from wig to toe.

'I wonder, do you think the *champagne* . . .?'

'Kitty.'

'Yes, Fanny, dear.'

'Kitty, I think, in fact, I am sure I have some sal volatile . . . Kitty, I thought that perhaps as you are nearer . . . it would really hardly be safe for me to try and descend . . . I might break a leg.'

'Not after *champagne*, Fanny, do you think?'

'But I need it. Of course, dear, *if it's too much trouble?*'

'Nothing is too much trouble, darling, you know that. But now I come to think of it, I remember, quite clearly, for a fact, that you did *not* pack the sal volatile.'

'Oh, Kitty, oh, Kitty, please . . . you would be sorry for this if I died . . . oh.'

'But I saw the sal volatile on your dressing-table after your luggage had gone down, dear. I remember thinking, I must take that down to Fanny, and then, dear, I got confused over the tips, so you see . . .'

'I . . . put . . . it . . . in . . . myself . . . Next to my brushes . . . you . . . beast.'

'Oh, Fanny . . .'

'Oh . . . Oh . . . Oh.'

To Father Rothschild no passage was worse than any other. He thought of the sufferings of the saints, the mutability of human nature, the Four Last Things, and between whiles repeated snatches of the penitential psalms.

The Leader of his Majesty's Opposition lay sunk in a rather glorious coma, made splendid by dreams of Oriental imagery – of painted paper houses; of golden dragons and gardens of almond blossom; of golden limbs and almond eyes, humble and caressing; of very small golden feet among almond blossoms; of little painted cups full of golden tea; of a golden voice singing behind a painted paper screen; of humble, caressing little golden hands and eyes shaped like almonds and the colour of night.

Outside his door two very limp detective sergeants had deserted their posts.

'The bloke as could make trouble on a ship like this 'ere deserves to get away with it,' they said.

The ship creaked in every plate, doors slammed, trunks fell about, the wind howled; the screw, now out of the water, now in, raced and churned, shaking down hatboxes like ripe apples; but above all the roar and clatter there rose from the second-class ladies' saloon the despairing voices of Mrs Ape's angels, in frequently broken unison, singing, singing, wildly, desperately, as though their hearts would break in the effort and their minds lose their reason, Mrs Ape's famous hymn, *There ain't no flies on the Lamb of God*.

The Captain and the Chief Officer sat on the bridge engrossed in a crossword puzzle.

'Looks like we may get some heavy weather if the wind gets up,' he said. 'Shouldn't wonder if there wasn't a bit of a sea running to-night.'

'Well, we can't always have it quiet like this,' said the Chief Officer. 'Word of eighteen letters meaning carnivorous mammal. Search me if I know how they do think of these things.'

Adam Fenwick-Symes sat among the good sailors in the smoking-room drinking his third Irish whisky and wondering how soon he would feel definitely ill. Already there was a vague depression gathering at the top of his head. There were thirty-five minutes more, probably longer with the head wind keeping them back.

Opposite him sat a much-travelled and chatty journalist telling him smutty stories. From time to time Adam interposed some more or less appropriate comment, 'No, I say that's a good one', or, 'I must remember that', or just 'Ha, Ha, Ha', but his mind was not really in a receptive condition.

Up went the ship, up, up, up, paused and then plunged down with a sidelong slither. Adam caught at his glass and saved it. Then shut his eyes.

'Now I'll tell you a drawing-room one,' said the journalist.

Behind them a game of cards was in progress among the commercial gents. At first they had rather a jolly time about it, saying, 'What ho, she bumps', or 'Steady, the Buffs', when the cards and glasses and ash-tray were thrown on to the floor, but in the last ten minutes they were growing notably quieter. It was rather a nasty kind of hush.

'. . . And forty aces and two-fifty for the rubber. Shall we cut again or stay as we are?'

'How about knocking off for a bit? Makes me tired – table moving about all the time.'

'Why, Arthur, you ain't feeling ill, surely?'

''Course I ain't feeling ill, only tired.'

'Well, of course, if Arthur's feeling ill . . .'

'Who'd have thought of old Arthur feeling ill?'

'I ain't feeling ill, I tell you. Just tired. But if you boys want to go on I'm not the one to spoil a game.'

'Good old Arthur. 'Course he ain't feeling ill. Look out for the cards, Bill, up she goes again.'

'What about one all round? Same again?'

'Same again.'

'Good luck, Arthur.' 'Good luck.' 'Here's fun.' 'Down she goes.'

'Whose deal? You dealt last, didn't you, Mr Henderson?'

'Yes, Arthur's deal.'

'Your deal, Arthur. Cheer up, old scout.'

'Don't you go doing that. It isn't right to hit a chap on the back like that.'

'Look out with the cards, Arthur.'

'Well, what d'you expect, being hit on the back like that. Makes me tired.'

'Here, I got fifteen cards.'

'I wonder if you've heard this one,' said the journalist. 'There was a man lived at Aberdeen, and he was terribly keen on fishing, so when he married, he married a woman with worms. That's rich, eh? You see he was keen on fishing, see, and she had worms, see, he lived in Aberdeen. That's a good one that is.'

'D'you know, I think I shall go on deck for a minute. A bit stuffy in here, don't you think?'

'You can't do that. The sea's coming right over it all the time. Not feeling queer, are you?'

'No, of course I'm not feeling queer. I only thought a little fresh air . . . Christ, why won't the damn thing stop?'

'Steady, old boy. I wouldn't go trying to walk about, not if I were you. Much better stay just where you are. What you want's a spot of whisky.'

'Not feeling ill, you know. Just stuffy.'

'That's all right, old boy. Trust Auntie.'

*

The bridge party was not being a success.

'Hullo, Mr Henderson. What's that spade?'

'That's the ace, that is.'

'I can see it's the ace. What I mean you didn't ought to have trumped that last trick not if you had a spade.'

'What d'you mean, didn't ought to have trumped it? Trumps led.'

'No, they did *not*. Arthur led a spade.'

'He led a trump, didn't you, Arthur?'

'Arthur led a spade.'

'He couldn't have led a spade because for why he put a heart on my king of spades when I thought he had the queen. He hasn't got no spades.'

'What d'you mean, not got no spades? I got the queen.'

'Arthur, old man, you *must* be feeling queer.'

'No, I ain't, I tell you, just tired. You'd be tired if you'd been hit on the back same as I was . . . anyway I'm fed up with this game . . . there go the cards again.'

This time no one troubled to pick them up. Presently Mr Henderson said, 'Funny thing, don't know why I feel all swimmy of a sudden. Must have ate something that wasn't quite right. You never can tell with foreign foods – all messed up like they do.'

'Now you mention it, I don't feel too spry myself. Damn bad ventilation on these Channel boats.'

'That's what it is. Ventilation. You said it.'

'You know I'm funny. I never feel sea-sick, mind, but I often find going on boats doesn't agree with me.'

'I'm like that, too.'

'Ventilation . . . a disgrace.'

'Lord, I shall be glad when we get to Dover. Home, sweet home, eh?'

Adam held on very tightly to the brass-bound edge of the table and felt a little better. He was *not* going to be sick, and that was that; not with that gargoyle of a man opposite anyway. They *must* be in sight of land soon.

It was at this time, when things were at their lowest, that Mrs

Ape reappeared in the smoking-room. She stood for a second or two in the entrance balanced between swinging door and swinging door-post; then as the ship momentarily righted herself, she strode to the bar, her feet well apart, her hands in the pockets of her tweed coat.

'Double rum,' she said and smiled magnetically at the miserable little collection of men seated about the room. 'Why, boys,' she said, 'but you're looking terrible put out over something. What's it all about? Is it your souls that's wrong or is it that the ship won't keep still? Rough? 'Course it's rough. But let me ask you this. If you're put out this way over just an hour's sea-sickness' ('Not sea-sick, ventilation,' said Mr Henderson mechanically), 'what are you going to be like when you make the mighty big journey that's waiting for us all? Are you right with God?' said Mrs Ape. 'Are you prepared for death?'

'Oh, am I not?' said Arthur. 'I 'aven't thought of nothing else for the last half-hour.'

'Now, boys, I'll tell you what we're going to do. We're going to sing a song together, you and me.' ('Oh, God,' said Adam.) 'You may not know it, but you are. You'll feel better for it body *and* soul. It's a song of Hope. You don't hear much about Hope these days, do you? Plenty about Faith, plenty about Charity. They've forgotten all about Hope. There's only one great evil in the world to-day. Despair. I know all about England, and I tell you straight, boys, I've got the goods for you. Hope's what you want and Hope's what I got. Here, steward, hand round these leaflets. There's the song on the back. Now all together . . . sing. Five bob for you, steward, if you can shout me down. Splendid, all together, boys.'

In a rich, very audible voice Mrs Ape led the singing. Her arms rose, fell and fluttered with the rhythm of the song. The bar steward was hers already – inaccurate sometimes in his reading of the words, but with a sustained power in the low notes that defied competition. The journalist joined in next and Arthur set up a little hum. Soon they were all at it, singing like blazes, and it is undoubtedly true that they felt the better for it.

Father Rothschild heard it and turned his face to the wall.

*

Kitty Blackwater heard it.

'Fanny.'

'Well.'

'Fanny, dear, do you hear singing?'

'Yes, dear, thank you.'

'Fanny, dear, I hope they aren't holding a *service*. I mean, dear, it sounds so like a hymn. Do you think, possibly, we are *in danger*? Fanny, are we going to be wrecked?'

'I should be neither surprised nor sorry.'

'Darling, how can you? . . . We should have heard it, shouldn't we, if we had actually *hit* anything? . . . Fanny, dear, if you like I will have a look for your sal volatile.'

'I hardly think that would be any help, dear, since you *saw* it on my dressing-table.'

'I may have been mistaken.'

'You *said* you *saw* it.'

The Captain heard it. 'All the time I been at sea,' he said, 'I never could stand for missionaries.'

'Word of six letters beginning with ZB,' said the Chief Officer, 'meaning "used in astronomic calculation".'

'Z can't be right,' said the Captain after a few minutes' thought.

The Bright Young People heard it. 'So like one's first parties,' said Miss Runcible, 'being sick with other people singing.'

Mrs Hoop heard it. 'Well,' she thought, 'I'm through with theosophy after this journey. Reckon I'll give the Catholics the once over.'

Aft, in the second-class saloon, where the screw was doing its worst, the angels heard it. It was some time since they had given up singing.

'Her again,' said Divine Discontent.

Mr Outrage alone lay happily undisturbed, his mind absorbed in lovely dream sequences of a world of little cooing voices, so caressing, so humble; and dark eyes, night-coloured, the shape of almonds over painted paper screens; little golden bodies, so flexible, so firm, so surprising in the positions they assumed.

They were still singing in the smoking-room when, in very little more than her usual time, the ship came into the harbour at Dover. Then Mrs Ape, as was her invariable rule, took round the hat and collected nearly two pounds, not counting her own five shillings which she got back from the bar steward. 'Salvation doesn't do them the same good if they think it's free,' was her favourite axiom.

Chapter Two

*

'Have you anything to declare?'

'Wings.'

'Have you wore them?'

'Sure.'

'That's all right, then.'

'Divine Discontent gets all the smiles all the time,' complained Fortitude to Prudence. 'Golly, but it's good to be on dry land.'

Unsteadily, but with renewed hope, the passengers had disembarked.

Father Rothschild fluttered a diplomatic *laissez-passer* and disappeared in the large car that had been sent to meet him. The others were jostling one another with their luggage, trying to attract the Customs officers and longing for a cup of tea.

'I got half a dozen of the best stowed away,' confided the journalist. 'They're generally pretty easy after a bad crossing.' And sure enough he was soon settled in the corner of a first-class carriage (for the paper was, of course, paying his expenses) with his luggage safely chalked in the van.

It was some time before Adam could get attended to.

'I've nothing but some very old clothes and some books,' he said.

But here he showed himself deficient in tact, for the man's casual air disappeared in a flash.

'Books, eh?' he said. 'And what sort of books, may I ask?'

'Look for yourself.'

'Thank *you*, that's what I mean to do. *Books*, indeed.'

Adam wearily unstrapped and unlocked his suitcase.

'Yes,' said the Customs officer menacingly, as though his worst suspicions had been confirmed, 'I should just about say you had got some books.'

One by one he took the books out and piled them on the counter. A copy of Dante excited his especial disgust.

'French, eh?' he said. 'I guessed as much, and pretty dirty, too, I shouldn't wonder. Now just you wait while I look up these here *books*' – how he said it! – 'in my list. Particularly against books the Home Secretary[2] is. If we can't stamp out literature in the country, we can at least stop its being brought in from outside. That's what he said the other day in Parliament, and I says "Hear, hear . . ." Hullo, hullo, what's this, may I ask?'

Gingerly, as though it might at any moment explode, he produced and laid on the counter a large pile of typescript.

'That's a book, too,' said Adam. 'One I've just written. It is my memoirs.'

'Ho, it is, is it? Well, I'll take that along, too, to the chief. You better come too.'

'But I've got to catch the train.'

'You come along. There's worse things than missing trains,' he hinted darkly.

They went together into an inner office, the walls of which were lined with contraband pornography and strange instruments, whose purpose Adam could not guess. From the next room came the shrieks and yells of poor Miss Runcible, who had been mistaken for a well-known jewel smuggler, and was being stripped to the skin by two terrific wardresses.

'Now then, what's this about books?' said the chief.

With the help of a printed list (which began 'Aristotle, Works of (Illustrated)') they went through Adam's books, laboriously, one at a time, spelling out the titles.

Miss Runcible came through the office, working hard with lipstick and compact.

'Adam, darling, I never saw you on the boat,' she said. 'My dear, I can't *tell* you the *things* that have been happening to me in there. The way they looked[3] . . . too, too shaming. Positively surgical, my dear, and *such* wicked old women, just like *Dowagers*, my dear. As soon as I get to London I shall ring up every Cabinet Minister and *all* the newspapers and give them all the most shy-making details.'

The chief was at this time engrossed in Adam's memoirs, giving vent at intervals to a sinister chuckling sound that was partly triumphant and partly derisive, but in the main genuinely appreciative.

'Coo, Bert,' he said. 'Look at this; that's rich, ain't it?'

Presently he collected the sheets, tied them together and put them on one side.

'Well, see here,' he said. 'You can take these books on architecture and the dictionary, and I don't mind stretching a point for once and letting you have the history books, too. But this book on Economics comes under Subversive Propaganda. That you leaves behind. And this here *Purgatorio* doesn't look right to me, so that stays behind, pending inquiries. But as for this autobiography, that's just downright dirt, and we burns that straight away, see.'

'But, good heavens, there isn't a word in the book – you must be misinterpreting it.'

'Not so much of it. I knows dirt when I sees it or I shouldn't be where I am to-day.'

'But do you realize that my whole livelihood depends on this book?'

'And *my* livelihood depends on stopping works like this coming into the country. Now 'ook it quick if you don't want a police-court case.'

'Adam, angel, don't fuss or we shall miss the train.'

Miss Runcible took his arm and led him back to the station and told him all about a lovely party that was going to happen that night.

'*Queer*, who felt queer?'

'You did, Arthur.'

'No I never . . . just tired.'

'It certainly was stuffy in there just for a bit.'

'Wonderful how that old girl cheered things up. Got a meeting next week in the Albert Hall.'

'Shouldn't be surprised if I didn't go. What do you say, Mr Henderson?'

'She got a troupe of angels, so she said. All dressed up in white with wings, lovely. Not a bad-looker herself, if it comes to that.'

'What did you put in the plate, Arthur?'

'Half-crown.'

'So did I. Funny thing, I ain't never give a half-crown like that before. She kind of draws it out of you, damned if she doesn't.'

'You won't get away from the Albert Hall not without putting your hand in your pocket.'

'No, but I'd like to see those angels dressed up, eh, Mr Henderson?'

'Fanny, surely that is Agatha Runcible, poor Viola Chasm's daughter?'

'I wonder Viola allows her to go about like that. If she were my daughter . . .'

'*Your* daughter, Fanny . . .'

'Kitty, that was not kind.'

'My dear, I only meant . . . have you, by the way, heard of her lately?'

'The last we heard was worse than anything, Kitty. She has left Buenos Aires. I am afraid she has severed her connection with Lady Metroland altogether. They think that she is in some kind of touring company.'

'Darling, I'm sorry. I should never have mentioned it, but whenever I see Agatha Runcible I can't help thinking . . . girls seem to know so much nowadays. We had to learn everything for ourselves, didn't we, Fanny, and it took so long. If I'd had Agatha Runcible's chances . . . Who is the young man with her?'

'I don't know, and frankly, I don't think, do you? . . . He has that self-contained look.'

'He has very nice eyes. And he moves well.'

'I dare say when it came to the point . . . Still, as I say, if I had had Agatha Runcible's advantages . . .'

'What are you looking for, darling?'

'Why, darling, such an extraordinary thing. Here *is* the sal volatile next to my brushes all the time.'

'Fanny, how awful of me, if I'd only known . . .'

'I dare say there must have been another bottle you saw on the dressing-table, sweetest. Perhaps the maid put it there. You never know at the Lotti, do you?'

'Fanny, forgive me . . .'

'But, dearest, what is there to forgive? After all, you *did see* another bottle, didn't you, Kitty darling?'

'Why, look, there's Miles.'

'Miles?'

'Your son, darling. My nephew, you know.'

'*Miles.* Do you know, Kitty, I believe it is. He never comes to see me now, the naughty boy.'

'My dear, he looks terribly *tapette*.'[4]

'Darling, I know. It is a great grief to me. Only I try not to think about it too much – he had so little chance with poor Throbbing what he was.'

'The sins of the fathers, Fanny . . .'

Somewhere not far from Maidstone Mr Outrage became fully conscious. Opposite him in the carriage the two detectives slept, their bowler hats jammed forwards on their foreheads, their mouths open, their huge red hands lying limply in their laps. Rain beat on the windows; the carriage was intensely cold and smelt of stale tobacco. Inside there were advertisements of horrible picturesque ruins; outside in the rain were hoardings advertising patent medicines and dog biscuits. 'Every Molassine dog cake wags a tail,' Mr Outrage read, and the train repeated over and over again, 'Right Honourable gent Right Honourable gent Right Honourable gentleman Right Honourable gent . . .'

Adam got into the carriage with the Younger Set. They still looked a bit queer, but they cheered up wonderfully when they heard about Miss Runcible's outrageous treatment at the hands of the Customs officers.

'*Well*,' they said. '*Well!* how too, too shaming, Agatha, darling,' they said. 'How devastating, how unpolicemanlike, how goat-like, how sick-making, how too, too awful.' And then they began talking about Archie Schwert's party that night.

'Who's Archie Schwert?' asked Adam.

'Oh, he's someone new since you went away. The *most* bogus man. Miles discovered him, and since then he's been climbing and climbing and *climbing*, my dear, till he hardly knows us. He's rather sweet, really, only too terribly common, poor darling. He lives at the Ritz, and I think that's rather grand, don't you?'

'Is he giving his party there?'

'My dear, of course not. In Edward Throbbing's house. He's Miles' brother, you know, only he's frightfully dim and political, and doesn't know anybody. He got ill and went to Kenya or some-where and left his perfectly sheepish house in Hertford Street, so we've all gone to live there. You'd better come, too. The caretakers didn't like it a bit at first, but we gave them drinks and things, and now they're simply thrilled to the marrow about it and spend all their time cutting out "bits", my dear, from the papers about our goings on.

'One awful thing is we haven't got a car. Miles broke it, Ed-ward's, I mean, and we simply can't afford to get it mended, so I think we shall have to move soon. Everything's getting rather broken up, too, and dirty, if you know what I mean. Because, you see, there aren't any servants, only the butler and his wife, and they are always tight now. So demoralizing. Mary Mouse has been a perfect angel, and sent us great hampers of caviare and things . . . She's paying for Archie's party to-night, of course.'

'Do you know, I rather think I'm going to be sick again?'

'Oh, Miles!'

(Oh, Bright Young People!)

Packed all together in a second-class carriage, the angels were late in recovering their good humour.

'She's taken Prudence off in her car again,' said Divine Dis-content, who once, for one delirious fortnight, had been Mrs Ape's favourite girl. 'Can't see what she sees in her. What's London like, Fortitude? I never been there but once.'

'Just exactly heaven. Shops and all.'

'What are the men like, Fortitude?'

'Say, don't you never think of nothing but *men*, Chastity?'

'I should say I do. I was only asking.'

'Well, they ain't much to look at, not after the shops. But they has their uses.'

'Say, did you hear that? You're a cute one, Fortitude. Did you hear what Fortitude said? She said "they have their uses".'

'What, shops?'

'No, silly, men.'

'*Men.* That's a good one, I should say.'

Presently the train arrived at Victoria, and all these passengers were scattered all over London.

Adam left his bag at Shepheard's Hotel, and drove straight to Henrietta Street to see his publishers. It was nearly closing time, so that most of the staff had packed up and gone home, but by good fortune Mr Sam Benfleet, the junior director with whom Adam always did his business, was still in his room correcting proofs for one of his women novelists. He was a competent young man, with a restrained elegance of appearance (the sten-ographer always trembled slightly when she brought him his cup of tea).

'No, she can't print that,' he kept saying, endorsing one after another of the printer's protests. 'No, damn it, she can't print *that.* She'll have us all in prison.' For it was one of his most exacting duties to 'ginger up' the more reticent of the manuscripts submit-ted and 'tone down' the more 'outspoken' until he had reduced them all to the acceptable moral standard of his day.

He greeted Adam with the utmost cordiality.

'Well, well, Adam, how are you? This is nice. Sit down. Have a cigarette. What a day to arrive in London. Did you have a good crossing?'

'Not too good.'

'I say, I *am* sorry. Nothing so beastly as a beastly crossing, is there? Why don't you come round to dinner at Wimpole Street to-night? I've got some rather nice Americans coming. Where are you staying?'

'At "Shepheard's" – Lottie Crump's.'

'Well, that's always fun. I've been trying to get an autobiography out of Lottie for ten years. And that reminds me. You're bringing us your manuscript, aren't you? Old Rampole was asking about it only the other day. It's a week overdue, you know. I hope you'll like the preliminary notices we've sent out. We've fixed the day of publication for the second week in December, so as to give it a fortnight's run before Johnnie Hoop's autobiography. That's going to be a seller. Sails a bit near the wind in places. We had to cut out some things – you know what old Rampole is. Johnnie didn't like it a bit. But I'm looking forward terribly to reading yours.'

'Well, Sam, rather an awful thing happened about that . . .'

'I say, I hope you're not going to say it's not finished. The date on the contract, you know . . .'

'Oh, it's finished all right. Burnt.'

'Burnt?'

'Burnt.'

'What an awful thing. I hope you are insured.'

Adam explained the circumstances of the destruction of his autobiography. There was a longish pause while Sam Benfleet thought.

'What worries me is how are we going to make that sound convincing to old Rampole.'

'I should think it sounded convincing enough.'

'You don't know old Rampole. It's sometimes very difficult for me, Adam, working under him. Now if I had my own way I'd say, "Take your own time. Start again. Don't worry . . ." But there's old Rampole. He's a devil for contracts, you know, and you did *say*, didn't you . . .? It's all very difficult. You know, I wish it hadn't happened.'

'So do I, oddly enough,' said Adam.

'There's another difficulty. You've had an advance already, haven't you? Fifty pounds, wasn't it? Well, you know, *that* makes things very difficult. Old Rampole never likes big advances like that to young authors. You know I hate to say it, but I can't help feeling that the best thing would be for you to repay the advance – plus interest, of course, old Rampole would insist on that – and cancel the contract. Then if you ever thought of rewriting the book, well, of course, we should be delighted to consider it. I suppose that – well, I mean, it *would* be quite *convenient*, and all that, to repay the advance?'

'Not only inconvenient, but impossible,' said Adam in no particular manner.

There was another pause.

'Deuced awkward,' said Sam Benfleet. 'It's a shame the way the Customs House officers are allowed to take the law into their own hands. Quite ignorant men, too. Liberty of the subject, I mean, and all that. I tell you what we'll do. We'll start a correspondence about it in the *New Statesman* . . . It is all so deuced awkward. But I think I can see a way out. I suppose you could get the book rewritten in time for the Spring List? Well, we'll cancel the contract and forget all about the advance. No, no, my dear fellow, don't thank me. If only I was alone here I'd be doing that kind of thing all day. Now instead we'll have a new contract. It won't be quite so good as the last, I'm afraid. Old Rampole wouldn't stand for that. I'll tell you what, we'll give you our standard first-novel contract. I've got a printed form here. It won't take a minute to fill up. Just sign here.'

'May I just see the terms?'

'Of course, my dear fellow. They look a bit hard at first, I know, but it's our usual form. We made a very special case for you, you know. It's very simple. No royalty on the first two thousand, then a royalty of two and a half per cent, rising to five per cent on the tenth thousand. We retain serial, cinema, dramatic, American, Colonial and translation rights, of course. And, of course, an option on your next twelve books on the same terms. It's a very straightforward arrangement really. Doesn't leave room for any of the disputes which embitter the relations of author and publisher. Most of our authors are working on a contract like that . . . Splendid. Now don't you bother any more about that advance. I understand *perfectly*, and I'll square old Rampole somehow, even if it comes out of my director's fees.'

'Square old Rampole,' repeated Mr Benfleet thoughtfully as Adam went downstairs. It was fortunate, he reflected, that none of the authors ever came across the senior partner, that benign old gentleman, who once a week drove up to board meetings from the country, whose chief interest in the business was confined to the progress of a little book of his own about bee-keeping, which they had published twenty years ago and, though he did not know it, allowed long ago to drop out of print. He often wondered in his uneasy moments what he would find to say when Rampole died.

It was about now that Adam remembered that he was engaged to be married. The name of his young lady was Nina Blount. So he went into a tube station to a telephone-box, which smelt rather nasty, and rang her up.

'Hullo.'

'Hullo.'

'May I speak to Miss Blount, please?'

'I'll just see if she's in,' said Miss Blount's voice. 'Who's speaking, please?' She was always rather snobbish about the fiction of having someone to answer the telephone.

'Mr Fenwick-Symes.'

'Oh.'

'Adam, you know . . . How are you, Nina?'

'Well, I've got rather a pain just at present.'

'Poor Nina. Shall I come round and see you?'

'No, don't do that, darling, because I'm just going to have a bath. Why don't we dine together?'

'Well, I asked Agatha Runcible to dinner.'

'Why?'

'She'd just had all her clothes taken off by some sailors.'

'Yes, I know, it's all in the evening paper to-night . . . Well, I'll tell you what. Let's meet at Archie Schwert's party. Are you going?'

'I rather said I would.'

'That's all right, then. Don't dress up. No one will, except Archie.'

'Oh, I say, Nina, there's one thing – I don't think I shall be able to marry you after all.'

'Oh, *Adam*, you are a bore. Why not?'

'They burnt my book.'

'Beasts. Who did?'

'I'll tell you about it to-night.'

'Yes, *do*. Good-bye, darling.'

'Good-bye, my sweet.'

He hung up the receiver and left the telephone-box. People had crowded into the Underground station for shelter from the rain, and were shaking their umbrellas and reading their evening papers. Adam could see the headlines over their shoulders.

PEER'S DAUGHTER'S DOVER ORDEAL

SERIOUS ALLEGATIONS BY SOCIETY BEAUTY

HON. A. RUNCIBLE SAYS

'TOO SHAMING'

'Poor pretty,' said an indignant old woman at his elbow. 'Disgraceful, I calls it. And such a good sweet face. I see her picture in the papers only yesterday. Nasty prying minds. That's what they got. And her poor father and all. Look, Jane, there's a piece about him, too. "Interviewed at the Carlton Club this evening, Lord Chasm", that's her dad, "refused to make a definite statement. 'The matter shall not be allowed to rest here,' he said." *And* quite right, too, I says. You know I feels about that girl just as though it was me own daughter. Seeing her picture so often and our Sarah having done the back stairs, Tuesdays, at them flats where her aunt used to live – the one as had that 'orrible divorce last year.'

Adam bought a paper. He had just ten shillings left in the world. It was too wet to walk, so he took a very crowded tube train to Dover Street and hurried across in the rain to Shepheard's Hotel (which, for the purposes of the narrative, may be assumed to stand at the corner of Hay Hill).

Chapter Three

*

Lottie Crump, proprietress of Shepheard's Hotel, Dover Street, attended invariably by two Cairn terriers, is a happy reminder to us that the splendours of the Edwardian era were not entirely confined to Lady Anchorage or Mrs Blackwater. She is a fine figure of a woman, singularly unscathed by any sort of misfortune and superbly oblivious of those changes in the social order which agitate the more observant *grandes dames* of her period. When the war broke out she took down the signed photograph of the Kaiser and, with some solemnity, hung it in the men-servants' lavatory; it was her one combative action; since then she has had her worries – income-tax forms and drink restrictions and young men whose fathers she used to know, who give her bad cheques, but these have been soon forgotten; one can go to Shepheard's parched with modernity any day, if Lottie likes one's face, and still draw up, cool and uncontaminated, great, healing draughts from the well of Edwardian certainty.

Shepheard's has a plain, neatly pointed brick front and large, plain doorway. Inside it is like a country house. Lottie is a great one for sales, and likes, whenever one of the great houses of her day is being sold up, to take away something for old times' sake. There is a good deal too much furniture at Shepheard's, some of it rare, some of it hideous beyond description; there is plenty of red plush and red morocco and innumerable wedding presents of the 'eighties; in particular many of those massive, mechanical devices covered with crests and monograms, and associated in some way with cigars. It is the sort of house in which one expects to find croquet mallets and polo sticks in the bathroom, and children's toys at the bottom of one's chest of drawers, and an estate map and an archery target – exuding straw – and a bicycle and one of those walking-sticks which turn into saws, somewhere in passages, between baize doors, smelling of damp. (As a matter of fact, all you are likely to find in your room at Lottie's is an empty champagne bottle or two and a crumpled camisole.)

The servants, like the furniture, are old and have seen aristocratic service. Doge, the head waiter, who is hard of hearing, partially blind, and tortured with gout, was once a Rothschild's butler. He had, in fact, on more than one occasion in Father Rothschild's youth, dandled him on his knee, when he came with his father (at one time the fifteenth richest man in the world) to visit his still richer cousins, but it would be unlike him to pretend that he ever really liked the embryo Jesuit who was 'too clever by half', given to asking extraordinary questions, and endowed with a penetrating acumen in the detection of falsehood and exaggeration.

Besides Doge, there are innumerable old housemaids always trotting about with cans of hot water and clean towels. There is also a young Italian who does most of the work and gets horribly insulted by Lottie, who once caught him powdering his nose, and will not let him forget it. Indeed, it is one of the few facts in Lottie's recent experience that seems always accessible.

Lottie's parlour, in which most of the life of Shepheard's centres, contains a comprehensive collection of signed photographs. Most of the male members of the royal families of Europe are represented (except the ex-Emperor of Germany, who has not been reinstated, although there was a distinct return of sentiment towards him on the occasion of his second marriage). There are photographs of young men on horses riding in steeplechases, of elderly men leading in the winners of 'classic' races, of horses alone and of young men alone, dressed in tight, white collars or in the uniform of the Brigade of Guards. There are caricatures by 'Spy', and photographs cut from illustrated papers, many of them with brief obituary notices, 'killed in action'. There are photographs of yachts in full sail and of elderly men in yachting caps; there are some funny pictures of the earliest kind of motor car. There are very few writers or painters and no actors, for Lottie is true to the sound old snobbery of pound sterling and strawberry leaves.[5]

Lottie was standing in the hall abusing the Italian waiter when Adam arrived.

'Well,' she said, 'you are a stranger. Come along in. We were just thinking about having a little drink. You'll find a lot of your friends here.'

She led Adam into the parlour, where they found several men, none of whom Adam had ever seen before.

'You all know Lord Thingummy, don't you?' said Lottie.

'Mr Symes,' said Adam.

'Yes, dear, that's what I said. Bless you, I knew you before you were born. How's your father? Not dead, is he?'

'Yes, I'm afraid he is.'

'Well, I never. I could tell you some things about him. Now let me introduce you – that's Mr What's-his-name, you remember him, don't you? And over there in the corner, that's the Major, and there's Mr What-d'you-call-him, and that's an American, and there's the King of Ruritania.'

'Alas, no longer,' said a sad, bearded man.

'Poor chap,' said Lottie Crump, who always had a weak spot for royalty, even when deposed. 'It's a shame. They gave him the boot after the war. Hasn't got a penny. Not that he ever did have much. His wife's locked up in a looney house, too.'

'Poor Maria Christina. It is true how Mrs Crump says. Her brains, they are quite gone out. All the time she thinks everyone is a bomb.'

'It's perfectly true, poor old girl,' said Lottie with relish. 'I drove the King down Saturday to see her . . . (I won't have him travelling third class). It fair brought tears to my eyes. Kept skipping about all the time, she did, dodging. Thought they were throwing things at her.'

'It is one strange thing, too,' said the King. 'All my family they have bombs thrown at them, but the Queen, never. My poor Uncle Joseph he blow all to bits one night at the opera, and my sister she find three bombs in her bed. But my wife, never. But one day her maid is brushing her hair before dinner, and she said, "Madam", she said, "the cook has had lesson from the cook at the French Legation" – the food at my home was not what you call *chic*. One day it was mutton hot, then mutton cold, then the same mutton hot again, but less nicer, not *chic*, you understand me – "he

32

has had lesson from the French cook", the maid say, "and he has made one big bomb as a surprise for your dinner-party to-night for the Swedish Minister." Then the poor Queen say "Oh", like so, and since then always her poor brains has was all nohow.'

The ex-King of Ruritania sighed heavily and lit a cigar.

'Well,' said Lottie, brushing aside a tear, 'what about a little drink? Here, you over there, your Honour Judge What's-your-name, how about a drink for the gentlemen?'

The American, who, like all the listeners, had been profoundly moved by the ex-King's recitation, roused himself to bow and say, 'I shall esteem it a great honour if His Majesty and yourself, Mrs Crump, and these other good gentlemen . . .'

'That's the way,' said Lottie. 'Hi, there, where's my Fairy Prince? Powdering hisself again, I suppose. Come here, Nancy, and put away the beauty cream.'

In came the waiter.

'Bottle of wine,' said Lottie, 'with Judge Thingummy there.'

(Unless specified in detail, all drinks are champagne in Lottie's parlour. There is also a mysterious game played with dice which always ends with someone giving a bottle of wine to everyone in the room, but Lottie has an equitable soul and she generally sees to it, in making up the bills, that the richest people pay for everything.)

After the third or fourth bottle of wine Lottie said, 'Who d'you think we've got dining upstairs to-night? *Prime Minister.*'

'Me, I have never liked Prime Ministers. They talk and talk and then they talk more. "Sir, you must sign that." "Sir, you must go here and there." "Sir, you must do up that button before you give audience to the black plenipotentiary from Liberia." Pah! After the war my people give me the bird, yes, but they throw my Prime Minister out of the window, bump right bang on the floor. Ha, ha.'

'He ain't alone either,' said Lottie with a terrific wink.

'What, Sir James Brown?' said the Major, shocked in spite of himself. 'I don't believe it.'

'No, name of Outrage.'

'He's not Prime Minister.'

'Yes, he is. I saw it in the paper.'

'No, he's not. He went out of office last week.'

'Well I never. How they keep changing. I've no patience with it. Doge. Doge. What's the Prime Minister's name?'

'Beg pardon, mum.'

'What's the name of the Prime Minister?'

'Not to-night, I don't think, mum, not as I've been informed anyway.'

'What's the name of the Prime Minister, you stupid old man?'

'Oh, I beg your pardon, mum. I didn't quite hear you. Sir James Brown, mum, Bart. A very nice gentleman, so I've been told. Conservative, I've heard said. Gloucestershire they come from, I think.'

'There, what did I say?' said Lottie triumphantly.

'It is one very extraordinary thing, your British Constitution,' said the ex-King of Ruritania. 'All the time when I was young they taught me nothing but British Constitution. My tutor had been a master at your Eton school. And now when I come to England always there is a different Prime Minister and no one knows which is which.'

'Oh, sir,' said the Major, 'that's because of the Liberal Party.'[6]

'Liberals? Yes. We, too, had Liberals. I tell you something now, I had a gold fountain-pen. My godfather, the good Archduke of Austria, give me one gold fountain-pen with eagles on him. I loved my gold fountain-pen.' (Tears stood in the King's eyes. Champagne was a rare luxury to him now.) 'I loved very well my pen with the little eagles. And one day there was a Liberal Minister. A Count Tampen, one man, Mrs Crump, of exceedingly evilness. He come to talk to me and he stood at my little escritoire and he thump and talk too much about somethings I not understand, and when he go – where was my gold fountain-pen with eagles – gone too.'

'Poor old King,' said Lottie. 'I tell you what. You have another drink.'

'. . . Esteem it a great honour,' said the American, 'if your Majesty and these gentlemen and Mrs Crump . . .'

'Doge, tell my little love-bird to come hopping in . . . you there, Judge wants another bottle of wine.'

'. . . Should honour it a great esteem . . . esteem it a great honour if Mrs Majesty and these gentlemen and His Crump . . .'

'That's all right, Judge. Another bottle coming.'

'. . . Should esteem it a great Crump if his honour and these Majesties and Mrs Gentlemen . . .'

'Yes, yes, that's all right, Judge. Don't let him fall down, boys. Bless me, how these Americans do drink.'

'. . . I should Crump it a great Majesty if Mrs Esteem . . .'

And his Honour Judge Skimp of the Federal High Court began to laugh rather a lot. (It must be remembered in all these people's favour that none of them had yet dined.)

Now there was a very bland, natty, moustachioed young man sitting there who had been drinking away quietly in the corner without talking to anyone except for an occasional 'Cheerioh' to Judge Skimp. Suddenly he got up and said:

'Bet-you-can't-do-this.'

He put three halfpennies on the table, moved them about very deliberately for a bit, and then looked up with an expression of pride. 'Only touched each halfpenny five times, and changed their positions twice,' he said. 'Do-it-again if you like.'

'Well, isn't he a clever boy?' said Lottie. 'Wherever did they teach you that?'

'Chap-in-a-train showed me,' he said.

'It didn't look very hard,' said Adam.

'Just-you-try. Bet-you-anything-you-like you can't do it.'

'How much will you bet?' Lottie loved this kind of thing.

'Anything-you-like. Five hundred pounds.'

'Go on,' said Lottie. 'You do it. He's got lots of money.'

'All right,' said Adam.

He took the halfpennies and moved them about just as the young man had done. When he finished he said, 'How's that?'

'Well I'm jiggered,' said the young man. 'Never saw anyone do it like that before. I've won a lot of money this week with that trick. Here you are.' And he took out a note-case and gave Adam a five-hundred-pound note.[7] Then he sat down in his corner again.

'Well,' said Lottie with approval, 'that's sporting. Give the boys a drink for that.'

So they all had another drink.

Presently the young man stood up again.

'Toss you double-or-quits,' he said. 'Best-out-of-three.'

'All right,' said Adam.

They tossed twice and Adam won both times.

'Well I'm jiggered,' said the young man, handing over another note. 'You're a lucky chap.'

'He's got pots of money,' said Lottie. 'A thousand pounds is nothing to him.'

(She liked to feel like that about all her guests. Actually in this young man's case she was wrong. He happened to have all that money in his pocket because he had just sold out his few remaining securities to buy a new motor car. So next day he bought a second-hand motor bicycle instead.)

Adam felt a little dizzy, so he had another drink.

'D'you mind if I telephone?' he said.

He rang up Nina Blount.

'Is that Nina?'

'Adam, dear, you're tight already.'

'How d'you know?'

'I can hear it. What is it? I'm just going out to dinner.'

'I just rang up to say that it's all right about our getting married. I've got a thousand pounds.'

'Oh, good. How?'

'I'll tell you when we meet. Where are you dining?'

'Ritz. Archie. Darling, I *am* glad about our getting married.'

'So am I. But don't let's get intense about it.'

'I wasn't, and anyway you're tight.'

He went back to the parlour. Miss Runcible had arrived and was standing in the hall very much dressed up.

'Who's that tart?' asked Lottie.

'That's not a tart, Lottie, that's Agatha Runcible.'

'Looks like a tart. How do you do, my dear, come in. We're just thinking of having a little drink. You know everyone here, of course, don't you? That's the King with the beard . . . No, dearie, the King of Ruritania. You didn't mind my taking you for a tart, did you, dear? You look so like one, got up like that. Of course, I can see you aren't now.'

'*My dear*,' said Miss Runcible, 'if you'd seen me this afternoon . . .' and she began to tell Lottie Crump about the Customs House.

'What would you do if you suddenly got a thousand pounds?' Adam asked.

'A thousand *pound*,' said the King, his eyes growing dreamy at this absurd vision. 'Well, first I should buy a house and a motor car and a yacht and a new pair of gloves, and then I would start one little newspaper in my country to say that I must come back and be the King, and then I don't know what I do, but I have such fun and grandness again.'

'But you can't do all that with a thousand pounds, you know, sir.'

'No . . . can't I not? . . . not with thousand pound . . . Oh, well, then I think I buy a gold pen with eagles on him like the Liberals stole.'

'I know what I'd do,' said the Major. 'I'd put it on a horse.'

'What horse?'

'I can tell you a likely outsider for the November Handicap. Horse named Indian Runner. It's at twenty to one at present, and the odds are likely to lengthen. Now if you were to put a thousand on him to win and he won, why you'd be rich, wouldn't you?'

'Yes, so I would. How marvellous. D'you know, I think I'll do that. It's a *very* good idea. How can I do it?'

'Just you give me the thousand and I'll arrange it.'

'I say, that's awfully nice of you.'

'Not at all.'

'No, really, I think that's frightfully nice of you. Look, here's the money. Have a drink, won't you?'

'No, you have one with me.'

'I said it first.'

'Let's both have one, then.'

'Wait a minute though, I must go and telephone about this.'

He rang up the Ritz and got on to Nina.

'Darling, you do telephone a lot, don't you?'

'Nina, I've something very important to say.'

'Yes, darling.'

'Nina, have you heard of a horse called Indian Runner?'

'Yes, I think so. Why?'

'What sort of a horse is it?'

'My dear, quite the worst sort of horse. Mary Mouse's mother owns it.'

'Not a good horse?'

'No.'

'Not likely to win the November Handicap, I mean.'

'Quite sure not to. I don't suppose it'll run even. Why?'

'I say, Nina, d'you know I don't think we shall be able to get married after all.'

'Why not, my sweet?'

'You see, I've put my thousand pounds on Indian Runner.'

'That was silly. Can't you get it back?'

'I gave it to a Major.'

'What sort of a Major?'

'Rather a drunk one. I don't know his name.'

'Well, I should try and catch him. I must go back and eat now. Good-bye.'

But when he got back to Lottie's parlour the Major was gone.

'What Major?' said Lottie, when he asked about him. 'I never saw a Major.'

'The one you introduced me to in the corner.'

'How d'you know he's a Major?'

'You said he was.'

'My dear boy, I've never seen him before. Now I come to think of it, he did look like a Major, didn't he? But this sweet little girlie here is telling me a story. Go on, my dear. I can hardly bear to hear it, it's so wicked.'

While Miss Runcible finished her story (which began to sound each time she told it more and more like the most lubricous kind of anti-Turkish propaganda) the ex-King of Ruritania told Adam about a Major *he* had known, who had come from Prussia to reorganize the Ruritanian Army. He had disappeared south, taking with him all the mess plate of the Royal Guard, and the Lord Chamberlain's wife, and a valuable pair of candlesticks from the Chapel Royal.

By the time Miss Runcible had finished, Lottie was in a high state of indignation.

'The very idea of it,' she said. 'The dirty hounds. And I used to know your poor father, too, before you were born *or* thought of. I'll talk to the Prime Minister about this,' she said, taking up the telephone. 'Give me Outrage,' she said to the exchange boy. 'He's up in number twelve with a Japanese.'

'Outrage isn't Prime Minister, Lottie.'

'Of course he is. Didn't Doge say so . . . Hullo, is that Outrage? This is Lottie. A fine chap you are, I don't think. Tearing the clothes off the back of a poor innocent girl.'

Lottie prattled on.

Mr Outrage had finished dinner, and, as a matter of fact, the phrasing of this accusation was not wholly inappropriate to his mood. It was some minutes before he began to realize that all this talk was only about Miss Runcible. By that time Lottie's flow of invective had come to an end, but she finished finely.

'Outrage your name, and Outrage your nature,' she said, banging down the receiver. 'And that's what I think of *him*. Now how about a little drink?'

But her party was breaking up. The Major was gone. Judge Skimp was sleeping, his fine white hair in an ash-tray. Adam and Miss Runcible were talking about where they would dine. Soon only the King remained. He gave her his arm with a grace he had acquired many years ago; far away in his sunny little palace, under a great chandelier which scattered with stars of light like stones from a broken necklace, a crimson carpet woven with a pattern of crowned ciphers.

So Lottie and the King went in to dinner together.

Upstairs in No. 12, which is a suite of notable grandeur, Mr Outrage was sliding back down the path of self-confidence he had so laboriously climbed. He really would have brought matters to a crisis if it had not been for that telephone, he told himself, but now

39

the Baroness was saying she was sure he was busy, must be wanting her to go: would he order her car.

It was so difficult. For a European the implications of an invitation to dinner *tête-à-tête* in a private room at Shepheard's were definitely[8] clear. Her acceptance on the first night of his return to England had thrown him into a flutter of expectation. But all through dinner she had been so self-possessed, so supremely social. Yet, surely, just before the telephone rang, surely then, when they left the table and moved to the fire, there had been *something* in the atmosphere. But you never know with Orientals. He clutched his knees and said in a voice which sounded very extraordinary to him, must she go, it was lovely after a fortnight, and then, desperately, he had thought of her in Paris such a lot. (Oh, for words, words! That massed treasury of speech that was his to squander at will, to send bowling and spinning in golden pieces over the floor of the House of Commons; that glorious largesse of vocables he cast far and wide, in ringing handfuls about his constituency!)

The little Baroness Yoshiwara, her golden hands clasped in the lap of her golden Paquin frock, sat where she had been sent, more puzzled than Mr Outrage, waiting for orders. What did the clever Englishman want? If he was busy with his telephone, why did he not send her away; tell her another time to come: if he wanted to be loved, why did he not tell her to come over to him? Why did he not pick her out of her red plush chair and sit her on his knee? Was she, perhaps, looking ugly to-night? She had thought not. It was so hard to know what these Occidentals wanted.

Then the telephone rang again.

'Will you hold on a minute? Father Rothschild wants to speak to you,' said a voice. '. . . Is that you, Outrage? Will you be good enough to come round and see me as soon as you can? There are several things which I must discuss with you.'

'Really, Rothschild . . . I don't see why I should. I have a guest.'

'The baroness had better return immediately. The waiter who brought you your coffee has a brother at the Japanese Embassy.'

'Good God, has he? But why don't you go and worry Brown? He's P.M., you know, not me.'

'You will be in office to-morrow . . . As soon as possible, please, at my usual address.'

'Oh, all right.'

'Why, of course.'

Chapter Four

*

At Archie Schwert's party the fifteenth Marquess of Vanburgh, Earl Vanburgh de Brendon, Baron Brendon, Lord of the Five Isles and Hereditary Grand Falconer to the Kingdom of Connaught, said to the eighth Earl of Balcairn, Viscount Erdinge, Baron Cairn of Balcairn, Red Knight of Lancaster, Count of the Holy Roman Empire and Chenonceaux Herald to the Duchy of Aquitaine, 'Hullo,' he said. 'Isn't this a repulsive party? What are you going to say about it?' for they were both of them, as it happened, gossip writers[9] for the daily papers.

'I've just telephoned my story through,' said Lord Balcairn. 'And now I'm going, thank God.'

'I can't think of what to say,' said Lord Vanburgh. 'My editress said yesterday she was tired of seeing the same names over and over again – and here they are again, all of them. There's Nina Blount's engagement being broken off, but she's not got any publicity value to speak of. Agatha Runcible's usually worth a couple of paragraphs, but they're featuring her as a front-page news story to-morrow over this Customs House business.'

'I made rather a good thing over Edward Throbbing being in a log shanty in Canada which he built himself with the help of one Red Indian. I thought that was fairly good because, you see, I could contrast that with Miles being dressed as a Red Indian to-night, don't you think so, or don't you?'

'I say, that's rather good, may I use it?'

'Well, you can have the shanty, but the Red Indian's mine.'

'Where is he actually?'

'Heaven knows. Government House at Ottawa, I think.'

'Who's that awful-looking woman? I'm sure she's famous in some way. It's not Mrs Melrose Ape, is it? I heard she was coming.'

'Who?'

'That one. Making up to Nina.'

'Good lord, no. She's no one. Mrs Panrast she's called now.'

'She seems to know you.'

'Yes, I've known her all my life. As a matter of fact, she's my mother.'

'My dear, how too shaming. D'you mind if I put that in?'

'I'd sooner you didn't. The family can't bear her. She's been divorced twice since then, you know.'

'My dear, of course not, I quite understand.'

Five minutes later he was busy at the telephone, dictating his story. '. . . Orchid stop, new paragraph. One of the most striking women in the room was Mrs Panrast – P-A-N-R-A-S-T, no, T for telephone, you know – formerly Countess of Balcairn. She dresses with that severely masculine chic, italics, which American women know so well how to assume, stop. Her son, comma, the present Earl, comma, was with her, stop. Lord Balcairn is one of the few young men about town . . .

'. . . the Hon. Miles Malpractice was dressed as a Red Indian. He is at present living in the house of his brother, Lord Throbbing, at which yesterday's party was held. His choice of costume was particularly – what shall I say? hullo, yes – was particularly piquant, italics, since the latest reports of Lord Throbbing say that he is living in a log shack in Canada which he built with his own hands, aided by one Red Indian servant, stop . . .'

You see, that was the kind of party Archie Schwert's party was.

Miss Mouse (in a very enterprising frock by Cheruit) sat on a chair with her eyes popping out of her head. She never *could* get used to so much excitement, never. To-night she had brought a little friend with her – a Miss Brown – because it was so much more fun if one had someone to talk to. It was too thrilling to see all that dull money her father had amassed, metamorphosed in this way into so much glitter and noise and so many bored young faces. Archie Schwert, as he passed, champagne bottle in hand, paused to say, 'How are you, Mary darling? Quite all right?'

'That's Archie Schwert,' said Miss Mouse to Miss Brown. 'Isn't he too clever?'

'Is he?' said Miss Brown, who would have liked a drink, but didn't know quite how to set about it. 'You *are* lucky to know such amusing people, Mary darling. I never see anyone.'

'Wasn't the invitation clever? Johnnie Hoop wrote it.'

'Well, yes, I suppose it was. But you know, was it dreadful of me, I hadn't heard of any of the names.'*

'My dear, of course you have,' said Miss Mouse, feeling somewhere in her depths – those unplumbed places in Miss Mouse's soul – a tiny, most unaccustomed flicker of superiority; for she had gone through that invitation word by word in papa's library some days ago and knew all about it.

She almost wished in this new mood of exaltation that she had come to the party in fancy dress. It was called a Savage party, that is to say that Johnnie Hoop had written on the invitation that they were to come dressed as savages. Numbers of them had done so; Johnnie himself in a mask and black gloves represented the Maharanee of Pukkapore, somewhat to the annoyance of the Maharajah, who happened to drop in. The real aristocracy, the younger members of those two or three great brewing families[11] which rule London, had done nothing about it. They had come on from a dance and stood in a little group by themselves, aloof, amused but not amusing. Pit-a-pat went the heart of Miss Mouse. How she longed to tear down her dazzling frock to her hips and dance like a Bacchante before them all. One day she would surprise them all, thought Miss Mouse.

There was a famous actor making jokes (but it was not so much what he said as the way he said it that made the people laugh who did laugh). 'I've come to the party as a wild widower,' he said.

---

* Perhaps it should be explained – there were at this time three sorts of formal invitation card; there was the nice sensible copy-book hand sort with a name and *At Home* and a date and time and address; then there was the sort that came from Chelsea, *Noel and Audrey are having a little whoopee on Saturday evening*: do please come and bring a bottle too, *if you can*; and finally there was the sort that Johnnie Hoop used to adapt from *Blast* and Marinetti's *Futurist Manifesto*. These had two columns of close print; in one was a list of all the things Johnnie hated, and in the other all the things he thought he liked. Most of the parties which Miss Mouse financed had invitations written by Johnnie Hoop.[10]

They were that kind of joke – but, of course, he made a droll face when he said it.

Miss Runcible had changed into Hawaiian costume and was the life and soul of the evening.

She had heard someone say something about an Independent Labour Party,[12] and was furious that she had not been asked.

There were two men with a lot of explosive powder taking photographs in another room. Their flashes and bangs had rather a disquieting effect on the party, causing a feeling of tension, because everyone looked negligent and said what a bore the papers were, and how *too* like Archie to let the photographers come, but most of them, as a matter of fact, wanted dreadfully to be photographed and the others were frozen with unaffected terror that they might be taken unawares and then their mamas would know where they had been when they said they were at the Bicesters' dance, and then there would be a row again, which was so *exhausting*, if nothing else.

There were Adam and Nina getting rather sentimental.

'D'you know,' she said, pulling out a lump, 'I'd quite made up my mind that your hair was dark?' Archie Schwert, pausing with a bottle of champagne, said, 'Don't be so sadistic, Nina.'

'Go away, hog's rump,' said Adam, in Cockney, adding, in softer tones, 'Are you disappointed?'

'Well, no, but it's rather disconcerting getting engaged to someone with dark hair and finding it's fair.'

'Anyway, we aren't engaged any more, are we – or are we?'

'I'm not sure that we're not. How much money *have* you, Adam?'

'Literally, none, my dear. Poor Agatha had to pay for dinner as it was, and God knows what I'm going to do about Lottie Crump's bill.'

'Of course, you know – Adam, don't fall asleep – there's always papa. I believe he's really much richer than he looks. He might give us some money until your books start paying.'

'You know, if I wrote a book a month I should be free of that contract in a year . . . I hadn't thought of that before. I don't at all see why I shouldn't do that, do you? . . . or do you?'

'Of course not, darling. I'll tell you what. We'll go down and see papa to-morrow, shall we?'

'Yes, that would be divine, darling.'

'Adam, don't go to sleep.'

'Sorry, darling, what I meant was that that would be divine.'

And he went to sleep for a little, with his head in her lap.

'Pretty as a picture,' said Archie, in Cockney, passing with a bottle of champagne in his hand.

'Wake up, Adam,' said Nina, pulling out more hair. 'It's time to go.'

'That would be divine . . . I say, have I been asleep?'

'Yes, for hours and hours. You looked rather sweet.'

'And you sat there . . . I say, Nina, you are getting sentimental . . . Where are we going?'

There were about a dozen people left at the party; that hard kernel of gaiety that never breaks. It was about three o'clock.

'Let's go to Lottie Crump's and have a drink,' said Adam.

So they all got into two taxicabs and drove across Berkeley Square to Dover Street. But at Shepheard's the night porter said that Mrs Crump had just gone to bed. He thought that Judge Skimp was still up with some friends; would they like to join them? They went up to Judge Skimp's suite, but there had been a disaster there with a chandelier that one of his young ladies had tried to swing on. They were bathing her forehead with champagne; two of them were asleep.

So Adam's party went out again, into the rain.

'Of course, there's always the Ritz,' said Archie. 'I believe the night porter can usually get one a drink.' But he said it in the sort of voice that made all the others say, no, the Ritz was too, too boring at that time of night.

They went to Agatha Runcible's house, which was quite near, but she found that she'd lost her latchkey, so that was no good. Soon someone would say those fatal words, 'Well, I think it's time for me to go to bed. Can I give anyone a lift to Knightsbridge?' and the party would be over.

But instead a little breathless voice said, 'Why don't you come to *my* house?'

It was Miss Brown.

So they all got into taxicabs again and drove rather a long way to Miss Brown's house. She turned on the lights in a sombre dining-room and gave them glasses of whisky and soda. (She turned out to be rather a good hostess, though over-zealous.) Then Miles said he wanted something to eat, so they all went downstairs into a huge kitchen lined with every shape of pot and pan and found some eggs and some bacon and Miss Brown cooked them. Then they had some more whisky upstairs and Adam fell asleep again. Presently Vanburgh said, 'D'you mind if I use the telephone? I must just send the rest of my story to the paper.' Miss Brown took him to a study that looked almost like an office, and he dictated the rest of his column, and then he came back and had some more whisky.

It was a lovely evening for Miss Brown. Flushed with successful hospitality, she trotted from guest to guest, offering here a box of matches, there a cigar, there a fruit from the enormous gilt dishes on the sideboard. To think that all these brilliant people, whom she had heard so much about, with what envy, from Miss Mouse, should be here in papa's dining-room, calling her 'my dear' and 'darling'. And when at last they said they really had to go, Miss Runcible said, 'Well, *I* can't go, because I've lost my latchkey. D'you mind awfully if I sleep here?'

Miss Brown, her heart in her mouth, but in the most natural way possible, said, 'Of course not, Agatha darling, that would be divine.'

And then Miss Runcible said, 'How too divine of you, darling.'
Rapture!

At half-past nine the next morning the Brown family came down to breakfast in the dining-room.

There were four quiet girls (of whom the Miss Brown who had given the party was the youngest), their brother worked in the motor shop and had had to get off early. They were seated at the table when their mama came down.

'Now, children,' she said, 'do try to remember to talk to your father at breakfast. He was quite hurt yesterday. He feels out of things. It's so easy to bring him into the conversation if you take a little trouble, and he does so enjoy hearing about everything.'

'Yes, Mama,' they said. 'We do try, you know.'

'And what was the Bicesters' dance like, Jane?' she said, pouring out some coffee. 'Did you have a good time?'

'It was just too divine,' said the youngest Miss Brown.

'It was *what*, Jane?'

'I mean it was *lovely*, Mama.'

'So I should think. You girls are very lucky nowadays. There were not nearly so many dances when I was your age. Perhaps two a week in the season, you know, but *none* before Christmas ever.'

'Mama.'

'Yes, Jane.'

'Mama. I asked a girl to stay the night.'

'Yes, dear. When? We're rather full up, you know.'

'Last night, Mama.'

'What an extraordinary thing to do. Did she accept?'

'Yes, she's here now.'

'*Well* . . . Ambrose, will you tell Mrs Sparrow to put on another egg?'

'I'm very sorry, my lady, Mrs Sparrow can't understand it, but there *are* no eggs this morning. She thinks there must have been burglars.'

'Nonsense, Ambrose, who ever heard of burglars coming into a house to steal eggs?'

'The shells were all over the floor, my lady.'

'I see. That's all, thank you, Ambrose. Well, Jane, has your guest eaten all our eggs too?'

'Well, I'm afraid she has . . . at least . . . I mean . . .'

At this moment Agatha Runcible came down to breakfast. She was not looking her best really in the morning light.

'Good morning, all,' she said in Cockney. 'I've found the right room at last. D'you know, I popped into a study or something. There was a sweet old boy sitting at a desk. He *did* look surprised to see me. Was it your papa?'

'This is Mama,' said Jane.

'How are you?' said Miss Runcible. 'I say, I think it's quite too sweet of you to let me come down to breakfast like this.' (It must be remembered that she was still in Hawaiian costume.) 'Are you sure you're not *furious* with me? All this is really much more embarrassing for *me*, isn't it, don't you think . . . or don't you?'

'Do you take tea or coffee?' at last Jane's mother managed to say. 'Jane, dear, give your friend some breakfast.' For in the course of a long public life she had formed the opinion that a judicious offer of food eased most social situations.

Then Jane's father came in.

'Martha, the most extraordinary thing! . . . I think I must be losing my reason. I was in my study just now going over that speech for this afternoon, when suddenly the door opened and in came a sort of dancing Hottentot woman half-naked. It just said, "Oh, how shy-making", and then disappeared, and . . . oh . . .' For he had suddenly caught sight of Miss Runcible '. . . oh . . . how do you do? . . . How . . .?'

'I don't think you have met my husband before.'

'Only for a second,' said Miss Runcible.

'I hope you slept well,' said Jane's father desperately. 'Martha never told me we had a guest. Forgive me if I appeared inhospitable . . . I – er . . . Oh, why doesn't somebody else say something?'

Miss Runcible, too, was feeling the strain. She picked up the morning paper.

'Here's something terribly funny,' she said, by way of making conversation. 'Shall I read it to you?'

'"*Midnight Orgies at No. 10.*" My dear, isn't that divine? Listen, "*What must be the most extraordinary party of the little season took place in the small hours of this morning at No. 10 Downing Street. At about 4 a.m. the policemen who are always posted outside the Prime Minister's residence were surprised to witness*" – Isn't this too amusing – "*the arrival of a fleet of taxis, from which emerged a gay throng in exotic fancy dress*" – How I should have loved to have seen it. Can't you imagine what they were like? – "*the hostess of what was described by one of the guests as the brightest party the Bright Young People have yet given, was no other than Miss Jane Brown, the youngest of the Prime Minister's four lovely daughters. The Honourable Agatha* . . ." Why, what an extraordinary thing . . . Oh, my God!'

Suddenly light came flooding in on Miss Runcible's mind as once when, in her débutante days, she had gone behind the scenes at a charity matinée, and returning had stepped through the wrong door and found herself in a blaze of flood-lights on the stage in the middle of the last act of *Othello*. 'Oh, my God!' she said, looking round the Brown breakfast table. 'Isn't that just too bad of Vanburgh. He's always doing that kind of thing. It really would serve him right if we complained and he lost his job, don't you think so, Sir James . . . or . . . don't you?'

Miss Runcible paused and met the eyes of the Brown family once more.

'Oh, dear,' she said, 'this really is all too bogus.'

Then she turned round and, trailing garlands of equatorial flowers, fled out of the room and out of the house to the huge delight and profit of the crowd of reporters and Press photographers who were already massed round the historic front door.

Chapter Five

*

Adam woke up feeling terribly ill. He rang his bell once or twice, but nobody came. Later he woke up again and rang the bell. The Italian waiter appeared, undulating slightly in the doorway. Adam ordered breakfast. Lottie came in and sat on his bed.

'Had a nice breakfast, dear?' she said.

'Not yet,' said Adam. 'I've only just woken up.'

'That's right,' said Lottie. 'Nothing like a nice breakfast. There was a young lady for you on the 'phone, but I can't remember what it was she said at the minute. We've all been upside down this morning. Such a fuss. Had the police in, we have, ever since I don't know what time, drinking up my wine and asking questions and putting their noses where they're not wanted. All because Flossie must needs go and swing on the chandelier. She never had any sense, Flossie. Well, she's learned her lesson now, poor girl. Whoever heard of such a thing – swinging on a chandelier. Poor Judge What's-his-name is in a terrible state about it. I said to him it's not so much the price of the chandelier, I said. What money can make, money can mend, I said, and that's the truth, isn't it, dear? But what I mind, I said, is having a death in the house and all the fuss. It doesn't do *anyone* any good having people killing theirselves in a house like Flossie did. Now what may *you* want, my Italian queen?' said Lottie as the waiter came in with a tray, the smell of kippers contending with *nuit de Noël* rather disagreeably.

'Gentleman's breakfast,' said the waiter.

'And how many *more* breakfasts do you think he wants, I should like to know? He's had his breakfast hours ago while you were powdering your nose downstairs, haven't you, dear?'

'No,' said Adam, 'as a matter of fact, no.'

'There, do you hear what the gentleman says? *He* doesn't want two breakfasts. Don't stand there wiggling your behind at me. Take it away quick or I'll catch you such a smack . . . That's just the way – once you get the police in everyone gets all upset. There's that boy brings you two breakfasts and I dare say there's some poor fellow along the passage somewhere who hasn't had any breakfast at all. You can't get anywhere without a nice breakfast. Half the young fellows as come here now don't have anything except a *cachet Faivre*[3] and some orange juice. It's not right,' said Lottie, 'and I've spoken to that boy about using scent twenty times if I've spoken once.'

The waiter's head appeared, and with it another wave of *nuit de Noël.*

'If you please, madam, the inspectors want to speak to you downstairs, madam.'

'All right, my little bird of paradise, I'll be there.'

Lottie trotted away and the waiter came sidling back bearing his tray of kippers and leering at Adam with a horrible intimacy.

'Turn on my bath, will you, please,' said Adam.

'Alas, there is a gentleman asleep in the bath. Shall I wake him?'

'No, it doesn't matter.'

'Will that be all, sir?'

'Yes, thank you.'

The waiter stood about fingering the brass knobs at the end of the bed, smiling ingratiatingly. Then he produced from under his coat a gardenia, slightly browned at the edges. (He had found it in an evening coat he had just been brushing.)

Would the signor perhaps like a buttonhole? ... Madame Crump was so severe . . . it was nice sometimes to be able to have a talk with the gentlemen . . .

'No,' said Adam. 'Go away.' For he had a headache.

The waiter sighed deeply, and walked with pettish steps to the door; sighed again and took the gardenia to the gentleman in the bathroom.

Adam ate some breakfast. No kipper, he reflected, is ever as good as it smells; how this too earthly contact with flesh and bone spoiled the first happy exhilaration; if only one could live, as Jehovah was said to have done, on the savour of burnt offerings. He lay back for a little in his bed thinking about the smells of food, of the greasy horror of fried fish and the deeply moving smell that came from it; of the intoxicating breath of bakeries and the dullness of buns . . . He planned dinners of enchanting aromatic foods that should be carried under the nose, snuffed and thrown to the dogs . . . endless dinners, in which one could alternate flavour with flavour from sunset to dawn without satiety, while one breathed great draughts of the bouquet of old brandy . . . Oh for the wings of a dove, thought Adam, wandering a little from the point as he fell asleep again (everyone is liable to this ninetyish feeling in the early morning after a party).

Presently the telephone by Adam's bed began ringing.

'Hullo, yes.'

'Lady to speak to you . . . Hullo, is that you, Adam?'

'Is that Nina?'

'How are you, my darling?'

'*Oh, Nina* . . .'

'My poor sweet, I feel like that, too. Listen, angel. You haven't forgotten that you're going to see my papa to-day, have you . . . or have you? I've just sent him a wire to say that you're going to lunch with him. D'you know where he lives?'

'But you're coming too?'

'Well, no. I don't think I will, if you don't mind . . . I've got rather a pain.'

'My dear, if you *knew* what a pain I've got . . .'

'Yes, but that's different, darling. Anyway, there's no object in our both going.'

'But what am I to say?'

'*Darling*, don't be tiresome. You know perfectly well. Just ask him for some money.'

'Will he like that?'

'Yes, darling, of course he will. Why will you go *on*? I've got to get up now. Good-bye. Take care of yourself . . . Ring me up when you get back and tell me what papa said. By the way, have you seen the paper this morning? – there's something so funny about last night. *Too* bad of Van. Good-bye.'

While Adam was dressing, he realized that he did not know

where he was to go. He rang up again. 'By the way, Nina, where does your papa live?'

'Didn't I tell you? It's a house called Doubting, and it's all falling down really. You go to Aylesbury by train and then take a taxi. They're the most expensive taxis in the world, too . . . Have you got any money?'

Adam looked on the dressing-table: 'About seven shillings,' he said.

'My dear, that's not enough. You'll have to make poor papa pay for the taxi.'

'Will he like that?'

'Yes, of course, he's an angel.'

'I wish you'd come too, Nina.'

'Darling, I told you. I've got such a pain.'

Downstairs, as Lottie had said, everything was upside down. That is to say that there were policemen and reporters teeming in every corner of the hotel, each with a bottle of champagne and a glass. Lottie, Doge, Judge Skimp, the Inspector, four plain-clothes men and the body were in Judge Skimp's suite.

'What is *not* clear to me, sir,' said the Inspector, 'is what *prompted* the young lady to swing on the chandelier. Not wishing to cause offence, sir, and begging your pardon, was she . . .?'

'Yes,' said Judge Skimp, 'she was.'

'*Exactly*,' said the Inspector. 'A clear case of misadventure, eh, Mrs Crump? There'll have to be an inquest, of course, but I think probably I shall be able to arrange things so that there is no mention of your name in the case, sir . . . well, that's very kind of you, Mrs Crump, perhaps just one more glass.'

'Lottie,' said Adam, 'can you lend me some money?'

'Money, dear? Of course. Doge, have you got any money?'

'I was asleep at the time myself, mum, and was not even made aware of the occurrence until I was called this morning. Being slightly deaf, the sound of the disaster . . .'

'Judge What's-your-name, got any money?'

'I should take it as a great privilege if I could be of any assistance . . .'

'That's right, give some to young Thingummy here. That all you want, deary? Don't run away. We're just thinking of having a little drink . . . No, not that wine, dear, it's what we keep for the police. I've just ordered a better bottle if my young butterfly would bring it along.'

Adam had a glass of champagne, hoping it would make him feel a little better. It made him feel much worse.

Then he went to Marylebone. It was Armistice Day, and they were selling artificial poppies in the streets. As he reached the station it struck eleven and for two minutes all over the country everyone was quiet and serious. Then he went to Aylesbury, reading on the way Balcairn's account of Archie Schwert's party. He was pleased to see himself described as 'the brilliant young novelist', and wondered whether Nina's papa read gossip paragraphs, and supposed not. The two women opposite him in the carriage obviously did.

'I no sooner opened the paper,' said one, 'than I was on the 'phone *at once* to all the ladies of the committee, and we'd sent off a wire to our Member before one o'clock. We know how to make things hum at the Bois. I've got a copy of what we sent. Look. *Members of the Committee of the Ladies' Conservative Association at Chesham Bois wish to express their extreme displeasure at reports in this morning's paper of midnight party at No. 10. They call upon Captain Crutwell* – that's our Member; such a nice stamp of man – *strenuously to withhold support to Prime Minister.* It cost nearly four shillings, but, as I said at the time, it was not a moment to spoil the ship for a ha'p'orth of tar. Don't you agree, Mrs Ithewaite?'

'I do, indeed, Mrs Orraway-Smith. It is clearly a case in which a mandate from the constituencies is required. I'll talk to our chairwoman at Wendover.'

'Yes, do, Mrs Ithewaite. It is in a case like this that the woman's vote can count.'

'If it's a choice between my moral judgment and the nationalization of banking, I prefer nationalization, if you see what I mean.'

'Exactly what I think. Such a terrible example to the lower classes, *apart from everything*.'

'That's what I mean. There's our Agnes, now. How can I stop her having young men in the kitchen when she knows that Sir James Brown has parties like that at all hours of the night . . .'

They were both wearing hats like nothing on earth, which bobbed and nodded as they spoke.

At Aylesbury Adam got into a Ford taxi and asked to be taken to a house called Doubting.

'Doubting 'All?'

'Well, I suppose so. Is it falling down?'

'Could do with a lick of paint,' said the driver, a spotty youth. 'Name of Blount?'

'That's it.'

'Long way from here Doubting 'All is. Cost you fifteen bob.'

'All right.'

'If you're a commercial, I can tell you straight it ain't no use going to 'im. Young feller asked me the way there this morning. Driving a Morris. Wanted to sell him a vacuum cleaner. Old boy 'ad answered an advertisement asking for a demonstration. When he got there the old boy wouldn't even look at it. Can you beat that?'

'No, I'm not trying to sell him anything – at least not exactly.'

'Personal visit, perhaps.'

'Yes.'

'Ah.'

Satisfied that his passenger was in earnest about the journey, the taxi-driver put on some coats – for it was raining – got out of his seat and cranked up the engine. Presently they started.

They drove for a mile or two past bungalows and villas and timbered public houses to a village in which every house seemed to be a garage and filling station. Here they left the main road and Adam's discomfort became acute.

At last they came to twin octagonal lodges and some heraldic gate-posts and large wrought-iron gates, behind which could be seen a broad sweep of ill-kept drive.

'Doubting 'All,' said the driver.

He blew his horn once or twice, but no lodge-keeper's wife,

aproned and appled-cheeked, appeared to bob them in. He got out and shook the gates reproachfully.

'Chained-and-locked,' he said. 'Try another way.'

They drove on for another mile; on the side of the Hall the road was bordered by dripping trees and a dilapidated stone wall; presently they reached some cottages and a white gate. This they opened and turned into a rough track, separated from the park by low iron railings. There were sheep grazing on either side. One of them had strayed into the drive. It fled before them in a frenzied trot, stopping and looking round over its dirty tail and then plunging on again until its agitation brought it to the side of the path, where they overtook it and passed it.

The track led to some stables, then behind rows of hothouses, among potting-sheds and heaps of drenched leaves, past non-descript outbuildings that had once been laundry and bakery and brewhouse and a huge kennel where once someone had kept a bear, until suddenly it turned by a clump of holly and elms and laurel bushes into an open space that had once been laid with gravel. A lofty Palladian façade stretched before them and in front of it an equestrian statue pointed a baton imperiously down the main drive.

''Ere y'are,' said the driver.

Adam paid him and went up the steps to the front door. He rang the bell and waited. Nothing happened. Presently he rang again. At this moment the door opened.

'Don't ring twice,' said a very angry old man. 'What do you want?'

'Is Mr Blount in?'

'There's no Mr Blount here. This is Colonel Blount's house.'

'I'm sorry . . . I think the Colonel is expecting me to luncheon.'

'Nonsense. I'm Colonel Blount,' and he shut the door.

The Ford had disappeared. It was still raining hard. Adam rang again.

'Yes,' said Colonel Blount, appearing instantly.

'I wonder if you'd let me telephone to the station for a taxi?'

'Not on the telephone . . . It's raining. Why don't you come in?

57

It's absurd to walk to the station in this. Have you come about the vacuum cleaner?'

'No.'

'Funny, I've been expecting a man all the morning to show me a vacuum cleaner. Come in, do. Won't you stay to luncheon?'

'I should love to.'

'Splendid. I get very little company nowadays. You must forgive me for opening the door to you myself. My butler is in bed to-day. He suffers terribly in his feet when it is wet. Both my footmen were killed in the war . . . Put your hat and coat here. I hope you haven't got wet . . . I'm sorry you didn't bring the vacuum cleaner . . . but never mind. How are you?' he said, suddenly holding out his hand.

They shook hands and Colonel Blount led the way down a long corridor, lined with marble busts on yellow marble pedestals, to a large room full of furniture, with a fire burning in a fine rococo fireplace. There was a large leather-topped walnut writing-table under a window opening on to a terrace. Colonel Blount picked up a telegram and read it.

'I'd quite forgotten,' he said in some confusion. 'I'm afraid you'll think me very discourteous, but it is, after all, impossible for me to ask you to luncheon. I have a guest coming on very intimate family business. You understand, don't you? . . . To tell you the truth, it's some young rascal who wants to marry my daughter. I must see him alone to discuss settlements.'

'Well, I want to marry your daughter, too,' said Adam.

'What an extraordinary coincidence. Are you sure you do?'

'Perhaps the telegram may be about me. What does it say?'

' "*Engaged to marry Adam Symes. Expect him luncheon. Nina.*" Are you Adam Symes?'

'Yes.'

'My dear boy, why didn't you say so before, instead of going on about a vacuum cleaner? How are you?'

They shook hands again.

'If you don't mind,' said Colonel Blount, 'we will keep our business until after luncheon. I'm afraid everything is looking very bare at present. You must come down and see the gardens in the summer. We had some lovely hydrangeas last year. I don't think I shall live here another winter. Too big for an old man. I was looking at some of the houses they're putting up outside Aylesbury. Did you see them coming along? Nice little red houses. Bathroom and everything. Quite cheap, too, and near the cinematographs. I hope you are fond of the cinematograph too? The Rector and I go a great deal. I hope you'll like the Rector. Common little man rather. But he's got a motor car, useful that. How long are you staying?'

'I promised Nina I'd be back to-night.'

'That's a pity. They change the film at the Electra Palace. We might have gone.'

An elderly woman servant came in to announce luncheon. 'What is at the Electra Palace, do you know, Mrs Florin?'

'Greta Garbo[14] in *Venetian Kisses*, I think, sir.'

'I don't really think I like Greta Garbo. I've tried to,' said Colonel Blount, 'but I just don't.'

They went in to luncheon in a huge dining-room dark with family portraits.

'If you don't mind,' said Colonel Blount, 'I prefer not to talk at meals.'

He propped a morocco-bound volume of *Punch* before his plate against a vast silver urn, from which grew a small castor-oil plant.

'Give Mr Symes a book,' he said.

Mrs Florin put another volume of *Punch* beside Adam.

'If you come across anything really funny read it to me,' said Colonel Blount.

Then they had luncheon.

They were nearly an hour over luncheon. Course followed course in disconcerting abundance while Colonel Blount ate and ate, turning the leaves of his book and chuckling frequently. They ate hare soup and boiled turbot and stewed sweetbreads and black Bradenham ham with Madeira sauce and roast pheasant and a rum omelette and toasted cheese and fruit. First they drank sherry, then claret, then port. Then Colonel Blount shut his book with a broad sweep of his arm rather as the headmaster of Adam's private school used to shut the Bible after evening prayers, folded his napkin carefully and stuffed it into a massive silver ring, muttered some words of grace and finally stood up, saying:

'Well, I don't know about you, but I'm going to have a little nap,' and trotted out of the room.

'There's a fire in the library, sir,' said Mrs Florin. 'I'll bring you your coffee there. The Colonel doesn't have coffee, he finds it interferes with his afternoon sleep. What time would you like your afternoon tea, sir?'

'I ought really to be getting back to London. How long will it be before the Colonel comes down, do you think?'

'Well, it all depends, sir. Not usually till about five or half-past. Then he reads until dinner at seven and after dinner he gets the Rector to drive him in to the pictures. A sedentary life, as you might say.'

She led Adam into the library and put a silver coffee-pot at his elbow.

'I'll bring you tea at four,' she said.

Adam sat in front of the fire in a deep armchair. Outside the rain beat on the double windows. There were several magazines in the library – mostly cheap weeklies devoted to the cinema. There was a stuffed owl and a case of early British remains, bone pins and bits of pottery and a skull, which had been dug up in the park many years ago and catalogued by Nina's governess. There was a cabinet containing the relics of Nina's various collecting fevers – some butterflies and a beetle or two, some fossils and some birds' eggs and a few postage stamps. There were some bookcases of superbly unreadable books, a gun, a butterfly net, an alpenstock in the corner. There were catalogues of agricultural machines and acetylene plants, lawn mowers, 'sports requisites'. There was a fire screen worked with a coat of arms. The chimney-piece was hung with the embroidered saddle-cloths of Colonel Blount's regiment of Lancers. There was an engraving of all the members of the Royal Yacht Squadron, with a little plan in the corner, marked to show who was who. There were many other things of equal interest besides, but before Adam had noticed any more he was fast asleep.

*

Mrs Florin woke him at four. The coffee had disappeared and its place was taken by a silver tray with a lace cloth on it. There was a silver tea-pot, and a silver kettle with a little spirit-lamp underneath, and a silver cream jug and a covered silver dish full of muffins. There was also hot buttered toast and honey and gentleman's relish and a chocolate cake, a cherry cake, a seed cake and a fruit cake and some tomato sandwiches and pepper and salt and currant bread and butter.

'Would you care for a lightly boiled egg, sir? The Colonel generally has one if he's awake.'

'No, thank you,' said Adam. He felt a thousand times better for his rest. When Nina and he were married, he thought, they would often come down there for the day after a really serious party. For the first time he noticed an obese liver-and-white spaniel, which was waking up, too, on the hearthrug.

'Please not to give her muffins,' said Mrs Florin, 'it's the one thing she's not supposed to have, and the Colonel will give them to her. He loves that dog,' she added with a burst of confidence. 'Takes her to the pictures with him of an evening. Not that she can appreciate them really like a human can.'

Adam gave her – the spaniel, not Mrs Florin – a gentle prod with his foot and a lump of sugar. She licked his shoe with evident cordiality. Adam was not above feeling flattered by friendliness in dogs.

He had finished his tea and was filling his pipe when Colonel Blount came into the library.

'Who the devil are you?' said his host.

'Adam Symes,' said Adam.

'Never heard of you. How did you get in? Who gave you tea? What do you want?'

'You asked me to luncheon,' said Adam. 'I came about being married to Nina.'

'My dear boy, of course. How absurd of me. I've such a bad memory for names. It comes of seeing so few people. How are you?'

They shook hands again.

'So you're the young man who's engaged to Nina,' said the Colonel, eyeing him for the first time in the way prospective sons-in-laws are supposed to be eyed. 'Now what in the world do you want to get married for? I shouldn't, you know, really I shouldn't. Are you rich?'

'No, not at present, I'm afraid, that's rather what I wanted to talk about.'

'How much money have you got?'

'Well, sir, actually at the moment I haven't got any at all.'

'When did you last have any?'

'I had a thousand pounds last night, but I gave it all to a drunk Major.'

'Why did you do that?'

'Well, I hoped he'd put it on Indian Runner for the November Handicap.'

'Never heard of the horse. Didn't he?'

'I don't think he can have.'

'When will you next have some money?'

'When I've written some books.'

'How many books?'

'Twelve.'

'How much will you have then?'

'Probably fifty pounds advance on my thirteenth book.'

'And how long will it take you to write twelve books?'

'About a year.'

'How long would it take most people?'

'About twenty years. Of course, put like that I do see that it sounds rather hopeless . . . but, you see, Nina and I hoped that you, that is, that perhaps for the next year until I get my twelve books written, that you might help us . . .'

'How could I help you? I've never written a book in my life.'

'No, we thought you might give us some money.'

'You thought that, did you?'

'Yes, that's what we thought . . .'

Colonel Blount looked at him gravely for some time. Then he said, 'I think that an admirable idea. I don't see any reason at all why I shouldn't. How much do you want?'

'That's really terribly good of you, sir . . . Well, you know, just enough to live on quietly for a bit. I hardly know . . .'

'Well, would a thousand pounds be any help?'

'Yes, it would indeed. We shall both be terribly grateful.'

'Not at all, my dear boy. Not at all. What did you say your name was?'

'Adam Symes.'

Colonel Blount went to the table and wrote out a cheque. 'There you are,' he said. 'Now don't go giving that away to another drunk major.'

'Really, sir! I don't know how to thank you. Nina . . .'

'Not another word. Now I expect that you will want to be off to London again. We'll send Mrs Florin across to the Rectory and make the Rector drive you to the station. Useful having a neighbour with a motor car. They charge fivepence on the buses from here to Aylesbury. *Robbers.*'

It does not befall many young men to be given a thousand pounds by a complete stranger twice on successive evenings. Adam laughed aloud in the Rector's car as they drove to the station. The Rector, who had been in the middle of writing a sermon and resented with daily increasing feeling Colonel Blount's neighbourly appropriation of his car and himself, kept his eyes fixed on the streaming windscreen, pretending not to notice. Adam laughed all the way to Aylesbury, sitting and holding his knees and shaking all over. The Rector could hardly bring himself to say good night when they parted in the station yard.

There was half an hour to wait for a train and the leaking roof and wet railway lines had a sobering effect on Adam. He bought an evening paper. On the front page was an exquisitely funny photograph of Miss Runcible in Hawaiian costume tumbling down the steps of No. 10 Downing Street. The Government had fallen that afternoon, he read, being defeated on a motion rising from the answer to a question about the treatment of Miss Runcible by Customs House officers. It was generally held in Parliamentary circles that the deciding factor in this reverse had been the revolt of the Liberals and the Nonconformist members at the revelations of the life that was led at No. 10 Downing Street, during

Sir James Brown's tenancy. The *Evening Mail* had a leading article, which drew a fine analogy between Public and Domestic Purity, between sobriety in the family and in the State.

There was another small paragraph which interested Adam.

'Tragedy in West-End Hotel

The death occurred early this morning at a private hotel in Dover Street of Miss Florence Ducane, described as being of independent means, following an accident in which Miss Ducane fell from a chandelier which she was attempting to mend. The inquest will be held to-morrow, which will be followed by the cremation at Golders Green. Miss Ducane, who was formerly connected with the stage, was well known in business circles.'

Which only showed, thought Adam, how much better Lottie Crump knew the business of avoiding undesirable publicity than Sir James Brown.

When Adam reached London the rain had stopped, but there was a thin fog drifting in belts before a damp wind. The station was crowded with office workers hurrying with attaché-cases and evening papers to catch their evening trains home, coughing and sneezing as they went. They still wore their poppies. Adam went to a telephone-box and rang up Nina. She had left a message for him that she was having cocktails at Margot Metroland's house. He drove to Shepheard's.

'Lottie,' he said, 'I've got a thousand pounds.'

'Have you, now,' said Lottie indifferently. She lived on the assumption that everyone she knew always had several thousand pounds. It was to her as though he had said, 'Lottie, I have a tall hat.'

'Can you lend me some money till to-morrow till I cash the cheque?'

'What a boy you are for borrowing. Just like your poor father. Here, you in the corner, lend Mr What-d'you-call-him some money.'

A tall Guardsman shook his retreating forehead and twirled his moustaches.

'No good coming to me, Lottie,' he said in a voice trained to command.

'Mean hound,' said Lottie. 'Where's that American?'

Judge Skimp, who, since his experiences that morning, had become profoundly Anglophile, produced two ten-pound notes. 'I shall be only too proud and honoured . . .' he said.

'Good old Judge Thingummy,' said Lottie. 'That's the way.'

Adam hurried out into the hall as another bottle of champagne popped festively in the parlour.

'Doge, ring up the Daimler Hire Company and order a car in my name. Tell it to go round to Lady Metroland's – Pastmaster House, Hill Street,' he said. Then he put on his hat and walked down Hay Hill, swinging an umbrella and laughing again, only more quietly, to himself.

At Lady Metroland's he kept on his coat and waited in the hall.

'Will you please tell Miss Blount I've called for her? No, I won't go up.'

He looked at the hats on the table. Clearly there was quite a party. Two or three silk hats of people who had dressed early, the rest soft and black like his own. Then he began to dance again, jigging to himself in simple high spirits.

In a minute Nina came down the broad Adam staircase.

'Darling, why didn't you come up? It's so rude. Margot is longing to see you.'

'I'm so sorry, Nina. I couldn't face a party. I'm so excited.'

'Why, what's happened?'

'Everything. I'll tell you in the car.'

'Car?'

'Yes, it'll be here in a minute. We're going down to the country for dinner. I can't tell you how clever I've been.'

'But what have you done, darling? Do stop dancing about.'

'Can't stop. You've no idea how clever I am.'

'Adam. Are you tight again?'

'Look out of the window and see if you can see a Daimler waiting.'

'Adam, what *have* you been doing? I will be told.'

'Look,' said Adam, producing the cheque. 'Whatcher think of that?' he added in Cockney.

'*My dear*, a thousand pounds. Did papa give you that?'

'I earned it,' said Adam. 'Oh, I earned it. You should have seen the luncheon I ate and the jokes I read. I'm going to be married to-morrow. Oh, Nina, would Margot hate it if I sang in her hall?'

'She'd simply loathe it, darling, and so should I. I'm going to take care of that cheque. You remember what happened the last time you were given a thousand pounds.'

'That's what your papa said.'

'Did you tell him that?'

'I told him everything – and he gave me a thousand pounds.'

'. . . Poor Adam . . .' said Nina suddenly.

'Why did you say that?'

'I don't know . . . I believe this is your car . . .'

'Nina, why did you say "Poor Adam"?'

'. . . Did I? . . . Oh, I don't know . . . Oh, I do adore you so.'

'I'm going to be married to-morrow. Are you?'

'Yes, I expect so, dear.'

The chauffeur got rather bored while they tried to decide where they would dine. At every place he suggested they gave a little wail of dismay. 'But that's sure to be full of awful people we know,' they said. Maidenhead, Thame, Brighton, he suggested. Finally they decided to go to Arundel.

'It'll be nearly nine before we get there,' the chauffeur said. 'Now there's a very nice hotel at Bray . . .'

But they went to Arundel.

'We'll be married to-morrow,' said Adam in the car. 'And we won't ask anybody to the wedding at all. And we'll go abroad at once, and just not come back till I've written all those books. Nina, isn't it divine? Where shall we go?'

'Anywhere you like, only rather warm, don't you think?'

'I don't believe you really think we are going to be married, Nina, do you, or do you?'

'I don't know . . . it's only that I don't believe that really divine things like that ever do happen . . . I don't know why . . . Oh, I do like you so much to-night. If only you *knew* how sweet you looked skipping about in Margot's hall all by yourself. I'd been watching you for hours before I came down.'

'I shall send the car back,' said Adam, as they drove through Pulborough. 'We can go home by train.'

'If there is a train.'

'There's bound to be,' said Adam. But this raised a question in both their minds that had been unobtrusively agitating them throughout the journey. Neither said any more on the subject, but there was a distinct air of constraint in the Daimler from Pulborough onwards.

This question was settled when they reached the hotel at Arundel.

'We want dinner,' said Adam, 'and a room for the night.'

'*Darling*, am I going to be seduced?'

'I'm afraid you are. Do you mind terribly?'

'Not as much as all that,' said Nina, and added in Cockney, 'Charmed, I'm sure.'

Everyone had finished dinner. They dined alone in a corner of the coffee-room, while the other waiters laid the tables for breakfast, looking at them resentfully. It was the dreariest kind of English dinner. After dinner the lounge was awful; there were some golfers in dinner-jackets playing bridge, and two old ladies. Adam and Nina went across the stable-yard to the tap-room and sat until closing-time in a warm haze of tobacco smoke listening to the intermittent gossip of the townspeople. They sat hand-in-hand, unembarrassed; after the first minute no one noticed them. Just before closing time Adam stood a round of drinks. They said:

'Good health, sir. Best respects, madam,' and the barman said, 'Come along, please. Finish your drinks, please,' in a peculiar singsong tone.

There was a clock chiming as they crossed the yard and a slightly drunk farmer trying to start up his car. Then they went up an oak staircase lined with blunderbusses and coaching prints to their room.

They had no luggage (the chambermaid remarked on this next

day to the young man who worked at the wireless shop, saying that that was the worst of being in a main-road hotel. You got all sorts).

Adam undressed very quickly and got into bed; Nina more slowly arranging her clothes on the chair and fingering the ornaments on the chimney-piece with less than her usual self-possession. At last she put out the light.

'Do you know,' she said, trembling slightly as she got into bed, 'this is the first time this has happened to me?'

'It's great fun,' said Adam, 'I promise you.'

'I'm sure it is,' said Nina seriously, 'I wasn't saying anything against it. I was only saying that it hadn't happened before . . . Oh, Adam . . .'

'And you said that really divine things didn't happen,' said Adam in the middle of the night.

'I don't think that this is at all divine,' said Nina. 'It's given me a pain. And – my dear, that reminds me. I've something terribly important to say to you in the morning.'

'What?'

'Not now, darling. Let's go to sleep for a little, don't you think?'

Before Nina was properly awake Adam dressed and went out into the rain to get a shave. He came back bringing two tooth-brushes and a bright red celluloid comb. Nina sat up in bed and combed her hair. She put Adam's coat over her back.

'My dear, you look exactly like *La Vie Parisienne*,' said Adam, turning round from brushing his teeth.

Then she threw off the coat and jumped out of bed, and he told her that she looked like a fashion drawing without the clothes. Nina was rather pleased about that, but she said that it was cold and that she still had a pain, only not so bad as it was. Then she dressed and they went downstairs.

Everyone else had had breakfast and the waiters were laying the tables for luncheon.

'By the way,' said Adam. 'You said there was something you wanted to say.'

'Oh, yes, so there is. My dear, something quite awful.'

'Do tell me.'

'Well, it's about that cheque papa gave you. I'm afraid it won't help us as much as you thought.'

'But, darling, it's a thousand pounds, isn't it?'

'Just look at it, my sweet.' She took it out of her bag and handed it across the table.

'I don't see anything wrong with it,' said Adam.

'Not the signature?'

'Why, good lord, the old idiot's signed it "Charlie Chaplin." '

'That's what I mean, darling.'

'But can't we get him to alter it? He must be dotty. I'll go down and see him again to-day.'

'I shouldn't do that, dear . . . don't you see . . . Of course, he's very old, and . . . I dare say you may have made things sound a little odd . . . don't you think, dear, *he* must have thought *you* a little dotty? . . . I mean . . . perhaps . . . that cheque was a kind of joke.'

'Well I'm damned . . . this really is a bore. When everything seemed to be going so well, too. When did you notice the signature, Nina?'

'As soon as you showed it to me, at Margot's. Only you looked so happy I didn't like to say anything . . . You did look happy, you know, Adam, and so sweet. I think I really fell in love with you for the first time when I saw you dancing all alone in the hall.'

'Well I'm damned,' said Adam again. 'The old devil.'

'Anyway, you've had some fun out of it, haven't you . . . or haven't you?'

'Haven't *you*?'

'My dear, I never hated anything so much in my life . . . still, as long as you enjoyed it that's something.'

'I say, Nina,' said Adam after some time, 'we shan't be able to get married after all.'

'No, I'm afraid not.'

'It *is* a bore, isn't it?'

Later he said, 'I expect that parson thought I was dotty too.'

And later, 'As a matter of fact, it's rather a good joke, don't you think?'

'I think it's divine.'

In the train Nina said: 'It's awful to think that I shall probably never, as long as I live, see you dancing like that again all by yourself.'

Chapter Six

*

That evening Lady Metroland gave a party for Mrs Melrose Ape. Adam found the telegram of invitation waiting for him on his return to Shepheard's. (Lottie had already used the prepaid reply to do some betting with. Someone had given her a tip for the November Handicap and she wanted to 'make her little flutter' before she forgot the name.) He also found an invitation to luncheon from Simon Balcairn.

The food at Shepheard's tends to be mostly game-pie – quite black inside and full of beaks and shot and inexplicable vertebrae – so Adam was quite pleased to lunch with Simon Balcairn, though he knew there must be some slightly sinister motive behind this sudden hospitality.

They lunched *Chez Espinosa*, the second most expensive restaurant in London; it was full of oilcloth and Lalique glass, and the sort of people who liked that sort of thing went there continually and said how awful it was.

'I hope you don't mind coming to this awful restaurant,' said Balcairn. 'The truth is that I get meals free if I mention them occasionally in my page. Not drinks, unfortunately. Who's here, Alphonse?' he asked the *maître d'hôtel*.

Alphonse handed him the typewritten slip that was always kept for gossip writers.

'H'm, yes. Quite a good list this morning, Alphonse. I'll do what I can about it.'

'Thank you, sir. A table for two? A cocktail?'

'No, I don't think I want a cocktail. I really haven't time. Will you have one, Adam? They aren't very good here.'

'No, thanks,' said Adam.

'Sure?' said Balcairn, already making for their table.

When they were being helped to caviare he looked at the wine list.

'The lager is rather good,' he said. 'What would you like to drink?'

'Whatever you're having . . . I think some lager would be lovely.'

'Two small bottles of lager, please . . . Are you sure you really like that better than anything?'

'Yes, really, thank you.'

Simon Balcairn looked about him gloomily, occasionally adding a new name to his list. (It is so depressing to be in a profession in which literally all conversation is 'shop'.)

Presently he said, with a deadly air of carelessness:

'Margot Metroland's got a party to-night, hasn't she? Are you going?'

'I think probably. I usually like Margot's parties, don't you?'

'Yes . . . Adam, I'll tell you a very odd thing. She hasn't sent me an invitation to this one.'

'I expect she will. I only got mine this morning.'

'. . . Yes . . . who's that woman just come in in the fur coat? I know her so well by sight.'

'Isn't it Lady Everyman?'

'Yes, of course.' Another name was added to the list. Balcairn paused in utmost gloom and ate some salad. 'The thing is . . . she told Agatha Runcible she wasn't *going* to ask me.'

'Why not?'

'Apparently she's in a rage about something I said about something she said about Miles.'

'People do take things so seriously,' said Adam encouragingly.

'It means ruin for me,' said Lord Balcairn. 'Isn't that Pamela Popham?'

'I haven't the least idea.'

'I'm sure it is . . . I must look up the spelling in the stud book when I get back. I got into awful trouble about spelling the other day . . . Ruin . . . She's asked Vanburgh.'

'Well, he's some sort of cousin, isn't he?'

'It's so damned unfair. All my cousins are in lunatic asylums or else they live in the country and do indelicate things with wild animals . . . except my mamma, and that's worse . . . They were furious at the office about Van getting that Downing Street "scoop". If I miss this party I may as well leave Fleet Street for good . . . I may as well put my head into a gas-oven and have done with it . . . I'm sure if Margot knew how much it meant to me she wouldn't mind my coming.'

Great tears stood in his eyes threatening to overflow.

'All this last week,' he said, 'I've been reduced to making up my page from the Court Circular and Debrett . . . No one ever asks me anywhere now . . .'

'I'll tell you what,' said Adam, 'I know Margot pretty well. If you like I'll ring her up and ask if I may bring you.'

'Will you? Will you, Adam? If only you really would. Let's go and do it at once. We've no time for coffee or liqueurs. Quick, we can telephone from my office . . . yes, that black hat and my umbrella, no, I've lost the number . . . there, no, there, oh do hurry . . . Yes, a taxi . . .'

They were out in the street and into a taxi before Adam had time to say any more. Soon they were embedded in a traffic block in the Strand, and after a time they reached Balcairn's office in Fleet Street.

They went up to a tiny room with 'Social' written on the glass of the door. Its interior seemed not to justify its name. There was one chair, a typewriter, a telephone, some books of reference and a considerable litter of photographs. Balcairn's immediate superior sat in the one chair.

'Hullo,' she said. 'So you're back. Where you been?'

'Espinosa. Here's the list.'

The social editress read it through. 'Can't have Kitty Blackwater,' she said. 'Had her yesterday. Others'll do. Write 'em down to a couple of paragraphs. Suppose you didn't notice what they were wearing?'

'Yes,' said Balcairn eagerly. 'All of them.'

'Well, you won't have room to use it. We got to keep everything down for Lady M.'s party. I've cut out the D. of Devonshire altogether. By the way, the photograph you used yesterday wasn't the present Countess of Everyman. It's an old one of the Dowager. We had 'em both on the 'phone about it, going on something awful. That's *you* again. Got your invite for to-night?'

'Not yet.'

'You better get it quick. I got to have a first-hand story before we go to press, see? By the way, know anything about this? Lady R.'s maid sent it in to-day.' She picked up a slip of paper: ' "Rumoured engagement broken off between Adam Fenwick-Symes, only son of the late Professor Oliver Fenwick-Symes, and Nina Blount, of Doubting Hall, Aylesbury". Never heard of either. Ain't even been announced, so far as I'm aware of.'

'You'd better ask him. This is Adam Symes.'

'Hullo, no offence meant, I'm sure . . . What about it?'

'It is neither announced nor broken off.'

'N.B.G. in fact, eh? Then *that* goes *there*.' She put the slip into the wastepaper basket. 'That girl's sent us a lot of bad stuff lately. Well, I'm off for a bit of lunch. I'll be over at the Garden Club if anything urgent turns up. So long.'

The editress went out, banging the door labelled 'Social', and whistled as she went down the passage.

'You see how they treat me,' said Lord Balcairn. 'They were all over me when I first arrived. I do so wish I were dead.'

'Don't cry,' said Adam, 'it's too shy-making.'

'I can't help it . . . oh, do come in.'

The door marked 'Social' opened and a small boy came in.

'Lord Circumference's butler downstairs with some engage-ments and a divorce.'

'Tell him to leave them.'

'Very good, my lord.'

'That's the only person in this office who's ever polite to me,' said Balcairn as the messenger disappeared. 'I wish I had some-thing to leave him in my will . . . Do ring up Margot. Then I shall at any rate know the worst . . . Come in.'

'Gentleman of the name of General Strapper downstairs. Wants to see you very particular.'

'What about?'

'Couldn't say, my lord, but he's got a whip. Seems very put out about something.'

'Tell him the social editor is having luncheon . . . Do ring up Margot.'

Adam said, 'Margot, may I bring someone with me to-night?'

'Well, Adam, I really don't think you can. I can't imagine how everyone's going to get in as it is. I'm terribly sorry, who is it?'

'Simon Balcairn. He's particularly anxious to come.'

'I dare say he is. I'm rather against that young man. He's written things about me in the papers.'

'*Please*, Margot.'

'Certainly not. I won't have him inside my house. I've only asked Van on the strictest understanding that he doesn't write anything about it. I don't wish to have anything more to do with Simon Balcairn.'

'My dear, how *rich* you sound.'

'I feel my full income when that young man is mentioned. Good-bye. See you to-night.'

'You needn't tell me,' said Balcairn. 'I know what she's said . . . it's no good, is it?'

'I'm afraid not.'

'Done for . . .' said Balcairn. '. . . End of the tether . . .' He turned over some slips of paper listlessly. 'Would it interest you to hear that Agatha and Archie are engaged?'

'I don't believe it.'

'Neither do I. One of our people has just sent it in. Half of what they send us is lies, and the other half libel . . . they sent us a long story about Miles and Pamela Popham having spent last night at Arundel . . . But we couldn't use it even if it were true, which it obviously isn't, knowing Miles. Thank you for doing what you could . . . good-bye.'

Downstairs in the outer office there was an altercation in progress.[15] A large man of military appearance was shaking and stamping in front of a middle-aged woman. Adam recognized the social editress.

'Answer me, yes or no,' the big man was saying. 'Are you or are you not responsible for this damnable lie about my daughter?'

(He had read in Simon Balcairn's column that his daughter had been seen at a night club. To anyone better acquainted with Miss Strapper's habits of life the paragraph was particularly reticent.)

'Yes or no,' cried the General, 'or I'll shake the life out of you.'

'No.'

'Then who is? Let me get hold of the cad who wrote it. Where is he?' roared the General.

'Upstairs,' the social editress managed to say.

'More trouble for Simon,' thought Adam.

Adam went to pick Nina up at her flat. They had arranged to go to a cinema together. She said, 'You're much later than you said. It's so boring to be late for a talkie.'

He said, 'Talkies are boring, anyhow.'

They treated each other quite differently after their night's experiences. Adam was inclined to be egotistical and despondent; Nina was rather grown-up and disillusioned and distinctly cross. Adam began to say that as far as he could see he would have to live on at Shepheard's now for the rest of his life, or at any rate for the rest of Lottie's life, as it wouldn't be fair to leave without paying the bill.

Then Nina said, 'Do be amusing, Adam. I can't bear you when you're not amusing.'

Then Adam began to tell her about Simon Balcairn and Margot's party. He described how he had seen Simon being horse-whipped in the middle of the office.

Nina said, 'Yes, that's amusing. Go on like that.'

The story of Simon's whipping lasted them all the way to the cinema. They were very late for the film Nina wanted to see, and that set them back again. They didn't speak for a long time. Then Nina said à propos of the film, 'All this fuss about sleeping together. For physical pleasure I'd sooner go to my dentist any day.'

Adam said, 'You'll enjoy it more next time.'

Nina said, '*Next time*,' and told him that he took too much for granted.

Adam said that was a phrase which only prostitutes used.

Then they started a real quarrel which lasted all through the film and all the way to Nina's flat and all the time she was cutting up a lemon and making a cocktail, until Adam said that if she didn't stop going on he would ravish her there and then on her own hearth-rug.

Then Nina went on.

But by the time that Adam went to dress she had climbed down enough to admit that perhaps love was a thing one could grow to be fond of after a time, like smoking a pipe.[16] Still she maintained that it made one feel very ill at first, and she doubted if it was worth it.

Then they began to argue at the top of the lift about whether acquired tastes were ever worth acquiring. Adam said it was imitation, and that it was natural to man to be imitative, so that acquired tastes were natural.

But the presence of the lift boy stopped that argument coming to a solution as the other had done.

'My, ain't this classy,' said Divine Discontent.

'It's all right,' said Chastity in a worldly voice. 'Nothing to make a song and dance about.'

'Who's making a song and dance? I just said it was classy – and it *is* classy, ain't it?'

'I suppose everything's classy to *some* people.'

'Now you two,' said Temperance, who had been put in charge of the angels for the evening, 'don't you start anything in here, not with your wings on. Mrs Ape won't stand for scrapping in wings, and you know it.'

'Who's starting anything?'

'Well, you are then.'

'Oh, it's no use talking to Chastity. She's too high and mighty to be an angel now. Went out for a drive with Mrs Panrast in a Rolls-Royce,' said Fortitude. 'I saw her. I was *so* sorry it rained all the time, or it might have been quite enjoyable, mightn't it, Chastity?'

'Well, you ought to be glad. Leaves the *men* for you, Fortitude. Only they don't seem to want to take advantage, do they?'

Then they talked about men for some time. Divine Discontent thought the second footman had nice eyes.

'And he knows it,' said Temperance.

They were all having supper together in what was still called the schoolroom in Lady Metroland's house. From the window they could see the guests arriving for the party. In spite of the rain quite a large crowd had collected on either side of the awning to criticize the cloaks with appreciative 'oohs' and 'ahs' or contemptuous sniffs. Cars and taxis drove up in close succession. Lady Circumference splashed up the street in goloshes, wearing a high fender of diamonds under a tartan umbrella. The Bright Young People came popping all together, out of someone's electric brougham[17] like a litter of pigs, and ran squealing up the steps. Some 'gate-crashers'[18] who had made the mistake of coming in Victorian fancy dress were detected and repulsed. They hurried home to change for a second assault. No one wanted to miss Mrs Ape's *début*.

But the angels were rather uneasy. They had been dressed ever since seven o'clock in their white shifts, gold sashes and wings. It was now past ten, and the strain was beginning to tell, for it was impossible to sit back comfortably in wings.

'Oh, I wish they'd hurry up so we could get it over,' said Creative Endeavour. 'Mrs Ape said we could have some champagne afterwards if we sang nice.'

'I don't mind betting *she's* doing herself pretty well, down there.'

'*Chastity!*'

'Oh, *all* right.'

Then the footman with the nice eyes came to clear the table. He gave them a friendly wink as he shut the door. 'Pretty creatures,' he thought. 'Blooming shame that they're so religious . . . wasting the best years of their lives.'

(There had been a grave debate in the servants' hall about the exact status of angels. Even Mr Blenkinsop, the butler, had been uncertain. 'Angels are certainly not guests,' he had said, 'and I don't think they are deputations. Nor they ain't governesses either, nor clergy not strictly speaking; they're not entertainers, because entertainers *dine* nowadays, the more's the pity.'

'I believe they're decorators,' said Mrs Blouse, 'or else charitable workers.'

'Charitable workers are governesses, Mrs Blouse. There is nothing to be gained by multiplying social distinctions indefinitely. Decorators are either guests or workmen.'

After further discussion the conclusion was reached that angels were nurses, and that became the official ruling of the household. But the second footman was of the opinion that they were just 'young persons', pure and simple, 'and very nice too', for nurses cannot, except in very rare cases, be winked at, and clearly angels could.)

'What we want to know, Chastity,' said Creative Endeavour, 'is how you come to take up with Mrs Panrast at all.'

'Yes,' said the Angels, 'yes. It's not like *you*, Chastity, to go riding in a motor car with a woman.' They fluttered their feathers in a menacing way. 'Let's third-degree her,' said Humility with rather nasty relish.

(There was a system of impromptu jurisdiction among the Angels which began with innuendo, went on to cross-examination, pinches and slaps and ended, as a rule, in tears and kisses.)

Faced by this circle of spiteful and haloed faces, Chastity began to lose her air of superiority.

'Why shouldn't I ride with a friend,' she asked plaintively, 'without all you girls pitching on me like this?'

'*Friend?*' said Creative Endeavour. 'You never saw her before to-day,' and she gave her a nasty pinch just above the elbow.

'*Ooooh!*' said Chastity. '*Ooh, please* . . . beast.'

Then they all pinched her all over, but precisely and judiciously, so as not to disturb her wings or halo, for this was no orgy (sometimes in their bedroom, they gave way, but not here, in Lady Metroland's schoolroom, before an important first night).

'Ooh,' said Chastity. '*Ooh, ow, ooh, ow. Please*, beasts, swine, cads . . . *please* . . . ooh . . . well, if you must know, I thought she *was* a man.'

'Thought she was a *man*, Chastity? That doesn't sound right to me.'

'Well, she looks like a man and – and she *goes on* like a man. I saw her sitting at a table in a tea-shop. She hadn't got a hat on, and I couldn't see her skirt . . . ooh . . . how can I tell you if you keep pinching . . . and she smiled and so, well, I went and had some tea with her, and she said would I go out with her in her motor car, and I said yes and, ooh, I wish I hadn't now.'

'What did she say in the motor car, Chastity?'

'I forget – nothing much.'

'Oh, what.' 'Do tell us.' 'We'll never pinch you again if you tell us.' 'I'm sorry if I hurt you, Chastity, do tell *me*.' 'You'd *better* tell us.'

'No, I can't, *really* – I don't remember, I tell you.'

'Give her another little nip, girls.'

'Ooh, ooh, ooh, *stop*. I'll tell you.'

Their heads were close together and they were so deeply engrossed in the story that they did not hear Mrs Ape's entry.

'Smut again,' said a terrible voice. 'Girls, I'm sick ashamed of you.'

Mrs Ape looked magnificent in a gown of heavy gold brocade embroidered with texts.

'I'm sick ashamed of you,' repeated Mrs Ape, 'and you've made Chastity cry again, just before the big act. If you must bully someone, *why* choose Chastity? You all know by this time that crying always gives her a red nose. How do *I* look, I should like to know, standing up in front of a lot of angels with red noses? You don't ever think of nothing but your own pleasures, do you? *Sluts*.' This last word was spoken with a depth of expression that set the angels trembling. 'There'll be no champagne for anyone to-night, see. And if you don't sing perfectly, I'll give the whole lot of you a good hiding, see. Now, come on, now, and for the love of the Lamb, Chastity, *do something to your nose*. They'll think it's a temperance meeting to see you like that.'

It was a brilliant scene into which the disconsolate angels trooped two minutes later. Margot Metroland shook hands with each of them as they came to the foot of the staircase, appraising them, one by one, with an expert eye.

'You don't look happy, my dear,' she found time to say to Chastity, as she led them across the ballroom to their platform, banked in orchids at the far end. 'If you feel you want a change, let me know later, and I can get you a job in South America. *I mean it*.'

'Oh, thank you,' said Chastity, 'but I could never leave Mrs Ape.'

'Well, think it over, child. You're far too pretty a girl to waste your time singing hymns. Tell that other girl, the red-headed one, that I can probably find a place for her, too.'

'What, Humility? Don't you have nothing to do with her. She's a fiend.'

'Well, some men like rough stuff, but I don't want anyone who makes trouble with the other girls.'

'She makes trouble all right. Look at that bruise.'

'My dear!'

Margot Metroland and Mrs Ape led the angels up the steps between the orchids and stood them at the back of the platform facing the room. Chastity stood next to Creative Endeavour.

'Please, Chastity, I'm sorry if we hurt you,' said Creative Endeavour. '*I* didn't pinch hard, did I?'

'Yes,' said Chastity. 'Like hell you did.'

A slightly sticky hand tried to take hers, but she clenched her fist. She would go to South America and work for Lady Metroland . . . and she wouldn't say anything about it to Humility either. She glared straight in front of her, saw Mrs Panrast and dropped her eyes.

The ballroom was filled with little gilt chairs and the chairs with people. Lord Vanburgh, conveniently seated near the door, through which he could slip away to the telephone, was taking them all in. They were almost all, in some way or another, notable. The motives for Margot Metroland's second marriage* had been mixed, but entirely worldly; chief among them had been the desire to re-establish her somewhat shaken social position, and her party that night testified to her success, for while many people can entertain the Prime Minister and the Duchess of Stayle and Lady Circumference, and anybody can, and often against her will does, entertain Miles Malpractice and Agatha Runcible, it is only a very confident hostess who will invite both these sets together at the same time, differing as they do upon almost all questions of

* See *Decline and Fall*.

principle and deportment. Standing near Vanburgh, by the door, was a figure who seemed in himself to typify the change that had come over Pastmaster House when Margot Beste-Chetwynde became Lady Metroland; an unobtrusive man of rather less than average height, whose black beard, falling in tight burnished curls, nearly concealed the order of St Michael and St George which he wore round his neck; he wore a large signet ring on the little finger of his left hand outside his white glove; there was an orchid in his buttonhole. His eyes, youthful but grave, wandered among the crowd; occasionally he bowed with grace and decision. Several people were asking about him.

'See the beaver with the medal,' said Humility to Faith.

'Who is that *very* important young man?' asked Mrs Blackwater of Lady Throbbing.

'I don't know, dear. He bowed to *you*.'

'He bowed to *you*, dear.'

'How very nice . . . I wasn't quite sure . . . He reminds me a little of dear Prince Anrep.'

'It's so nice in these days, isn't it, dearest, to see someone who really looks . . . don't you think?'

'You mean the beard?'

'*The beard among other things*, darling.'

Father Rothschild was conspiring with Mr Outrage and Lord Metroland. He stopped short in the middle of his sentence.

'Forgive me,' he said, 'but there are spies everywhere. That man with the beard, do you know him?'

Lord Metroland thought vaguely he had something to do with the Foreign Office; Mr Outrage seemed to remember having seen him before.

'*Exactly*,' said Father Rothschild. 'I think it would be better if we continued our conversation in private. I have been watching him. *He is bowing across the room to empty places and to people whose backs are turned to him*.' The Great Men withdrew to Lord Metroland's study. Father Rothschild closed the door silently and looked behind the curtains.

'Shall I lock the door?' asked Lord Metroland.

'No,' said the Jesuit. 'A lock does not prevent a spy from hearing; but it does hinder us, inside, from catching the spy.'

'Well, I should never have thought of that,' said Mr Outrage in frank admiration.

'How pretty Nina Blount is,' said Lady Throbbing, busy from the front row with her lorgnette, 'but don't you think, a little changed; almost as though . . .'

'You notice everything, darling.'

'When you get to our age, dear, there is so little left, but I do believe Miss Blount must have had an *experience* . . . she's sitting next to Miles. You know I heard from Edward to-night. He's on his way back. It will be a great blow for Miles because he's been living in Edward's house all this time. To tell you the truth I'm a little glad because from what I hear from Anne Opalthorpe, who lives opposite, the things that go on . . . he's got a friend staying there now. Such an odd man . . . a dirt-track racer. But then it's no use attempting to disguise the fact, *is* there . . . There's Mrs Panrast . . . yes, dear, of course you know her, she used to be Eleanor Balcairn . . . now *why* does dear Margot ask anyone like that, do you think? . . . it is not as though Margot was so innocent . . . and there's Lord Monomark . . . yes, the man who owns those *amusing* papers . . . they say that he and Margot, but *before* her marriage, of course (her second marriage, I mean), but you never know, do you, how things *crop* up again? . . . I wonder where Peter Pastmaster is? . . . he never stays to Margot's parties . . . he was at dinner, of course, and, my dear, *how* he drank. . . . He can't be more than twenty-one . . . Oh, so that is Mrs Ape. What a coarse face . . . no dear, of course she can't hear . . . she looks like a *procureuse* . . . but perhaps I shouldn't say that *here*, should I?'

Adam came and sat next to Nina.

'Hullo,'[19] they said to each other.

'My dear, do look at Mary Mouse's new young man,' said Nina.

Adam looked and saw that Mary was sitting next to the Maharajah of Pukkapore.

'I call that a pretty pair,' he said.

'Oh, how bored I feel,' said Nina.

Mr Benfleet was there talking to two poets. They said '. . . and I wrote to tell William that I didn't write the review, but it was true that Tony did read me the review over the telephone when I was very sleepy before he sent it in. I thought it was best to tell him the truth because he would hear it from Tony anyway. Only I said I advised him not to publish it just as I had advised William not to publish the book in the first place. Well Tony rang up Michael and told him that I'd said that William thought Michael had written the review because of the reviews I had written of Michael's book last November, though, as a matter of fact, it was Tony himself who wrote it . . .'

'Too bad,' said Mr Benfleet. 'Too bad.'

'. . . but is that any reason, even if I had written it, why Michael should tell Tony that I had stolen five pounds from William?'

'Certainly not,' said Mr Benfleet. 'Too bad.'

'Of course, they're *simply* not *gentlemen*, either of them. That's all it is, only one's shy of saying it nowadays.'

Mr Benfleet shook his head sadly and sympathetically.

Then Mrs Melrose Ape stood up to speak. A hush fell in the gilt ballroom beginning at the back and spreading among the chairs until only Mrs Blackwater's voice was heard exquisitely articulating some details of Lady Metroland's past. Then she, too, was silent and Mrs Ape began her oration about Hope.

'Brothers and Sisters,' she said in a hoarse, stirring voice. Then she paused and allowed her eyes, renowned throughout three continents for their magnetism, to travel among the gilded chairs. (It was one of her favourite openings.) '*Just you look at yourselves,*' she said.

Magically, self-doubt began to spread in the audience. Mrs Panrast stirred uncomfortably; had that silly little girl been talking, she wondered.

'Darling,' whispered Miss Runcible, 'is my nose awful?'

Nina thought how once, only twenty-four hours ago, she had

been in love. Mr Benfleet thought should he have made it three per cent on the tenth thousand. The gate-crashers wondered whether it would not have been better to have stayed at home. (Once in Kansas City Mrs Ape had got no further than these opening words; there had been a tornado of emotion and all the seats in the hall had been broken to splinters. It was there that Humility had joined the Angels.) There were a thousand things in Lady Throbbing's past ... Every heart found something to bemoan.

'She's got 'em again,' whispered Creative Endeavour. 'Got 'em stiff.'

Lord Vanburgh slipped from the room to telephone through some racy paragraphs about fashionable piety.

Mary Mouse shed two little tears and felt for the brown, be-jewelled hand of the Maharajah.

But suddenly on that silence vibrant with self-accusation broke the organ voice of England, the hunting-cry of the *ancien régime*. Lady Circumference gave a resounding snort of disapproval:

'What a damned impudent woman,' she said.

Adam and Nina and Miss Runcible began to giggle, and Margot Metroland for the first time in her many parties was glad to realize that the guest of the evening was going to be a failure. It had been an awkward moment.

In the study Father Rothschild and Mr Outrage were plotting with enthusiasm. Lord Metroland was smoking a cigar and wondering how soon he could get away. He wanted to hear Mrs Ape and to have another look at those Angels. There was one with red hair ... Besides, all this statesmanship and foreign policy had always bored him. In his years in the Commons he had always liked a good scrap, and often thought a little wistfully of those orgies of competitive dissimulation in which he had risen to eminence. Even now, when some straightforward, easily intelligible subject was under discussion, such as poor people's wages or public art, he enjoyed from time to time making a sonorous speech to the Upper House. But this sort of thing was not at all in his line.

Suddenly Father Rothschild turned out the light.

'There's someone coming down the passage,' he said. 'Quick, get behind the curtains.'

'Really, Rothschild . . .' said Mr Outrage.

'I say . . .' said Lord Metroland.

'*Quick*,' said Father Rothschild.

The three statesmen hid themselves. Lord Metroland, still smoking, his head thrown back and his cigar erect. They heard the door open. The light was turned on. A match was struck. Then came the slight tinkle of the telephone as someone lifted the receiver.

'Central ten thousand,' said a slightly muffled voice.

'*Now*,' said Father Rothschild, and stepped through the curtain.

The bearded stranger who had excited his suspicions was standing at the table smoking one of Lord Metroland's cigars and holding the telephone.

'Oh, hullo,' he said, 'I didn't know you were here. Just thought I'd use the telephone. So sorry. Won't disturb you. Jolly party, isn't it? Good-bye.'

'Stay exactly where you are,' said Father Rothschild, 'and take off that beard.'

'Damned if I do,' said the stranger crossly. 'It's no use talking to me as though I were one of your choir boys . . . you old *bully*.'

'Take off that beard,' said Father Rothschild.

'Take off that beard,' said Lord Metroland and the Prime Minister, emerging suddenly from behind the curtain.

This concurrence of Church and State, coming so unexpectedly after an evening of prolonged embarrassment, was too much for Simon.

'Oh, all right,' he said, 'if you *will* make such a *thing* about it . . . it hurts too frightfully, if you knew . . . it ought to be soaked in hot water . . . ooh . . . ow.'

He gave some tugs at the black curls, and bit by bit they came away.

'*There*,' he said. 'Now I should go and make Lady Throbbing take off her wig . . . I should have a really jolly evening while you're about it, if I were you.'

'I seem to have over-estimated the gravity of the situation,' said Father Rothschild.

'Who is it, after all this?' said Mr Outrage. 'Where are those detectives? What does it all mean?'

'That,' said Father Rothschild bitterly, 'is *Mr Chatterbox*.'

'Never heard of him. I don't believe there is such a person . . . *Chatterbox*, indeed . . . you make us hide behind a curtain and then you tell us that some young man in a false beard is called Chatterbox. Really, Rothschild . . .'

'Lord Balcairn,' said Lord Metroland, 'will you kindly leave my house immediately?'

'*Is* this young man called Chatterbox or is he not? . . . Upon my soul, I believe you're all crazy.'

'Oh yes, I'm going,' said Simon. 'You didn't think I was going to go back to the party like this, did you? – or did you?' Indeed, he looked very odd with little patches of black hair still adhering to parts of his chin and cheeks.

'Lord Monomark is here this evening. I shall certainly inform him of your behaviour . . .'

'He writes for the papers,' Father Rothschild tried to explain to the Prime Minister.

'Well, damn it, so do I, but I don't wear a false beard and call myself Chatterbox . . . I simply do not understand what has happened . . . Where are those detectives? . . . Will no one explain? . . . *You treat me like a child*,' he said. It was all like one of those Cabinet meetings, when they all talked about something he didn't understand and paid no attention to him.

Father Rothschild led him away, and attempted with almost humiliating patience and tact to make clear to him some of the complexities of modern journalism.

'I don't believe a word of it,' the Prime Minister kept saying. 'It's all humbug. You're keeping something back . . . *Chatterbox*, indeed.'

Simon Balcairn was given his hat and coat and shown to the door. The crowd round the awning had dispersed. It was still raining. He walked back to his little flat in Bourdon Street. The rain washed a few of the remaining locks from his face; it dripped down his collar.

They were washing a car outside his front door; he crept between it and his dustbin, fitted his latchkey in the lock and went upstairs. His flat was like *Chez Espinosa* – all oilcloth and Lalique glass; there were some enterprising photographs by David Lennox, a gramophone (on the instalment system) and numberless cards of invitation on the mantelpiece. His bath towel was where he had left it on his bed.

Simon went to the ice box in the kitchen and chipped off some ice. Then he made himself a cocktail. Then he went to the telephone.

'Central ten thousand . . .' he said '. . . Give me Mrs Brace. Hullo, this is Balcairn.'

'Well . . . gotcher story?'

'Oh yes, I've got my story, only this isn't gossip, it's news – front page. You'll have to fill up the Chatterbox page on Espinosa's.'

'Hell!'

'Wait till you see the story . . . Hullo, give me news, will you . . . This is Balcairn. Put on one of the boys to take this down, will you? . . . ready? All right.'

At his glass-topped table, sipping his cocktail, Simon Balcairn dictated his last story.

'*Scenes of wild religious enthusiasm, comma, reminiscent of a negro camp-meeting in Southern America, comma, broke out in the heart of Mayfair yesterday evening at the party given for the famous American Revivalist Mrs Ape by the Viscountess Metroland, formerly the Hon. Mrs Beste-Chetwynde, at her historic mansion, Pastmaster House, stop. The magnificent ballroom can never have enshrined a more brilliant assembly . . .*'

It was his swan-song. Lie after monstrous lie bubbled up in his brain.

'*. . . The Hon. Agatha Runcible joined Mrs Ape among the orchids and led the singing, tears coursing down her face . . .*'

Excitement spread at the *Excess* office. The machines were stopped. The night staff of reporters, slightly tipsy, as always at that hour, stood over the stenographer as he typed. The compositors snatched the sheets of copy as they came. The sub-editors began ruthlessly cutting and scrapping; they suppressed important political announcements, garbled the evidence at a murder trial, reduced the dramatic criticism to one caustic paragraph, to make room for Simon's story.

It came through 'hot and strong, as nice as mother makes it', as one of them remarked.

'Little Lord Fauntleroy's on a good thing at last,' said another.

'What-ho,' said a third appreciatively.

'. . . *barely had Lady Everyman finished before the Countess of Throbbing rose to confess her sins, and in a voice broken with emotion disclosed the hitherto unverified details of the parentage of the present Earl . . .*'

'Tell Mr Edwardes to look up photographs of all three of 'em,' said the assistant news editor.

'. . . *The Marquess of Vanburgh, shaken by sobs of contrition . . . Mrs Panrast, singing feverishly . . . Lady Anchorage with downcast eyes . . .*'

'. . . *The Archbishop of Canterbury, who up to now had remained unmoved by the general emotion, then testified that at Eton in the eighties he and Sir James Brown. . . .*'

'. . . *the Duchess of Stayle next threw down her emerald and diamond tiara, crying "a Guilt Offering", an example which was quickly followed by the Countess of Circumference and Lady Brown, until a veritable rain of precious stones fell on to the parquet flooring, heirlooms of priceless value rolling among Tecla[20] pearls and Chanel diamonds. A blank cheque fluttered from the hands of the Maharajah of Pukkapore . . .*'

It made over two columns, and when Simon finally rang off, after receiving the congratulations of his colleagues, he was for the first time in his journalistic experience perfectly happy about his work. He finished the watery dregs of the cocktail shaker and went into the kitchen. He shut the door and the window and opened the door of the gas oven. Inside it was very black and dirty and smelled of meat. He spread a sheet of newspaper on the lowest tray and lay down, resting his head on it. Then he noticed that by some mischance he had chosen Vanburgh's gossip-page in the *Morning Despatch.* He put in another sheet. (There were crumbs on the floor.) Then he turned on the gas. It came surprisingly with a loud roar; the wind of it stirred his hair and the remaining particles of his beard. At first he held his breath. Then he thought that was silly and gave a sniff. The sniff made him cough, and coughing made him breathe, and breathing made him feel very ill; but soon he fell into a coma and presently died.

So the last Earl of Balcairn went, as they say, to his fathers (who had fallen in many lands and for many causes, as the eccentricities of British Foreign Policy and their own wandering natures had directed them; at Acre and Agincourt and Killiecrankie, in Egypt and America. One had been picked white by fishes as the tides rolled him among the tree-tops of a submarine forest; some had grown black and unfit for consideration under tropical suns; while many of them lay in marble tombs of extravagant design).

At Pastmaster House, Lady Metroland and Lord Monomark were talking about him. Lord Monomark was roaring with boyish laughter.

'That's a great lad,' he said. 'Came in a false beard, did he? That's peppy. What'd you say his name was? I'll raise him tomorrow first thing.'

And he turned to give Simon's name to an attendant secretary.

And when Lady Metroland began to expostulate, he shut her up rather discourteously.

'Shucks, Margot,' he said. 'You know better than to get on a high horse with me.'

Chapter Seven

*

Then Adam became Mr Chatterbox.

He and Nina were lunching at Espinosa's and quarrelling half-heartedly when a business-like, Eton-cropped woman came across to their table, whom Adam recognized as the social editress of the *Daily Excess*.

'See here,' she said, 'weren't you over at the office with Balcairn the day he did himself in?'

'Yes.'

'Well, a pretty mess he's let us in for. Sixty-two writs for libel up to date and more coming in. And that's not the worst. Left me to do his job and mine. I was wondering if you could tell me the names of any of these people and anything about them.'

Adam pointed out a few well-worn faces.

'Yes, they ain't no good. They're on the black list. You see, Monomark was in an awful way about Balcairn's story of Lady Metroland's party, and he's sent down a chit that none of the people who are bringing actions against the paper can be mentioned again. Well, I ask you, what's one to do? It's just bricks without straw. Why, we can't even mention the Prime Minister or the Archbishop of Canterbury. I suppose you don't know of anyone who'd care to take on the job? They'd have to be a pretty good mutt, if they would.'

'What do they pay?'

'Ten pounds a week and expenses. Know anyone?'

'I'd do it myself for that.'

'*You?*' The social editress looked at him sceptically. 'Would you be any good?'

'I'll try for a week or two.'

'That's about as long as anyone sticks it. All right, come back to the office with me when you've finished lunch. You can't cause more trouble than Balcairn, anyhow, and he looked the goods at first.'

'Now we can get married,' said Nina.

Meanwhile the libel actions against the authors, printers and publishers of Simon Balcairn's last story practically paralysed the judicial system of the country. The old brigade, led by Mrs Blackwater, threw themselves with relish into an orgy of litigation such as they had not seen since the war (one of the younger counsel causing Lady Throbbing particular delight . . . 'I do think, when you get to my age, dear, there is something *sympathique* about a wig, don't you? . . .'). The younger generation for the most part allowed their cases to be settled out of court and later gave a very delightful party on the proceeds in a captive dirigible. Miss Runcible, less well advised, filled two albums with Press cuttings portraying her various appearances at the Law Courts, sometimes as plaintiff, sometimes as witness, sometimes (in a hat borrowed from Miss Mouse) as part of the queue of 'fashionably dressed women waiting for admission', once as an intruder being removed by an usher from the Press gallery, and finally as a prisoner being sentenced to a fine of ten pounds or seven days' imprisonment for contempt of court.

The proceedings were considerably complicated by the behaviour of Mrs Ape, who gave an interview in which she fully confirmed Simon Balcairn's story. She also caused her Press agent to wire a further account to all parts of the world. She then left the country with her angels, having received a sudden call to ginger up the religious life of Oberammergau.

At intervals letters arrived from Buenos Aires in which Chastity and Divine Discontent spoke rather critically of Latin American entertainment.

'They didn't know when they was well off,' said Mrs Ape.

'It don't sound much different from us,' said Creative Endeavour wistfully.

'They won't be dead five minutes before *they* see the difference,' said Mrs Ape.

Edward Throbbing and two secretaries returned to Hertford

Street somewhat inopportunely for Miles and his dirt-track racer, who were obliged to move into Shepheard's. Miles said that the thing he resented about his brother's return was not so much the inconvenience as the expense. For some weeks Throbbing suffered from the successive discoveries by his secretaries of curious and compromising things in all parts of the house; his butler, too, seemed changed. He hiccoughed heavily while serving dinner to two Secretaries of State, complained of spiders in his bath and the sound of musical instruments, and finally had 'the horrors', ran mildly amok in the pantry with the kitchen poker, and had to be taken away in a van. Long after these immediate causes of distress had been removed, the life of Throbbing's secretaries was period-ically disturbed by ambiguous telephone calls and the visits of menacing young men who wanted new suits or tickets to America, or a fiver to go on with.

But all these events, though of wide general interest, are of necessity a closed book to the readers of Mr Chatterbox's page.

Lord Monomark's black list had made a devastating change in the personnel of the *Daily Excess* gossip. In a single day Mr Chatterbox's readers found themselves plunged into a murky underworld of nonentities. They were shown photographs of the misshapen daughters of backwoods peers carrying buckets of meal to their fathers' chickens; they learned of the engagement of the younger sister of the Bishop of Chertsey and of a dinner party given in Elm Park Gardens by the widow of a High Commissioner to some of the friends she had made in their colony. There were details of the blameless home life of women novelists, photo-graphed with their spaniels before rose-covered cottages; stories of undergraduate 'rags' and regimental reunion dinners; anecdotes from Harley Street and the Inns of Court; snaps and snippets about cocktail parties given in basement flats by spotty announcers at the B.B.C., of tea dances in Gloucester Terrace and jokes made at High Table by dons.

Urged on by the taunts of the social editress, Adam brought new enterprise and humanity into this sorry column. He started a series of 'Notable Invalids', which was, from the first, wildly successful. He began chattily. '*At a dinner party the other evening my neighbour and I began to compile a list of the most popular deaf peeresses. First, of course, came old Lady —. . .'*

Next day he followed it up with a page about deaf peers and statesmen; then about the one-legged, blind and bald. Postcards of appreciation poured in from all over the country.

'I have read your column for many years now,' wrote a correspondent from Bude, *'but this is the first time I have really enjoyed it. I have myself been deaf for a long time, and it is a great comfort to me to know that my affliction is shared by so many famous men and women. Thank you, Mr Chatterbox, and good luck to you.'*

Another wrote: *'Ever since childhood I have been cursed with abnormally large ears which have been a source of ridicule to me and a serious handicap in my career (I am a chub fuddler).[21] I should be so glad to know whether any great people have suffered in the same way.'*

Finally, he ransacked the lunatic asylums and mental houses of the country, and for nearly a week ran an extremely popular series under the heading 'Titled Eccentrics'.[22]

'It is not generally known that the Earl of —, who lives in strict retirement, has the unusual foible of wearing costume of the Napoleonic Period. So great, indeed, is his detestation of modern dress that on one occasion . . .'

'Lord —, whose public appearances are regrettably rare nowadays, is a close student of comparative religions. There is an amusing story of how, when lunching with the then Dean of Westminster, Lord — startled his host by proclaiming that so far from being of divine ordinance, the Ten Commandments were, in point of fact, composed by himself and delivered by him to Moses on Sinai . . .'

'Lady —, whose imitations of animal sounds are so lifelike that she can seldom be persuaded to converse in any other way . . .'

And so on.

Besides this, arguing that people did not really mind *whom* they read about provided that a kind of vicarious inquisitiveness into the lives of others was satisfied, Adam began to invent people.

He invented a sculptor called Provna, the son of a Polish nobleman, who lived in a top-floor studio in Grosvenor House. Most of his work (which was all in private hands) was constructed in cork, vulcanite and steel. The Metropolitan Museum at New York, Mr Chatterbox learned, had been negotiating for some time to purchase a specimen, but so far had been unable to out-bid the collectors.

Such is the power of the Press, that soon after this a steady output of early Provnas began to travel from Warsaw to Bond Street and from Bond Street to California, while Mrs Hoop announced to her friends that Provna was at the moment at work on a bust of Johnny, which she intended to present to the nation (a statement which Adam was unable to record owing to the presence of Mrs Hoop's name on the black list, but which duly appeared, under a photograph of Johnny, in the Marquess of Vanburgh's rival column).

Encouraged by his success, Adam began gradually to introduce to his readers a brilliant and lovely company. He mentioned them casually at first in lists of genuine people. There was a popular young attaché at the Italian Embassy called Count Cincinnati. He was descended from the famous Roman Consul, Cincinnatus, and bore a plough as his crest. Count Cincinnati was held to be the best amateur 'cellist in London. Adam saw him one evening dancing at the Café de la Paix. A few evenings later Lord Vanburgh noticed him at Covent Garden, remarking that his collection of the original designs for the Russian ballet was unequalled in Europe. Two days later Adam sent him to Monte Carlo for a few days' rest, and Vanburgh hinted that there was more in this visit than met the eye, and mentioned the daughter of a well-known American hostess who was staying there at her aunt's villa.

There was a Captain Angus Stuart-Kerr, too, whose rare appearances in England were a delight to his friends; unlike most big-game hunters, he was an expert and indefatigable dancer. Much to Adam's disgust he found Captain Stuart-Kerr taken up by an unknown gossip-writer in a twopenny illustrated weekly, who saw him at a point-to-point meeting, and remarked that he was well known as the hardest rider in the Hebrides. Adam put a stop to that next day.

'*Some people,*' he wrote, '*are under the impression that Captain Angus Stuart-Kerr, whom I mentioned on this page a short time ago, is a keen rider. Perhaps they are confusing him with Alastair Kerr-Stuart, of Inverauchty, a very distant cousin. Captain Stuart-Kerr never rides, and for a very interesting* *reason. There is an old Gaelic rhyme repeated among his clansmen which says in rough translation "the Laird rides well on two legs". Tradition has it that when the head of the house mounts a horse the clan will be dispersed.'**

But Adam's most important creation was Mrs Andrew Quest. There was always some difficulty about introducing English people into his column as his readers had a way of verifying his references in Debrett (as he knew to his cost, for one day, having referred to the engagement of the third and youngest daughter of a Welsh baronet, he received six postcards, eighteen telephone calls, a telegram and a personal visit of protest to inform him that there are two equally beautiful sisters still in the schoolroom. The social editress had been scathing about this). However, he put Imogen Quest down one day, quietly and decisively, as the most lovely and popular of the younger married set. And from the first she exhibited signs of a marked personality. Adam wisely eschewed any attempts at derivation, but his readers nodded to each other and speedily supplied her with an exalted if irregular origin. Everything else Adam showered upon her. She had slightly more than average height, and was very dark and slim, with large Laurencin eyes and the negligent grace of the trained athlete (she fenced with the sabre for half an hour every morning before breakfast). Even Provna, who was notoriously indifferent to conventional beauty, described her as 'justifying the century'.

Her clothes were incomparable, with just that suggestion of the haphazard which raised them high above the mere *chic* of the mannequin.

Her character was a lovely harmony of contending virtues – she was witty and tender-hearted; passionate and serene, sensual and temperate, impulsive and discreet.

Her set, the most intimate and brilliant in Europe, achieved a superb mean between those two poles of savagery Lady Circumference and Lady Metroland.

---

* This story, slightly expanded, found its way later into a volume of Highland Legends called *Tales from the Mist*, which has been approved to be read in elementary schools. This shows the difference between what is called a 'living' as opposed to a 'dead' folk tradition.

Soon Imogen Quest became a byword for social inaccessibility – the final goal for all climbers.

Adam went one day to a shop in Hanover Square to watch Nina buy some hats and was seriously incommoded by the heaps of bandboxes disposed on the chairs and dressing-tables ostentatiously addressed to Mrs Andrew Quest. He could hear her name spoken reverently in cocktail clubs, and casually let slip in such phrases as 'My dear, I never see Peter now. He spends all his time with Imogen Quest', or 'As Imogen would say . . .' or 'I think the Quests have got one like that. I must ask them where it came from'. And this knowledge on the intangible Quest set, moving among them in uncontrolled dignity of life, seemed to leaven and sweeten the lives of Mr Chatterbox's readers.

One day Imogen gave a party, the preparations for which occupied several paragraphs. On the following day Adam found his table deep in letters of complaint from gate-crashers who had found the house in Seamore Place untenanted.

Finally a message came down that Lord Monomark was interested in Mrs Quest; could Mr Chatterbox arrange a meeting. That day the Quests sailed for Jamaica.

Adam also attempted in an unobtrusive way to exercise some influence over the clothes of his readers. '*I noticed at the Café de la Paix yesterday evening,*' he wrote, '*that two of the smartest men in the room were wearing black suède shoes with their evening clothes – one of them, who shall be nameless, was a Very Important Person indeed. I hear that this fashion, which comes, like so many others, from New York, is likely to become popular over here this season.*' A few days later he mentioned Captain Stuart-Kerr's appearance at the Embassy '*wearing, of course, the ultra-fashionable black suède shoes*'. In a week he was gratified to notice that Johnny Hoop and Archie Schwert had both followed Captain Stuart-Kerr's lead, while in a fortnight the big emporiums of ready-made clothes in Regent Street had transposed their tickets in the windows and arranged rows of black suède shoes on a silver step labelled 'For evening wear'.

His attempt to introduce a bottle-green bowler hat, however, was not successful; in fact, a 'well-known St James's Street hatter', when interviewed by an evening paper on the subject, said that he had never seen or heard of such a thing, and though he would not refuse to construct one if requested to by an old customer, he was of the opinion that no old customer of his would require a hat of that kind (though there was a sad case of an impoverished old beau who attempted to stain a grey hat with green ink, as once in years gone by he had been used to dye the carnation[23] for his buttonhole).

As the days passed, Mr Chatterbox's page became almost wholly misleading. With sultanesque caprice Adam would tell his readers of inaccessible eating-houses which were now the centre of fashion; he drove them to dance in temperance hotels in Bloomsbury. In a paragraph headed 'Montparnasse in Belgravia', he announced that the buffet at Sloane Square tube station had become the haunt of the most modern artistic coterie (Mr Benfleet hurried there on his first free evening, but saw no one but Mrs Hoop and Lord Vanburgh and a plebeian toper with a celluloid collar).

As a last resort, on those hopeless afternoons when invention failed and that black misanthropy settled on him which waits alike on gossip writer and novelist, Adam sometimes found consolation in seizing upon some gentle and self-effacing citizen and trans-figuring him with a blaze of notoriety.

He did this with a man called Ginger.

As part of his duties, which led him into many unusual places, Adam and Nina went up to Manchester for the November Handi-cap. Here they had the disheartening experience of seeing Indian Runner come in an easy winner and the totalisator paying out thirty-five to one. It was during the bottle-green bowler campaign, and Adam was searching in vain for any sign of his influence when, suddenly, among the crowd, he saw the genial red face of the drunk Major to whom he had entrusted his thousand pounds at Lottie's. It seemed odd that a man so bulky could be so elusive. Adam was not sure whether the Major saw him, but in some mysterious way Adam's pursuit coincided with the Major's com-plete disappearance. The crowd became very dense, brandishing flasks and sandwiches. When Adam reached the spot where the Major had stood he found two policemen arresting a pickpocket.

''Ere, who are you pushing?' asked the spectators.

'Have you seen a drunk Major anywhere?' asked Adam.

But no one could help him, and he returned disconsolately to Nina, whom he found in conversation with a young man with a curly red moustache.

The young man said he was fed up with racing, and Adam said he was too; so the young man said why didn't they come back to London in his bus, so Adam and Nina said they would. The bus turned out to be a very large, brand-new racing car, and they got to London in time for dinner. Nina explained that the young man used to play with her as a child, and that he had been doing something military in Ceylon for the last five years. The young man's name was Eddy Littlejohn, but over dinner he said, look here, would they call him Ginger; everyone else did. So they began to call him Ginger, and he said wouldn't it be a good idea if they had another bottle of fizz, and Nina and Adam said yes, it would, so they had a magnum and got very friendly.

'You know,' said Ginger, 'it was awful luck meeting you two to-day. I was getting awfully fed up with London. It's so damn slow. I came back meaning to have a good time, you know, paint the place a bit red, and all that. Well, the other day I was reading the paper, and there was a bit that said that the posh place to go to dance nowadays was the Casanova Hotel in Bloomsbury. Well, it seemed a bit rum to me – place I'd never heard of, you know – but, still, I'd been away for some time and places change and all that, so I put on my bib and tucker and toddled off, hoping for a bit of innocent amusement. Well, I mean to say, you never saw such a place. There were only about three people dancing, so I said, "Where's the bar?" And they said, "Bar!" And I said, "You know, for a drink." And they said, well, they could probably make me some coffee. And I said, "No, not coffee." And then they said they hadn't got a licence for what they called alcohol. Well, I mean to say, if that's the best London can do, give me Colombo. I wonder who writes things like that in the papers?'

'As a matter of fact, *I* do.'

'I say no, do you? You must be frightfully brainy. Did you write all that about the green bowlers?'

'Yes.'

'Well, I mean to say, whoever heard of a green bowler, I mean . . . I tell you what, you know, I believe it was all a leg pull. You know, I think that's damn funny. Why, a whole lot of poor mutts may have gone and bought green bowlers.'

After this they went on to the Café de la Paix, where they met Johnny Hoop, who asked them all to the party in a few days' time in the captive balloon.

But Ginger was not to be had twice.

'Oh, no you know,' he said, 'not in a captive balloon. You're trying to pull the old leg again. Whoever heard of a party in a captive balloon? I mean to say, suppose one fell out, I mean?'

Adam telephoned his page through to the *Excess*, and soon after this a coloured singer appeared, paddling his black suède shoes in a pool of limelight, who excited Ginger's disapproval. He didn't mind niggers, Ginger said; remarking justly that niggers were all very well in their place, but, after all, one didn't come all the way from Colombo to London just to see niggers. So they left the Café de la Paix, and went to Lottie's, where Ginger became a little moody, saying that London wasn't home to him any more and that things were changed.

'You know,' said Ginger, 'all the time I've been out in Ceylon I've always said to myself, "As soon as the governor kicks the bucket, and I come in for the family doubloons and pieces of eight, I'm going to come back to England and have a real old bust." And now when it comes to the point there doesn't seem to be anything I much want to do.'

'How about a little drink?' said Lottie.

So Ginger had a drink, and then he and an American sang the Eton Boating Song several times. At the end of the evening he admitted that there was some life left in the jolly old capital of the Empire.

Next day Mr Chatterbox's readers learned that: '*Captain "Ginger" Littlejohn, as he is known to his intimates, was one of the well-*

known sporting figures at the November Handicap who favoured the new bottle-green bowler. Captain Littlejohn is one of the wealthiest and best-known bachelors in Society, and I have lately heard his name spoken of in connection with the marriage of the daughter of a famous ducal house. He came all the way to yesterday's races in his own motor omnibus, which he drives himself . . .'

For some days Ginger's name figured largely on Adam's page, to his profound embarrassment. Several engagements were predicted for him, it was rumoured that he had signed a contract with a film company, that he had bought a small island in the Bristol Channel which he proposed to turn into a country club, and that his forthcoming novel about Singhalese life contained many very thinly disguised portraits of London celebrities.

But the green bowler joke had gone too far. Adam was sent for by Lord Monomark.

'Now see here, Symes,' said the great man, 'I like your page. It's peppy; it's got plenty of new names in it and it's got the intimate touch I like. I read it every day and so does my daughter. Keep on that way and you'll be all right. But *what's all this about bottle-green bowlers?*'

'Well, of course, sir, they're only worn by a limited number of people at present, but . . .'

'Have you got one? Show me a green bowler.'

'I don't wear one myself, I'm afraid.'

'Well, where d'you see 'em? I haven't seen one yet. My daughter hasn't seen one. Who does wear 'em? Where do they buy 'em? That's what I want to know. Now see here, Symes, I don't say that there ain't any such thing as a green bowler;[24] there may be and again there mayn't. But from now on there are going to be no more bottle-green bowlers in my paper. See. And another thing. This Count Cincinnati. I don't say *he* doesn't exist. He may do and he mayn't. But the Italian Ambassador doesn't know anything about him and the Almanak de Gotha[25] doesn't. So as far as my paper goes that's good enough for him. And I don't want any more about Espinosa's. They made out my bill wrong last night.

'Got those three things clear? Tabulate them in the mind – 1, 2,

3, that's the secret of memory. Tab-u-late. All right, then, run along now and tell the Home Secretary he can come right in. You'll find him waiting in the passage – ugly little man with a pince-nez.'

Chapter Eight

*

Two nights later Adam and Nina took Ginger to the party in the captive dirigible. It was not a really good evening. The long drive in Ginger's car to the degraded suburb where the airship was moored chilled and depressed them, dissipating the gaiety which had flickered rather spasmodically over Ginger's dinner.

The airship seemed to fill the whole field, tethered a few feet from the ground by innumerable cables over which they stumbled painfully on the way to the steps. These had been covered by a socially minded caterer with a strip of red carpet.

Inside, the saloons were narrow and hot, communicating to each other by spiral staircases and metal alleys. There were protrusions at every corner, and Miss Runcible had made herself a mass of bruises in the first half-hour. There was a band and a bar and all the same faces. It was the first time that a party was given in an airship.

Adam went aloft to a kind of terrace. Acres of inflated silk blotted out the sky, stirring just perceptibly in the breeze. The lights of other cars arriving lit up the uneven grass. A few louts had collected round the gates to jeer. There were two people making love to each other near him on the terrace, reclining on cushions. There was also a young woman he did not know, holding one of the stays and breathing heavily; evidently she felt unwell. One of the lovers lit a cigar and Adam observed that they were Mary Mouse and the Maharajah of Pukkapore.

Presently Nina joined him. 'It seems such a waste,' she said, thinking of Mary and the Maharajah, 'that two very rich people like that should fall in love with each other.'

'Nina,' said Adam, 'let's get married soon, don't you think?'

'Yes, it's a bore not being married.'

The young woman who felt ill passed by them, walking shakily, to try and find her coat and her young man to take her home.

'. . . I don't know if it sounds absurd,' said Adam, 'but I do feel that a marriage ought to *go on* – for quite a long time, I mean. D'you feel that too, at all?'

'Yes, it's one of the things about a marriage!'

'I'm glad you feel that. I didn't quite know if you did. Otherwise it's all rather bogus, isn't it?'

'I think you ought to go and see papa again,' said Nina. 'It's never any good writing. Go and tell him that you've got a job and are terribly rich and that we're going to be married before Christmas!'[26]

'All right. I'll do that.'

'. . . D'you remember last month we arranged for you to go and see him the first time? . . . just like this . . . it was at Archie Schwert's party . . .'

'Oh, Nina, *what a lot of parties.*'

(. . . Masked parties, Savage parties, Victorian parties, Greek parties, Wild West parties, Russian parties, Circus parties, parties where one had to dress as somebody else, almost naked parties in St John's Wood, parties in flats and studios and houses and ships and hotels and night clubs, in windmills and swimming-baths, tea parties at school where one ate muffins and meringues and tinned crab, parties at Oxford where one drank brown sherry and smoked Turkish cigarettes, dull dances in London and comic dances in Scotland and disgusting dances in Paris – all that succession and repetition of massed humanity . . . Those vile bodies . . .)

He leant his forehead, to cool it, on Nina's arm and kissed her in the hollow of her forearm.

'I *know*, darling,' she said, and put her hand on his hair.

Ginger came strutting jauntily by, his hands clasped under his coat-tails.

'Hullo, you two,' he said. 'Pretty good show this, what.'

'Are you enjoying yourself, Ginger?'

'*Rather*. I say, I've met an awful good chap called Miles. Regular topper. You know, *pally*. That's what I like about a really decent party – you meet such topping fellows. I mean some chaps it takes absolutely years to know but a chap like Miles I feel is a pal straight away.'

*

Presently cars began to drive away again. Miss Runcible said that she had heard of a divine night club near Leicester Square some- where where you could get a drink at any hour of the night. It was called the St Christopher's Social Club.

So they all went there in Ginger's car.

On the way Ginger said, 'That cove Miles, you know, he's awfully *queer* . . .'[27]

St Christopher's Social Club took some time to find.

It was a little door at the side of a shop, and the man who opened it held his foot against it and peeped round.

They paid ten shillings each and signed false names in the vis- itors' book. Then they went downstairs to a very hot room full of cigarette smoke; there were unsteady tables with bamboo legs round the walls and there were some people in shirt sleeves dancing on a shiny linoleum floor.

There was a woman in a yellow beaded frock playing a piano and another in red playing the fiddle.

They ordered some whisky. The waiter said he was sorry, but he couldn't oblige, not that night he couldn't. The police had just rung up to say that they were going to make a raid any minute. If they liked they could have some nice kippers.

Miss Runcible said that kippers were not very drunk-making and that the whole club seemed bogus to her.

Ginger said well anyway they had better have some kippers now they were there. Then he asked Nina to dance and she said no. Then he asked Miss Runcible and she said no, too.

Then they ate kippers.

Presently one of the men in shirt sleeves (who had clearly had a lot to drink before the St Christopher Social Club knew about the police) came up to their table and said to Adam:

'You don't know me. I'm Gilmour. I don't want to start a row in front of ladies, but when I see a howling cad I like to tell him so.'

Adam said, 'Why do you spit when you talk?'

Gilmour said, 'That is a very unfortunate physical disability, and it shows what a howling cad you are that you mention it.'

Then Ginger said, 'Same to you, old boy, with knobs on.'

Then Gilmour said, 'Hullo, Ginger, old scout.'

And Ginger said, 'Why, it's Bill. You mustn't mind Bill. Awfully stout chap. Met him on the boat.'

Gilmour said, 'Any pal of Ginger's is a pal of mine.'

So Adam and Gilmour shook hands.

Gilmour said, 'This is a pretty low joint, anyhow. You chaps come round to my place and have a drink.'

So they went to Gilmour's place.

Gilmour's place was a bed-sitting-room in Ryder Street.

So they sat on the bed in Gilmour's place and drank whisky while Gilmour was sick next door.

And Ginger said, 'There's nowhere like London really you know.'

That same evening while Adam and Nina sat on the deck of the dirigible a party of quite a different sort was being given at Anchorage House. This last survivor of the noble town houses of London was, in its time, of dominating and august dimensions, and even now, when it had become a mere 'picturesque bit' lurking in a ravine between concrete skyscrapers, its pillared façade, standing back from the street and obscured by railings and some wisps of foliage, had grace and dignity and other-worldliness enough to cause a flutter or two in Mrs Hoop's heart as she drove into the forecourt.

'Can't you just see the *ghosts*?' she said to Lady Circumference on the stairs. 'Pitt and Fox and Burke and Lady Hamilton and Beau Brummel and Dr Johnson' (a concurrence of celebrities, it may be remarked, at which something memorable might surely have occurred). 'Can't you just *see* them – in their buckled shoes?'

Lady Circumference raised her lorgnette and surveyed the stream of guests debouching from the cloak-rooms like City workers from the Underground. She saw Mr Outrage and Lord Metroland in consultation about the Censorship Bill (a statesmanlike and much-needed measure which empowered a committee of five atheists to destroy all books, pictures and films they considered undesirable, without any nonsense about defence or appeal). She saw both Archbishops, the Duke and Duchess of Stayle, Lord Vanburgh and Lady Metroland, Lady Throbbing and Edward

Throbbing and Mrs Blackwater, Mrs Mouse and Lord Monomark and a superb Levantine, and behind and about them a great concourse of pious and honourable people (many of whom made the Anchorage House reception the one outing of the year), their women-folk well gowned in rich and durable stuffs, their men-folk ablaze with orders; people who had represented their country in foreign places and sent their sons to die for her in battle, people of decent and temperate life, uncultured, unaffected, unembarrassed, unassuming, unambitious people, of independent judgment and marked eccentricities, kind people who cared for animals and the deserving poor, brave and rather unreasonable people, that fine phalanx of the passing order, approaching, as one day at the Last Trump they hoped to meet their Maker, with decorous and frank cordiality to shake Lady Anchorage by the hand at the top of her staircase. Lady Circumference saw all this and sniffed the exhalation of her own herd. But she saw no ghosts.

'That's all my eye,' she said.

But Mrs Hoop ascended step by step in a confused but very glorious dream of eighteenth-century elegance.

The Presence of Royalty was heavy as thunder in the drawing-room.

The Baroness Yoshiwara and the Prime Minister met once more.

'I tried to see you twice this week,' she said, 'but always you were busy. We are leaving London. Perhaps you heard? My husband has been moved to Washington. It was his wish to go . . .'

'No. I say, Baroness . . . I had no idea. That's very bad news. We shall all miss you terribly.'

'I thought perhaps I would come to make my adieux. One day next week.'

'Why, yes, of course, that would be delightful. You must both come to dine. I'll get my secretary to fix something up to-morrow.'

'It has been nice being in London . . . you were kind.'

'Not a bit. I don't know what London would be without our guests from abroad.'

'Oh, twenty damns to your great pig-face,' said the Baroness suddenly and turned away.

Mr Outrage watched her bewildered. Finally he said, 'For East is East and West is West and never the twain shall meet' (which was a poor conclusion for a former Foreign Secretary).

Edward Throbbing stood talking to the eldest daughter of the Duchess of Stayle. She was some inches taller than he and inclined slightly so that, in the general murmur of conversation, she should not miss any of his colonial experiences. She wore a frock such as only duchesses can obtain for their elder daughters, a garment curiously puckered and puffed up and enriched with old lace at improbable places, from which her pale beauty emerged as though from a clumsily tied parcel. Neither powder, rouge nor lipstick had played any part in her toilet and her colourless hair was worn long and bound across her forehead in a broad fillet. Long pearl drops hung from her ears and she wore a tight little collar of pearls round her throat. It was generally understood that now Edward Throbbing was back these two would become engaged to be married.

Lady Ursula was acquiescent if unenthusiastic. When she thought about marriage at all, which was rarely (for her chief interests were a girls' club in Canning Town and a younger brother at school), she thought what a pity it was that one had to be so ill to have children. Her married friends spoke of this almost with relish and her mother with awe.

An innate dilatoriness of character rather than any doubt of the ultimate issue kept Edward from verbal proposal. He had decided to arrange everything before Christmas and that was enough. He had no doubt that a suitable occasion would soon be devised for him. It was clearly suitable that he should marry before he was thirty. Now and then when he was with Ursula he felt a slight quickening of possessive impulse towards her fragility and distance; occasionally when he read some rather lubricous novel or saw much love-making on the stage he would translate the characters in his mind and put Lady Ursula, often incongruously, in the place of the heroine. He had no doubt that he was in love.

Perhaps he would propose this very evening and get it over. It was up to Lady Ursula to engineer an occasion. Meanwhile he kept the conversation on to the subject of labour problems in Montreal, about which his information was extensive and accurate.

'He's a nice, steady boy,' said the Duchess, 'and it's a comfort, nowadays, to see two young people so genuinely fond of each other. Of course, nothing is actually arranged yet, but I was talking to Fanny Throbbing yesterday, and apparently Edward has already spoken to her on the subject. I think that everything will be settled before Christmas. Of course, there's not a great deal of money, but one's learnt not to expect that nowadays, and Mr Outrage speaks very highly of his ability. Quite one of the coming men in the party.'

'Well,' said Lady Circumference, 'you know your own business, but if you ask me I shouldn't care to see a daughter of mine marry into that family. Bad hats every one of them. Look at the father and the sister, and from all I hear the brother is rotten all through.'

'I don't say it's a match I should have chosen myself. There's certainly a bad strain in the Malpractices . . . but you know how headstrong children are nowadays, and they seem so fond of each other . . . and there seem so few young men about. At least I never seem to see any.'

'Young toads, the whole lot of them,' said Lady Circumference.

'And these *terrible* parties which I'm told they give. I don't know what I should have done if Ursula had ever wanted to go to them . . . the poor Chasms . . .'

'If I were Viola Chasm I'd give that girl a thunderin' good hidin'.'

The topic of the Younger Generation spread through the company like a yawn. Royalty remarked on their absence and those happy mothers who had even one docile daughter in tow swelled with pride and commiseration.

'I'm told that they're having another of their parties,' said Mrs Mouse, 'in an aeroplane this time.'

'In an aeroplane? How very extraordinary.'

'Of course, I never hear a word from Mary, but her maid told my maid . . .'

'What I always wonder, Kitty dear, is what they actually *do* at these parties of theirs. I mean, *do* they . . .?'

'My dear, from all I hear, I think they do.'

'Oh, to be young again, Kitty. When I think, my dear, of all the trouble and exertion which we had to go through to be even moderately bad . . . those passages in the early morning, and mama sleeping next door.'

'And yet, my dear, I doubt very much whether they really *appreciate* it all as much as we should . . . young people take things so much for granted. *Si la jeunesse savait.*'

'*Si la vieillesse pouvait,* Kitty.'

Later that evening Mr Outrage stood almost alone in the supper-room drinking a glass of champagne. Another episode in his life was closed, another of those tantalizing glimpses of felicity capriciously withdrawn. Poor Mr Outrage, thought Mr Outrage; poor, poor old Outrage, always just on the verge of revelation, of some sublime and transfiguring experience; always frustrated . . . Just Prime Minister, nothing more, bullied by his colleagues, a source of income to low caricaturists. Was Mr Outrage an immortal soul, thought Mr Outrage; had he wings, was he free and unconfined, was he born for eternity? He sipped his champagne, fingered his ribbon of the Order of Merit, and resigned himself to the dust.

Presently he was joined by Lord Metroland and Father Rothschild.

'Margot's left – gone on to some party in an airship. I've been talking to Lady Anchorage for nearly an hour about the younger generation.'

'Everyone seems to have been talking about the younger generation to-night. The most boring subject I know.'

'Well, after all, what does all this stand for if there's going to be no one to carry it on?'

'All what?' Mr Outrage looked round the supper-room, deserted save for two footmen who leant against the walls looking as waxen as the clumps of flowers sent up that morning from hot-houses in the country. 'What does all what stand for?'

'All this business of government.'

'As far as I'm concerned it stands for a damned lot of hard work and precious little in return. If those young people can find a way to get on without it, good luck to them.'

'I see what Metroland means,' said Father Rothschild.

'Blessed if I do. Anyway I've got no children myself, and I'm thankful for it. I don't understand them, and I don't want to. They had a chance after the war that no generation has ever had. There was a whole civilization to be saved and remade – and all they seem to do is to play the fool. Mind you, I'm all in favour of them having a fling. I dare say that Victorian ideas *were* a bit strait-laced. Saving your cloth, Rothschild, it's only human nature to run a bit loose when one's young. But there's something wanton about these young people to-day. That stepson of yours, Metroland, and that girl of poor old Chasm's and young Throbbing's brother.'

'Don't you think,' said Father Rothschild gently, 'that perhaps it is all in some way historical? I don't think people ever *want* to lose their faith either in religion or anything else. I know very few young people, but it seems to me that they are all possessed with an almost fatal hunger for permanence. I think all these divorces show that. People aren't content just to muddle along nowadays . . . And this word "bogus" they all use . . . They won't make the best of a bad job nowadays. My private schoolmaster used to say, "If a thing's worth doing at all, it's worth doing well." My Church has taught that in different words for several centuries. But these young people have got hold of another end of the stick, and for all we know it may be the right one. They say, "If a thing's not worth doing well, it's not worth doing at all." It makes everything very difficult for them.'

'Good heavens, I should think it did. What a darned silly principle. I mean to say, if one didn't do anything that wasn't worth doing well – why, what *would* one do? I've always maintained that success in this world depends on knowing exactly how little effort each job is worth . . . distribution of energy . . . And, I suppose, most people would admit that I was a pretty successful man.'

'Yes, I suppose they would, Outrage,' said Father Rothschild, looking at him rather quizzically.

But that self-accusing voice in the Prime Minister's heart was silent. There was nothing like a little argument for settling the mind. Everything became so simple as soon as it was put into words.

'And anyway, what do you mean by "historical"?'

'Well, it's like this war that's coming . . .'

'*What war?*' said the Prime Minister sharply. 'No one has said anything to me about a war. I really think I should have been told. I'll be damned,' he said defiantly, 'if they shall have a war without consulting me. What's a Cabinet for if there's not more mutual confidence than that? What do they want a war for, anyway?'

'That's the whole point. No one talks about it, and no one wants it. No one talks about it *because* no one wants it. They're all afraid to breathe a word about it.'

'Well, hang it all, if no one wants it, who's going to make them have it?'

'Wars don't start nowadays because people want them. We long for peace, and fill our newspapers with conferences about disarmament and arbitration, but there is a radical instability in our whole world-order, and soon we shall all be walking into the jaws of destruction again, protesting our pacific intentions.'

'Well, you seem to know all about it,' said Mr Outrage, 'and I think I should have been told sooner. This will have to mean a coalition with that old wind-bag Brown, I suppose.'

'Anyhow,' said Lord Metroland, 'I don't see how all that explains why my stepson should drink like a fish and go about everywhere with a negress.'

'I think they're connected, you know,' said Father Rothschild. 'But it's all very difficult.'

Then they separated.

Father Rothschild pulled on a pair of overall trousers in the forecourt and, mounting his motor cycle, disappeared into the night, for he had many people to see and much business to transact before he went to bed.

Lord Metroland left the house in some depression. Margot had taken the car, but it was scarcely five minutes' walk to Hill Street.

He took a vast cigar from his case, lit it and sank his chin in the astrakhan collar of his coat, conforming almost exactly to the popular conception of a highly enviable man. But his heart was heavy. What a lot of nonsense Rothschild had talked. At least he hoped it was nonsense.

By ill-fortune he arrived on the doorstep to find Peter Pastmaster fumbling with the lock, and they entered together. Lord Metroland noticed a tall hat on the table by the door. 'Young Trumpington's, I suppose,' he thought. His stepson did not once look at him, but made straight for the stairs, walking unsteadily, his hat on the back of his head, his umbrella still in his hand.

'Good night, Peter,' said Lord Metroland.

'Oh, go to hell,' said his stepson thickly, then, turning on the stairs, he added, 'I'm going abroad to-morrow for a few weeks. Will you tell my mother?'[28]

'Have a good time,' said Lord Metroland. 'You'll find it just as cold everywhere, I'm afraid. Would you care to take the yacht? No one's using it.'

'Oh, go to hell.'

Lord Metroland went into the study to finish his cigar. It would be awkward if he met young Trumpington on the stairs. He sat down in a very comfortable chair . . . A radical instability, Rothschild had said, radical instability . . . He looked round his study and saw shelves of books – the *Dictionary of National Biography*, the *Encyclopaedia Britannica* in an early and very bulky edition, *Who's Who*, Debrett, Burke, Whitaker, several volumes of Hansard, some Blue Books and Atlases – a safe in the corner painted green with a brass handle, his writing-table, his secretary's table, some very comfortable chairs and some very business-like chairs, a tray with decanters and a plate of sandwiches, his evening mail laid out on the table . . . radical instability, indeed. How like poor old Outrage to let himself get taken in by that charlatan of a Jesuit.

He heard the front door open and shut behind Alastair Trumpington.

Then he rose and went quietly upstairs, leaving his cigar smouldering in the ash-tray, filling the study with fragrant smoke.

*

Quarter of a mile away the Duchess of Stayle went, as she always did, to say good night to her eldest daughter. She crossed the room and drew up the window a few inches, for it was a cold and raw night. Then she went over to the bed and smoothed the pillow.

'Good night, dear child,' she said. 'I thought you looked sweet to-night.'

Lady Ursula wore a white cambric night-gown with a little yoke collar and long sleeves. Her hair hung in two plaits.

'Mama,' she said. 'Edward proposed to me to-night.'

'*Darling*. What a funny girl you are. Why didn't you tell me before? You weren't frightened, were you? You know that your father and I are delighted at anything that makes our little girl happy.'

'Well, I said I wouldn't marry him . . . I'm sorry.'

'But, my dear, it's nothing to be sorry about. Leave it to your old mother. I'll put it all right for you in the morning.'

'But, Mama, I don't want to marry him. I didn't know until it actually came to the point. I'd always meant to marry him, as you know. But somehow, when he actually asked me . . . I just couldn't.'

'There, dear child, you mustn't worry any more. You know perfectly well, don't you, that your father and I would not let you do anything you didn't want. It's a matter that only you can decide. After all, it's your life and your happiness at stake, not ours, isn't it, Ursula? . . . but I *think* you'd better marry Edward.'

'But, Mama, I don't want to . . . I couldn't . . . it would kill me!'

'Now, now, my pet mustn't worry her head about it any more. You know your father and I only want *your* happiness, dear one. No one is going to make my darling girl do anything she doesn't want to . . . Papa shall see Edward in the morning and make everything all right . . . dear Lady Anchorage was only saying to-night what a lovely bride you will make.'

'But, Mama . . .'

'Not another word, dear child. It's very late and you've got to look your best for Edward to-morrow, haven't you, love?'

The Duchess closed the door softly and went to her own room. Her husband was in his dressing-room.

'Andrew.'

'What is it, dear? I'm saying my prayers.'

'Edward proposed to Ursula to-night.'

'Ah!'

'Aren't you glad?'

'I told you, dear, I'm trying to say my prayers.'

'It's a real joy to see the dear children so happy.'

Chapter Nine

*

At luncheon-time next day Adam rang up Nina.

'Nina, darling, are you awake?'

'Well, I wasn't . . .'

'Listen, do you really want me to go and see your papa to-day?'

'Did we say you were going to?'

'Yes.'

'Why?'

'To say could we be married now I had a job.'

'I remember . . . yes, go and see him, darling. It would be nice to be married.'

'But, listen, what about my page?'

'What page, angel?'

'My page in the *Excess* . . . my job, you know.'

'Oh . . . well, look . . . Ginger and I will write that for you.'

'Wouldn't that be a bore?'

'I think it would be divine. I know just the sort of things you say . . . I expect Ginger does too by now, the poor angel . . . how he did enjoy himself last night . . . I'm going to sleep now . . . such a pain . . . good-bye, my sweet.'

Adam had some luncheon. Agatha Runcible was at the next table with Archie Schwert. She said they were all going to some motor races next day. Would Adam and Nina come, too. Adam said yes. Then he went to Aylesbury.

There were two women on the other side of the carriage, and they, too, were talking about the Younger Generation.

'. . . and it's a very good position, too, for a boy of that age, and I've told him and his father told him. "You ought to think yourself lucky," I've said, "to get a good position like that in these days, particularly when it's so hard to get a position at all of any kind *or* sort." And there's Mrs Hemingway with her son next door who left school eighteen months ago, and there he is kicking his heels about the house all day and doing nothing, and taking a correspondence course in civil engineering. "It's a very good position", I told him, "and, of course, you can't expect *work* to be interesting, though no doubt after a time you get used to it just as your father's done, and would probably miss it if you hadn't it to do" – you know how Alfred gets on his holidays, doesn't know what to do with himself half the time, just looks at the sea and says, "Well, this *is* a change", and then starts wondering how things are at the office. Well, I told Bob that, but it's no good, and all he wants to do is to go into the motor business; well, as I said to him, the motor business is all right for them that have influence, but what could Bob hope to do throwing up a good job, too, and with nothing to fall back on supposing things did go wrong. But, no, Bob is all for motors, and, of course, you know it doesn't really do having him living at home. He and his father don't get on. You can't have two men in a house together and both wanting the bath at the same time, and I suppose it's only natural that Bob should feel he ought to have his own way a bit more now that he's earning his own money. But, then, what is he to do? He can't go and live on his own with his present salary, and I shouldn't be any too pleased to see him doing it even if he could afford it – you know what it is with young people, how easy it is to get into mischief when they're left to themselves. And there are a great many of Bob's friends now that I don't really approve of, not to have in and out of the house, you know the way they do come. He meets them at the hockey club he goes to Saturdays. And they're most of them earning more money than he is, or, at any rate, they seem to have more to throw about, and it isn't good for a boy being about with those that have more money than him. It only makes him discontented. And I did think at one time that perhaps Bob was thinking of Betty Rylands, you know Mrs Rylands' girl at the Laurels, such nice people, and they used to play tennis together and people remarked how much they were about, but now he never seems to pay any attention to her, it's all his hockey friends, and I said one Saturday, "Wouldn't you like to ask Betty over to tea?" and he said, "Well, you can if you like", and she came looking ever so sweet, and, would you believe it, Bob went out and didn't come in at all until supper-time. Well, you can't expect any girl to put up with that, and now she's practically engaged to that young Anderson boy who's in the wireless business.'

'Well, and there's our Lily now. You know how she would go in for being a manicurist. Her father didn't like it, and for a long time he wouldn't have it at all. He said it was just an excuse for holding hands, but, anyway, I said, "If that's what the girl wants to do, and if she can make good money doing it, I think you ought to be able to trust your own daughter better than to stand in her way." I'm a modern, you see. "We're not living in the Victorian Age," I told him. Well, she's in a very nice job. Bond Street – and they treat her very fair, and we've no complaints on that score, but now there's this man she's met there – he's old enough to be her father – well, middle-aged anyway – but very smart, you know, neat little grey moustache, absolute gentleman, with a Morris Oxford saloon. And he comes and takes her out for drives Sundays, and sometimes he fetches her after work and takes her to the pictures, and always most polite and well spoken to me and my husband, just as you'd expect, seeing the sort of man he is, and he sent us all tickets for the theatre the other night. Very affable, calls me "Ma", if you please . . . and, anyway, I *hope* there's no harm in it . . .'

'Now our Bob . . .'

They got out at Berkhamsted, and a man got in who wore a bright brown suit and spent his time doing sums, which never seemed to come right, in a little note-book with a stylographic pen. 'Has he given all to his daughters?' thought Adam.

He drove out to Doubting by a bus which took him as far as the village of petrol pumps. From there he walked down the lane to the park gates. To his surprise these stood open, and as he approached he narrowly missed being run down by a large and ramshackle car which swept in at a high speed; he caught a glimpse of two malignant female eyes which glared contemptuously at him from the small window at the back. Still more surprising was a large notice which hung on the central pier of the gates and said: 'No ADMITTANCE EXCEPT ON BUSINESS'. As Adam walked up the drive two lorries thundered past him. Then a man appeared with a red flag.

'Hi! You can't go that way. They're shooting in front. Go round by the stables, whoever you are.'

Wondering vaguely what kind of sport this could be, Adam followed the side path indicated. He listened for sounds of firing, but hearing nothing except distant shouting and what seemed to be a string band, he concluded that the Colonel was having a poor day. It seemed odd, anyway, to go shooting in front of one's house with a string band, and automatically Adam began making up a paragraph about it:

'*Colonel Blount, father of the lovely Miss Nina Blount referred to above, rarely comes to London nowadays. He devotes himself instead to shooting on his estate in Buckinghamshire. The coverts, which are among the most richly stocked in the country, lie immediately in front of the house, and many amusing stories are related of visitors who have inadvertently found themselves in the line of fire . . . Colonel Blount has the curious eccentricity of being unable to shoot his best except to the accompaniment of violin and 'cello. (Mr "Ginger" Littlejohn has the similar foible that he can only fish to the sound of the flageolet . . .)*'[29]

He had not gone very far in his detour before he was again stopped, this time by a man dressed in a surplice, episcopal lawn sleeves and scarlet hood and gown; he was smoking a cigar.

'Here, what in hell do *you* want?' said the Bishop.

'I came to see Colonel Blount.'

'Well, you can't, son. They're just shooting him now.'

'Good heavens. What for?'

'Oh, nothing important. He's just one of the Wesleyans, you know – we're trying to polish off the whole crowd this afternoon while the weather's good.'

Adam found himself speechless before this cold-blooded bigotry.

'What d'you want to see the old geezer about, anyway?'

'Well, it hardly seems any good now. I came to tell him that I'd got a job on the *Excess*.'

'The devil you have. Why didn't you say so before? Always pleased to see gentlemen of the Press. Have a weed?' A large cigar-case appeared from the recesses of the episcopal bosom. 'I'm Bishop Philpotts, you know,' he said, slipping a voluminously clothed arm through Adam's. 'I dare say you'd like to come round to the front and see the fun. I should think they'd be just singing their last hymn now. It's been uphill work,' he confided as they walked round the side of the house, 'and there's been some damned bad management. Why, yesterday, they kept Miss La Touche waiting the whole afternoon, and then the light was so bad when they did shoot her that they made a complete mess of her – we had the machine out and ran over all the bits carefully last night after dinner – you never saw such rotten little scraps – quite unrecognizable half of them. We didn't dare show them to her husband – he'd be sick to death about it – so we just cut out a few shots to keep and threw away the rest. I say, you're not feeling queer, are you? You look all green suddenly. Find the weed a bit strong?'

'Was – was she a Wesleyan too?'

'My dear boy, she's playing lead . . . she's Selina, Countess of Huntingdon . . . There, now you can see them at work.'

They had rounded the wing and were now in full view of the front of the house, where all was activity and animation. A dozen or so men and women in eighteenth-century costume were standing in a circle singing strongly, while in their centre stood a small man in a long clerical coat and a full white wig, conducting them. A string band was playing not far off, and round the singers clustered numerous men in shirt-sleeves bearing megaphones, cinematograph cameras, microphones, sheaves of paper and arc lamps. Not far away, waiting their turn to be useful, stood a coach and four, a detachment of soldiers and some scene shifters with the transept of Exeter Cathedral in sections of canvas and match-boarding.

'The Colonel's somewhere in that little crowd singing the hymn,' said the Bishop. 'He was crazy to be allowed to come on as a super, and as he's letting us the house dirt cheap Isaacs said he might. I don't believe he's ever been so happy in his life.'

As they approached the hymn stopped.

'All right,' said one of the men with megaphones. 'You can beat it. We'll shoot the duel now. I shall want two supers to carry the body. The rest of you are through for the afternoon.'

A man in a leather apron, worsted stockings and flaxen wig emerged from the retreating worshippers.

'Oh, please, Mr Isaacs,' he said, 'please may *I* carry the body?'

'All right, Colonel, if you want to. Run in and tell them in the wardrobe to give you a smock and a pitchfork.'

'Thank you so much,' said Colonel Blount, trotting off towards his house. Then he stopped. 'I suppose,' he said, 'I suppose it wouldn't be better for me to carry a sword?'

'No, pitchfork, and hurry up about it or I shan't let you carry the body at all; someone go and find Miss La Touche.'

The young lady whom Adam had seen in the motor car came down the steps of the house in a feathered hat, riding-habit and braided cape. She carried a hunting-crop in her hand. Her face was painted very yellow.

'Do I or do I not have a horse in this scene, Mr Isaacs? I've been round to Bertie and he says all the horses are needed for the coach.'

'I'm sorry, Effie, you do *not* and it's no good taking on. We only got four horses and you know that, and you saw what it was like when we tried to move the coach with two. So you've just got to face it. You comes across the fields on foot.'

'Dirty Yid,' said Effie La Touche.

'The trouble about this film,' said the Bishop, 'is that we haven't enough capital. It's heart-breaking. Here we have a first-rate company, first-rate producer, first-rate scene, first-rate story and the whole thing being hung up for want of a few hundred pounds. How can he expect to get the best out of Miss La Touche if they won't give her a horse? No girl will stand for that sort of treatment. If I were Isaacs I'd scrap the whole coach sooner. It's no sense getting a star and not treating her right. Isaacs is putting everyone's back up the way he goes on. Wanted to do the whole of my cathedral scene with twenty-five supers. But you're here to give us a write-up, aren't you? I'll call Isaacs across and let him give you the dope . . . *Isaacs*!'

'Yuh?'

'*Daily Excess* here.'

'Where?'

'Here.'

'I'll be right over.' He put on his coat, buttoned it tightly at the waist and strode across the lawn, extending a hand of welcome. Adam shook it and felt what seemed to be a handful of rings under his fingers. 'Pleased to meet you, Mister. Now just you ask me anything you want about this film because I'm just here to answer. Have you got my name? Have a card. That's the name of the company in the corner. Not the one that's scratched out. The one written above. *The Wonderfilm Company of Great Britain.* Now this film,' he said, in what seemed a well-practised little speech, 'of which you have just witnessed a mere fragment marks a stepping stone in the development of the British Film Industry. It is the most important All-Talkie super-religious film to be produced solely in this country by British artists and management and by British capital. It has been directed throughout regardless of difficulty and expense, and supervised by a staff of expert historians and theologians. Nothing has been omitted that would contribute to the meticulous accuracy of every detail. The life of that great social and religious reformer John Wesley[30] is for the first time portrayed to a British public in all its humanity and tragedy . . . Look here, I've got all this written out. I'll have them give you a copy before you go. Come and see the duel . . .

'That's Wesley and Whitefield just going to start. Of course, it's not them really. Two fencing instructors we got over from the gym at Aylesbury. That's what I mean when I say we spare no expense to get the details accurate. Ten bob each we're paying them for the afternoon.'

'But did Wesley and Whitefield fight a duel?'

'Well, it's not actually recorded, but it's known that they quarrelled and there was only one way of settling quarrels in those days. They're both in love with Selina, Countess of Huntingdon, you see. She comes to stop them, but arrives too late. Whitefield has escaped in the coach and Wesley is lying wounded. That's a scene that'll go over big. Then she takes him back to her home and nurses him back to health. I tell you, this is going to make film history. D'you know what the Wesleyan population of the British Isles is? Well nor do I, but I've been told and *you'd be surprised.* Well every one of those is going to come and see this film and there's going to be discussions about it in all the chapels. We're recording extracts from Wesley's sermons and we're singing all his own hymns. I'm glad your paper's interested. You can tell them from me that we're on a big thing . . . There's one thing though,' said Mr Isaacs, suddenly becoming confidential, 'which I shouldn't tell many people. But I think you'll understand because you've seen some of our work here and the sort of scale it's on, and you can imagine that expenses are pretty heavy. Why, I'm paying Miss La Touche alone over ten pounds a week. And the truth is – I don't mind telling you – we're beginning to feel the wind a bit. It's going to be a big success *when* and *if* it's finished. Now, suppose there was someone – yourself, for instance, or one of your friends – who had a little bit of loose capital he wanted to invest – a thousand pounds, say – well, I wouldn't mind selling him a half share. It's not a gamble, mind – it's a certain winner. If I cared to go into the open market with it, it would be snapped up before you could say knife. But I don't want to do that and I'll tell you why. This is a British company and I don't want to let any of those foreign speculators in on it, and once you let the shares get into the open market you can't tell who's buying them, see. Now why leave money idle bringing in four and a half or five per cent when you might be doubling it in six months?'

'I'm afraid it's no use coming to me for capital,' said Adam. 'Do you think I could possibly see Colonel Blount?'

'One of the things I hate in life,' said Mr Isaacs, 'is seeing anyone lose an opportunity. Now listen, I'll make you a fair offer. I can see you're interested in this film. Now I'll sell you the whole thing – film we've made up to date, artists' contracts, copyright of scenario, everything for five hundred quid. Then all you have to do is to finish it off and your fortune's made and I shall be cursing for not having held on longer. How about it?'

'It's very good of you, but really I don't think I can afford it at the moment.'

'Just as you like,' said Mr Isaacs airily. 'There's many who *can* who'd jump at the offer, only I thought I'd let you in on it first because I could see you were a smart kid . . . Tell you what I'll do.

I'll let you have it for four hundred. Can't say fairer than that, can I? And wouldn't do it for anyone but you.'

'I'm terribly sorry, Mr Isaacs, but I didn't come to buy your film. I came to see Colonel Blount.'

'Well, I shouldn't have thought you were the sort of chap to let an opportunity like that slip through your fingers. Now I'll give you one more chance and after that, mind, the offer is closed. I'll sell you it for three-fifty. Take it or leave it. That's my last word. Of course, you're not in any way obliged to buy,' said Mr Isaacs rather haughtily, 'but I assure you that you'll regret it from the bottom of your heart if you don't.'

'I'm sorry,' said Adam, 'I think it's a wonderfully generous offer, but the truth is I simply don't want to buy a film at all.'

'In that case,' said Mr Isaacs, 'I shall return to my business.'

Not till sunset did the Wonderfilm Company of Great Britain rest. Adam watched them from the lawn. He saw the two fencing instructors in long black coats and white neck bands lunging and parrying manfully until one of them fell; then the cameras stopped and his place was taken by the leading actor (who had been obliged through the exigencies of the wardrobe to lend his own coat). Whitefield took the place (and the wig) of the victor and fled to the coach. Effie La Touche appeared from the shrubbery still defiantly carrying her hunting-crop. Close-ups followed of Effie and Wesley and Effie and Wesley together. Then Colonel Blount and another super appeared as yokels and carried the wounded preacher back to the house. All this took a long time as the action was frequently held up by minor mishaps and once when the whole scene had been triumphantly enacted the chief cameraman found that he had forgotten to put in a new roll of film ('Can't think how I come to make a mistake like that, Mr Isaacs'). Finally the horses were taken out of the coach and mounted by grenadiers and a few shots taken of them plunging despairingly up the main drive.

'Part of Butcher Cumberland's army,' explained Mr Isaacs. 'It's always good to work in a little atmosphere like that. Gives more educational value. Besides we hire the horses by the day so we might as well get all we can out of them while they're here. If we don't use 'em in Wesley we can fit 'em in somewhere else. A hundred feet or so of galloping horses is always useful.'

When everything was over Adam managed to see Colonel Blount, but it was not a satisfactory interview.

'I'm afraid I've really got very little time to spare,' he said. 'To tell you the truth, I'm at work on a scenario of my own. They tell me you come from the *Excess* and want to write about the film. It's a glorious film, isn't it? Of course, you know, I have very little to do with it really. I have let them the house and have acted one or two small parts in the crowd. I don't have to pay for them though.'

'No, I should think not.'

'My dear boy, all the others have to. I knocked a little off the rent of the house, but I don't actually *pay*. In fact, you might almost say I was a professional already. You see, Mr Isaacs is the principal of the National Academy of Cinematographic Art. He's got a little office in Edgware Road, just one room, you know, to interview candidates in. Well, if he thinks that they're promising enough – he doesn't take anyone, mind, only a chosen few – he takes them on as pupils. As Mr Isaacs says, the best kind of training is practical work, so he produces a film straight away and pays the professionals out of the pupil's fees. It's really a very simple and sensible plan. All the characters in "John Wesley" are pupils, except Wesley himself and Whitefield and the Bishop and, of course, Miss La Touche – she's the wife of the man who looks after the Edgware Road office when Mr Isaacs is away. Even the cameramen are only learning. It makes everything so exciting, you know. This is the third film Mr Isaacs has produced. The first went wrong, through Mr Isaacs trusting one of the pupils to develop it. Of course, he made him pay damages – that's in the contract they all have to sign – but the film was ruined, and Mr Isaacs said it was disheartening – he nearly gave up the cinema altogether. But then a lot more pupils came along, so they produced another, which was *very* good indeed. Quite a revolution in Film Art, Mr Isaacs said, but that was boycotted through professional jealousy. None of the theatres would show it. But that's been made all right now. Mr Isaacs has got in with the ring, he says, and this is going to establish Wonderfilms as the leading company in the country.

What's more, he's offered me a half share in it for five thousand pounds. It's wonderfully generous, when he might keep it all to himself, but he says that he must have someone who understands *acting* from the practical side on the board of directors. Funnily enough, my bank manager is very much against my going in for it. In fact, he's putting every obstacle in my way . . . But I dare say Mr Isaacs would sooner you didn't put any of this into your paper.'

'What I really came about was your daughter, Nina.'

'Oh, she's not taking any part in the film at all. To tell you the truth, I very much doubt whether she has any real talent. It's funny how these things often skip a generation. My father, now, was a very bad actor indeed – though he always used to take a leading part when we had theatricals at Christmas. Upon my soul, he used to make himself look quite ridiculous sometimes. I remember once he did a skit of Henry Irving in *The Bells* . . .'

'I'm afraid you've forgotten me, sir, but I came here last month to see you about Nina. Well, she wanted me to tell you that I'm Mr Chatterbox now . . .'

'Chatterbox . . . no, my boy, I'm afraid I don't remember you. My memory's not what it was . . . There's a Canon Chatterbox at Worcester I used to know . . . he was up at New College with me . . . unusual name.'

'Mr Chatterbox on the *Daily Excess*.'

'No, no, my dear boy, I assure you not. He was ordained just after I went down and was chaplain somewhere abroad – Bermuda, I think. Then he came home and went to Worcester. He was never on the *Daily Excess* in his life.'

'No, no, sir, *I'm* on the *Daily Excess*.'

'Well, you ought to know your own staff, certainly. He *may* have left Worcester and taken to journalism. A great many parsons do nowadays, I know. But I must say that he's the last fellow I should have expected it of. Awful stupid fellow. Besides, he must be at least seventy . . . Well, well . . . who would have thought it. Good-bye, my boy, I've enjoyed our talk.'

'Oh, sir,' cried Adam, as Colonel Blount began to walk away. 'You don't understand – I want to marry Nina.'

'Well, it's no good coming here,' said the Colonel crossly. 'I told you, she's somewhere in London. She's got nothing to do with the film at all. You'll have to go and ask her about it. Anyway, I happen to know she's engaged already. There was a young ass of a chap down here about it the other day . . . the Rector said he was off his head. Laughed the whole time – bad sign that – still, Nina wants to marry him for some reason. So I'm afraid you're too late, my boy. I'm sorry . . . and, anyway, the Rector's behaved very badly about this film. Wouldn't lend his car. I suppose it's because of the Wesleyanism. Narrow-minded, that . . . Well, good-bye. So nice of you to come. Remember me to Canon Chatterbox. I must look him up next time I come to London and pull his leg about it . . . Writing for the papers, indeed, at his age.'

And Colonel Blount retired victorious.

Late that evening Adam and Nina sat in the gallery of the Café de la Paix eating oysters.

'Well we won't bother any more about papa,' she said. 'We'll just get married at once.'

'We shall be terribly poor.'

'Well, we shan't be any poorer than we are now . . . I think it will be divine . . . Besides, we'll be terribly economical. Miles says he's discovered a place near Tottenham Court Road where you can get oysters for three and six a dozen.'

'Wouldn't they be rather ill-making?'

'Well, Miles said the only odd thing about them is that they all taste a little different . . . I had lunch with Miles to-day. He rang up to find where you were. He wanted to sell Edward Throbbing's engagement to the *Excess*. But Van offered him five guineas for it, so he gave it to them.'

'I'm sorry we missed that. The editor will be furious. By the way, how did the gossip page go? Did you manage to fill it all right?'

'My dear, I think I did rather well. You see Van and Miles didn't know I was in the trade, so they talked about Edward's engagement a whole lot, so I went and put it in . . . was that very caddish? . . . and I wrote a lot about Edward and the girl he's to marry. I used to know her when I came out, and that took up half the page.

So I just put in a few imaginary ones like you do, so then it was finished.'

'What did you say in the imaginary ones?'

'Oh, I don't know. I said I saw Count Cincinnati going into Espinosa's in a green bowler . . . things like that.'

'*You said that?*'

'Yes, wasn't it a good thing to say . . . Angel, is anything wrong?'

'Oh, God.'

Adam dashed to the telephone.

'Central ten thousand . . . put me through to the night editor . . . Look here, I've got to make a correction in the Chatterbox page . . . it's urgent.'

'Sorry, Symes. Last edition went to bed half an hour ago. Got everything made up early to-night.'

So Adam went back to finish his oysters.

'Bad tabulation there,' said Lord Monomark next morning, when he saw the paragraph.

So Miles Malpractice became Mr Chatterbox.

'Now we can't be married,' said Nina.

Chapter Ten

*

Adam and Miss Runcible and Miles and Archie Schwert went up to the motor races in Archie Schwert's car. It was a long and cold drive. Miss Runcible wore trousers and Miles touched up his eye-lashes in the dining-room of the hotel where they stopped for luncheon. So they were asked to leave. At the next hotel they made Miss Runcible stay outside, and brought her cold lamb and pickles in the car. Archie thought it would be nice to have champagne, and worried the wine waiter about dates (a subject which had always been repugnant to him). They spent a long time over luncheon because it was warm there, and they drank Kümmel over the fire until Miss Runcible came in very angrily to fetch them out.

Then Archie said he was too sleepy to drive any more, so Adam changed places with him and lost the way, and they travelled miles in the wrong direction down a limitless bye-pass road.

And then it began to be dark and the rain got worse. They stopped for dinner at another hotel, where everyone giggled at Miss Runcible's trousers in a dining-room hung with copper warming pans.

Presently they came to the town where the race was to be run. They drove to the hotel where the dirt-track racer was staying. It was built in the Gothic style of 1860, large, dark and called the Imperial.

They had wired him to book them rooms, but 'Bless you', said the woman at the counter marked 'Reception', 'all our rooms have been booked for the last six months. I couldn't fit you in any-where, not if you was the Speed Kings themselves, I couldn't. I don't suppose you'll find anything in the town to-night. You might try at the Station Hotel. That's your only chance.'

At the Station Hotel they made Miss Runcible wait outside, but with no better success.

'I might put one of you on the sofa in the bar parlour, there's only a married couple in there at present and two little boys, or if you didn't mind sitting up all night, there's always the palm lounge.' As for a bed, that was out of the question. They might try at the 'Royal George', but she doubted very much whether they'd *like* that even if there was room, which she was pretty sure there was not.

Then Miss Runcible thought that she remembered that there were some friends of her father who lived quite near, so she found out their telephone number and rang them up, but they said no, they were sorry, but they had a completely full house and practically no servants, and that as far as they knew they had never heard of Lord Chasm. So that was no good.

Then they went to several more hotels, sinking through the various gradations of Old Established Family and Commercial, plain Commercial, High Class Board Residence pension terms, Working Girls' Hostel, plain Pub and Clean Beds: Gentlemen Only. All were full. At last, by the edge of a canal, they came to the 'Royal George'. The landlady stood at the door and rounded off an argument with an elderly little man in a bowler hat.

'First 'e takes off 'is boots in the saloon bar,' she said, enlisting the sympathy of her new audience, 'which is not the action of a gentleman.'

'They was wet,' said the little man, 'wet as 'ell.'

'Well, and who wants your wet boots on the counter, I should like to know. Then, if you please, he calls me a conspiring woman because I tells him to stop and put them on before he goes 'ome.'

'Want to go 'ome,' said the little man. ''Ome to my wife and kids. *Trying to keep a man from 'is wife.*'

'No one wants to keep you from your wife, you old silly. All I says is for Gawd's sake put on your boots before you go 'ome. What'll your wife think of you comin' 'ome without boots.'

'She won't mind 'ow I come 'ome. Why, bless you, I ain't been 'ome at all for five years. It's 'ard to be separated from a wife and kids by a conspiring woman trying to make yer put on yer boots.'

'My dear, she's quite right, you know,' said Miss Runcible. 'You'd far better put on your boots.'

'There, 'ear what the lady says. Lady says you've to put on your boots.'

The little man took his boots from the landlady, looked at Miss Runcible with a searching glance, and threw them into the canal. '*Lady*,' he said with feeling. '*Trousers*,' and then he paddled[31] off in his socks into the darkness.

'There ain't no 'arm in 'im really,' said the landlady, 'only he do get a bit wild when he's 'ad the drink. Wasting good boots like that . . . I expect he'll spend the night in the lock-up.'

'Won't he get back to his wife, poor sweet?'

'Lor' bless you, no. She lives in London.'

At this stage Archie Schwert, whose humanitarian interests were narrower than Miss Runcible's, lost interest in the discussion.

'The thing we want to know is, can you let us have beds for the night?'

The landlady looked at him suspiciously.

'Bed or beds?'

'Beds.'

'Might do.' She looked from the car to Miss Runcible's trousers and back to the car again, weighing them against each other. 'Cost you a quid each,' she said at last.

'Can you find room for us all?'

'Well,' she said, 'which of you's with the young lady?'

'I'm afraid I'm all alone,' said Miss Runcible. 'Isn't it too shaming?'

'Never you mind, dearie, luck'll turn one day. Well, now, how can we all fit in? There's one room empty. I can sleep with our Sarah, and that leaves a bed for the gentlemen – then if the young lady wouldn't mind coming in with me and Sarah . . .'

'If you don't think it rude, I think I'd sooner have the empty bed,' said Miss Runcible, rather faintly. 'You see,' she added, with tact, 'I snore so terribly.'

'Bless you, so does our Sarah. *We* don't mind . . . still, if you'd *rather* . . .'

'Really, I think I should,' said Miss Runcible.

'Well then, I could put Mr Titchcock on the floor, couldn't I?'

'Yes,' said Miles, 'just you put Mr Titchcock on the floor.'

'And if the other gentleman don't mind going on the landing . . . Well, we'll manage somehow, see if we don't.'

So they all drank some gin together in the back parlour and they woke Mr Titchcock up and made him help with the luggage and they gave him some gin, too, and he said it was all the same to him whether he slept on the floor or in bed, and he was very pleased to be of any service to anyone and didn't mind if he did have another drop just as a night-cap, as they might say; and at last they all went to bed, very tired, but fairly contented, and oh, how they were bitten by bugs all that night.

Adam had secured one of the bedrooms. He awoke early to find rain beating on the window. He looked out and saw a grey sky, some kind of factory and the canal from whose shallow waters rose little islands of scrap-iron and bottles; a derelict perambulator lay partially submerged under the opposite bank. In his room stood a chest of drawers full of horrible fragments of stuff, a washhand stand with a highly coloured basin, an empty jug and an old toothbrush. There was also a rotund female bust covered in shiny red material, and chopped off short, as in primitive martyr-doms, at neck, waist and elbows; a thing known as a dressmaker's 'dummy' (there had been one of these in Adam's home which they used to call 'Jemima' – one day he stabbed 'Jemima' with a chisel and scattered stuffing over the nursery floor and was punished. A more enlightened age would have seen a complex in this action and worried accordingly. Anyway he was made to sweep up all the stuffing himself).

Adam was very thirsty, but there was a light green moss in the bottom of the water bottle that repelled him. He got into bed again and found someone's handkerchief (presumably Mr Titch-cock's) under the pillow.

He woke again a little later to find Miss Runcible dressed in pyjamas and a fur coat sitting on his bed.

'Darling,' she said, 'there's no looking-glass in my room and no bath anywhere, and I trod on someone cold and soft asleep in the passage, and I've been awake all night killing bugs with drops of face lotion, and everything smells, and I feel so low I could die.'

'For heaven's sake let's go away,' said Adam.

So they woke Miles and Archie Schwert, and ten minutes later they all stole out of the 'Royal George' carrying their suitcases.

'I wonder, do you think we ought to leave some money?' asked Adam, but the others all said no.

'Well, perhaps we ought to pay for the gin,' said Miss Runcible.

So they left five shillings on the bar and drove away to the 'Imperial'.

It was still very early, but everyone seemed to be awake, running in and out of the lifts carrying crash helmets and overalls. Miles' friend, they were told, had been out before dawn, presumably at his garage. Adam met some reporters whom he used to see about the *Excess* office. They told him that it was anyone's race, and that the place to see the fun was Headlong Corner, where there had been three deaths the year before, and it was worse this year, because they'd been putting down wet tar. It was nothing more or less than a death trap, the reporters said. Then they went away to interview some more drivers. All teams were confident of victory, they said.

Meanwhile Miss Runcible discovered an empty bathroom, and came down half an hour later all painted up and wearing a skirt and feeling quite herself again and ready for anything. So they went in to breakfast.

The dining-room was very full indeed. There were Speed Kings of all nationalities, unimposing men mostly with small moustaches and apprehensive eyes; they were reading the forecasts in the morning papers and eating what might (and in some cases did) prove to be their last meal on earth. There were a great number of journalists making the best of an 'out-of-town' job; there were a troop of nondescript 'fans', knowledgeable young men with bright jumpers tucked inside their belted trousers, old public-school ties, check tweeds, loose mouths and scarcely discernible Cockney accents; there were R.A.C. officials and A.A. officials, and the representatives of oil firms and tyre manufacturers. There was one disconsolate family who had come to the town for the christening of a niece. (No one had warned them that there was a motor race on; their hotel bill *was* a shock.)

'Very better-making,' said Miss Runcible with approval as she ate her haddock.

Scraps of highly technical conversation rose on all sides of them.

'. . . Changed the whole engine over after they'd been scruti-neered.[32] Anyone else would have been disqualified . . .'

'. . . just cruising round at fifty . . .'

'. . . stung by a bee just as he was taking the corner, missed the tree by inches and landed up in the Town Hall. There was a Riley coming up behind, spun round twice, climbed the bank, turned right over and caught fire . . .'

'. . . local overheating at the valve-heads. It's no sense putting a supercharger in that engine at all . . .'

'. . . Headlong Corner's jam. All you want to do is to brake right down to forty or forty-five at the white cottage, then rev up oppos-ite the pub and get straight away in second on the near side of the road. A child could do it. It's the double bend just after the rail-way bridge where you'll get the funny stuff.'

'. . . kept flagging him down from the pits. I tell you that bunch don't want him to win.'

'. . . She wouldn't tell me her name, but she said she'd meet me at the same place to-night and gave me a sprig of white heather for the car. I lost it, like a fool. She said she'd look out for it too . . .'

'. . . Only offers a twenty pound bonus this year . . .'

'. . . lapped at seventy-five . . .'

'. . . Burst his gasket and blew out his cylinder heads . . .'

'. . . Broke both arms and cracked his skull in two places . . .'

'. . . Tailwag . . .'

'. . . Speed-wobble . . .'

'. . . Merc . . .'

'. . . Mag . . .'

'. . . crash . . .'

When they finished breakfast Miss Runcible and Adam and Archie Schwert and Miles went to the garage to look for their Speed King. They found him hard at work listening to his engine. A corner of the garage had been roped off and the floor strewn with sand as though for a boxing match.

Outside this ring clustered a group of predatory little boys with autograph albums and leaking fountain-pens, and inside, surrounded by attendants, stood the essential parts of a motor car. The engine was running and the whole machine shook with fruitless exertion. Clouds of dark smoke came from it, and a shattering roar which reverberated from concrete floor and corrugated iron roof into every corner of the building so that speech and thought became insupportable and all the senses were numbed. At frequent intervals this high and heartbreaking note was varied by sharp detonations, and it was these apparently which were causing anxiety, for at each report Miles' friend, who clearly could not have been unduly sensitive to noise, gave a little wince and looked significantly at his head mechanic.

Apart from the obvious imperfection of its sound, the car gave the impression to an uninstructed observer of being singularly unfinished. In fact, it was obviously still under construction. It had only three wheels; the fourth being in the hands of a young man in overalls, who, in the intervals of tossing back from his eyes a curtain of yellow hair, was beating it with a hammer. It also had no seats, and another mechanic was screwing down slabs of lead ballast in the place where one would have expected to find them. It had no bonnet; that was in the hands of a sign painter, who was drawing a black number 13 in a white circle. There was a similar number on the back, and a mechanic was engaged in fixing another number board over one of the headlights. There was a mechanic, too, making a windscreen of wire gauze, and a mechanic lying flat doing something to the back axle with a tin of grate polish and a rag. Two more mechanics were helping Miles' friend to listen to the bangs. 'As if we couldn't have heard them from Berkeley Square,' said Miss Runcible.

(The truth is that motor cars offer a very happy illustration of the metaphysical distinction between 'being' and 'becoming'. Some cars, mere vehicles with no purpose above bare locomotion, mechanical drudges such as Lady Metroland's Hispano Suiza, or Mrs Mouse's Rolls-Royce, or Lady Circumference's 1912 Daimler, or the 'general reader's' Austin Seven, these have definite 'being' just as much as their occupants. They are bought all screwed up and numbered and painted, and there they stay through various declensions of ownership, brightened now and then with a lick of paint or temporarily rejuvenated by the addition of some minor organ, but still maintaining their essential identity to the scrap heap.

Not so the *real* cars, that become masters of men; those vital creations of metal who exist solely for their own propulsion through space, for whom their drivers, clinging precariously at the steering-wheel, are as important as his stenographer to a stock-broker. These are in perpetual flux; a vortex of combining and disintegrating units; like the confluence of traffic at some spot where many roads meet, streams of mechanism come together, mingle and separate again.)

Miles' friend, even had it been possible in the uproar, seemed indisposed to talk. He waved abstractedly and went on with his listening. Presently he came across and shouted:

'Sorry I can't spare a moment, I'll see you in the pits. I've got you some brassards.'

'My dear, what *can* that be?'

He handed them each a strip of white linen, terminating in tape.

'For your arms,' he shouted. 'You can't get into the pits without them.'

'My dear, what bliss! Fancy their having pits.'

Then they tied on their brassards. Miss Runcible's said, 'SPARE DRIVER'; Adam's, 'DEPOT STAFF'; Miles', 'SPARE MECHANIC' and Archie's, 'OWNER'S REPRESENTATIVE'.

Up till now the little boys round the rope had been sceptical of the importance of Miss Runcible and her friends, but as soon as they saw these badges of rank they pressed forward with their autograph books. Archie signed them all with the utmost complaisance, and even drew a slightly unsuitable picture in one of them. Then they drove away in Archie's car.

The race was not due to start until noon, but any indecision which they may have felt about the employment of the next few hours was settled for them by the local police, who were engaged in directing all traffic, irrespective of its particular inclinations, on the road to the course. No pains had been spared about this point of organization; several days before, the Chief Constable had issued a little route map which was to be memorized by all constables on point duty, and so well had they learned their lesson that from early that morning until late in the afternoon no vehicle approaching the town from any direction escaped being drawn into that broad circuit marked by the arrows and dotted line A-B which led to the temporary car park behind the Grand Stand. (Many doctors, thus diverted, spent an enjoyable day without apparent prejudice to their patients.)

The advance of the spectators had already assumed the form of a slow and unbroken stream. Some came on foot from the railway station, carrying sandwiches and camp stools; some on tandem bicycles; some in 'runabouts' or motor cycle side-car combinations, but most were in modestly priced motor cars. Their clothes and demeanour proclaimed them as belonging to the middle rank; a few brought portable wireless sets with them and other evidence of gaiety, but the general air of the procession was one of sobriety and purpose. This was no Derby day holiday-making; they had not snatched a day from the office to squander it among gypsies and roundabouts and thimble-and-pea men. They were there for the race. As they crawled along in bottom gear in a fog of exhaust gas, they discussed the technicalities of motor car design and the possibilities of bloodshed, and studied their maps of the course to pick out the most dangerous corners.

The detour planned by the Chief Constable was a long one, lined with bungalows and converted railway carriages. Banners floated over it between the telegraph posts, mostly advertising the *Morning Despatch*, which was organizing the race and paying for the victor's trophy – a silver gilt figure of odious design, symbolizing Fame embracing Speed. (This at the moment was under careful guard in the steward's room, for the year before it had been stolen on the eve of the race by the official timekeeper, who pawned it for a ridiculously small sum in Manchester, and was subsequently deprived of his position and sent to gaol.) Other advertisements proclaimed the superiorities of various sorts of petrol and sparking plugs, while some said '£100 FOR LOSS OF LIMB. INSURE

To-day'. There was also an elderly man walking among the motor cars with a blue and white banner inscribed, 'Without Shedding of Blood is no Remission of Sin', while a smartly dressed young man was doing a brisk trade in bogus tickets for the Grand Stand.

Adam sat in the back of the car with Miles, who was clearly put out about his friend's lack of cordiality. 'What I can't make out,' he said, 'is why we came to this beastly place at all. I suppose I ought to be thinking of something to write for the *Excess*. I *know* this is just going to be the most dreary day we've ever spent.'

Adam felt inclined to agree. Suddenly he became aware that someone was trying to attract his attention.

'There's an awful man shouting "Hi" at you,' said Miles. 'My dear, *your friends*.'

Adam turned and saw not three yards away, separated from him by a young woman riding a push-bicycle in khaki shorts, her companion, who bore a knapsack on his shoulders, and a small boy selling programmes, the long-sought figure of the drunk Major. He looked sober enough this morning, dressed in a bowler hat and Burberry, and he was waving frantically to Adam from the dicky[33] of a coupé car.

'Hi!' cried the drunk Major. 'Hi! I've been looking for you everywhere.'

'I've been looking for you,' shouted Adam. 'I want some money.'

'Can't hear – what do you want?'

'Money.'

'It's no good – these infernal things make too much noise. What's your name? Lottie had forgotten.'

'Adam Symes.'

'Can't hear.'

The line of traffic, creeping forward yard by yard, had at last reached the point B on the Chief Constable's map, where the dotted lines diverged. A policeman stood at the crossing directing the cars right and left, some to the parking place behind the Grand Stand, others to the mound above the pits. Archie turned off to the left. The drunk Major's car accelerated and swept away to the right.

'*I must know your name*,' he cried. All the drivers seemed to choose this moment to sound their horns; the woman cyclist at Adam's elbow rang her bell; the male cyclist tooted a little horn like a Paris taxi, and the programme boy yelled in his ear, 'Official programme – map of the course – all the drivers.'

'Adam Symes,' he shouted desperately, but the Major threw up his hands in despair and he disappeared in the crowd.

'*The way you pick people up* . . .' said Miles, startled into admiration.

'The pits' turned out to be a line of booths, built of wood and corrugated iron immediately opposite the Grand Stand. Many of the cars had already arrived and stood at their 'pits', surrounded by a knot of mechanics and spectators; they seemed to be already under repair. Busy officials hurried up and down, making entries in their lists. Over their heads a vast loud speaker was relaying the music of a military band.

The Grand Stand was still fairly empty, but the rest of the course was already lined with people. It stretched up and down hill for a circle of thirteen or fourteen miles, and those who were fortunate enough to own cottages or public houses at the more dangerous corners had covered their roofs with unstable wooden forms, and were selling tickets like very expensive hot cakes. A grass-covered hill rose up sharply behind the pits. On this had been erected a hoarding where a troop of Boy Scouts were preparing to score the laps, passing the time contentedly with ginger beer, toffee, and rough-and-tumble fights. Behind the hoarding was a barbed-wire fence, and behind that again a crowd of spectators and several refreshment tents. A wooden bridge, advertising the *Morning Despatch*, had been built on the road. At various points officials might be seen attempting to understand each other over a field telephone. Sometimes the band would stop and a voice would announce, 'Will Mr So-and-So kindly report at once to the timekeeper's office'; then the band would go on.

Miss Runcible and her party found their way to the pit

numbered 13 and sat on the matchboard counter smoking and signing autograph books. An official bore down on them.

'No smoking in the pits, please.'

'My dear, I'm terribly sorry. I didn't know.'

There were six open churns behind Miss Runcible, four containing petrol and two water. She threw her cigarette over her shoulder, and by a beneficent attention of Providence which was quite rare in her career it fell into the water. Had it fallen into the petrol it would probably have been all up with Miss Runcible.

Presently No. 13 appeared. Miles' friend and his mechanic, wearing overalls, crash-helmets, and goggles, jumped out, opened the bonnet and began to reconstruct it again.

'They didn't ought to have a No. 13 at all,' said the mechanic. 'It isn't fair.'

Miss Runcible lit another cigarette.

'No smoking in the pits, *please*,' said the official.

'My dear, how *awful* of me. I quite forgot.'

(This time it fell in the mechanic's luncheon basket and lay smouldering quietly on a leg of chicken until it had burnt itself out.)

Miles' friend began filling up his petrol tank with the help of a very large funnel.

'Listen,' he said. 'You're not allowed to hand me anything direct, but if Edwards holds up his left hand as we come past the pits, that means we shall be stopping next lap for petrol. So what you've got to do is to fill up a couple of cans and put them on the shelf with the funnel for Edwards to take. If Edwards holds up his right hand . . .' elaborate instructions followed. 'You're in charge of the depôt,' he said to Archie. 'D'you think you've got all the signals clear? The race may depend on them, remember.'

'What does it mean if I wave the blue flag?'

'That you want me to stop.'

'Why should I want you to stop?'

'Well, you might see something wrong – leaking tank or anything like that, or the officials might want the number plate cleaned.'

'I think perhaps I won't do anything much about the blue flag. It seems rather too bogus for me.'

Miss Runcible lit another cigarette.

'Will you kindly leave the pits if you wish to smoke?' said the official.

'What a damned rude man,' said Miss Runcible. 'Let's go up to that divine tent and get a drink.'

They climbed the hill past the Boy Scouts, found a gate in the wire fence, and eventually reached the refreshment tent. Here an atmosphere of greater geniality prevailed. A profusion of men in plus-fours were having 'quick-ones' before the start. There was no nonsense about not smoking. There was a middle-aged woman sitting on the grass with a bottle of stout and a baby.

'Home from home,' said Miss Runcible.

Suddenly the military band stopped and a voice said, 'Five minutes to twelve. All drivers and mechanics on the other side of the track, please.'

There was a hush all over the course, and the refreshment tent began to empty quickly.

'Darling, we shall miss the start.'

'Still, a drink *would* be nice.'

So they went into the tent.

'Four whiskies, please,' said Archie Schwert.

'You'll miss the start,' said the barmaid.

'What a pig that man was,' said Miss Runcible. 'Even if we weren't supposed to smoke, he might at least have asked us politely.'

'My dear, it was only you.'

'Well, I think that made it worse.'

'Lor', Miss,' said the barmaid. 'You surely ain't going to miss the start?'

'It's the one thing I want to see more than anything . . . my dear, I believe they're off already.'

The sudden roar of sixty high-power engines rose from below. 'They *have* started . . . how too shaming.' They went to the door of the tent. Part of the road was visible over the heads of the specta-tors, and they caught a glimpse of the cars running all jammed together like pigs being driven through a gate; one by one they shook themselves free and disappeared round the bend with a high shriek of acceleration.

'They'll be round again in quarter of an hour,' said Archie. 'Let's have another drink.'

'Who was ahead?' asked the barmaid anxiously.

'I couldn't see for certain,' said Miss Runcible, 'but I'm fairly sure it was No. 13.'

'*My!*'

The refreshment tent soon began to fill up again. The general opinion seemed to be that it was going to be a close race between No. 13 and No. 28, a red Omega car, driven by Marino, the Italian 'ace'.

'Dirtiest driver I ever seen,' said one man with relish.

'Why, over at Belfast 'e was just tipping 'em all into the ditches, just like winking.'

'There's one thing you *can* be sure of. They won't *both* finish.'

'It's sheer murder the way that Marino drives – a fair treat to see 'im.'

'He's a one all right – a real artist and no mistake about it.'

Adam and Miss Runcible and Archie and Miles went back to their pit.

'After all,' said Miss Runcible, 'the poor sweet may be wanting all sorts of things and signalling away like mad, and no one there to pay any attention to him – so discouraging.'

By this time the cars were fairly evenly spread out over the course. They flashed by intermittently with dazzling speed and a shriek; one or two drew into their pits and the drivers leapt out, trembling like leaves, to tinker with the works. One had already come to grief – a large German whose tyre had burst – punctured, some said, by a hireling of Marino's. It had left the road and shot up a tree like a cat chased by a dog. Two little American cars had failed to start; their team worked desperately at them amid derisive comments from the crowd. Suddenly two cars appeared coming down the straight, running abreast within two feet of each other.

'It's No. 13,' cried Miss Runcible, really excited at last. 'And there's that Italian devil just beside it. Come on, thirteen! Come on!' she cried, dancing in the pit and waving a flag she found at hand. 'Come on. Oh! Well done, thirteen.'

The cars were gone in a flash and succeeded by others.

'Agatha, darling, you shouldn't have waved the blue flag.'

'My dear, how awful. Why not?'

'Well, that means that he's to stop next lap.'

'Good God. Did I wave a blue flag?'

'My dear, you know you did.'

'*How* shaming. What *am* I to say to him?'

'Let's all go away before he comes back.'

'D'you know, I think we'd better. He might be furious, mightn't he? Let's go to the tent and have another drink – don't you think, or don't you?'

So No. 13 pit was again deserted.

'What did I say?' said the mechanic. 'The moment I heard we'd drawn this blinkin' number I knew we was in for trouble.'

The first person they saw when they reached the refreshment tent was the drunk Major.

'Your boy friend again,' said Miles.

'Well, there you are,' said the Major. 'D'you know I've been chasing you all over London. What have you been doing with yourself all this time?'

'I've been staying at Lottie's.'

'Well, she said she'd never heard of you. You see, I don't mind admitting I'd had a few too many that night, and to tell you the truth I woke up with things all rather a blur. Well then I found a thousand pounds in my pocket, and it all came back to me. There'd been a cove at Lottie's who gave me a thousand pounds to put on Indian Runner. Well, as far as I knew, Indian Runner was no good. I didn't want to lose your money for you, but the devil of it was I didn't know you from Adam.' ('I think that's a perfect joke,'[34] said Miss Runcible.) 'And apparently Lottie didn't either. You'd have thought it was easy enough to trace the sort of chap who deals out thousands of pounds to total strangers, but I couldn't find one fingerprint.'

'Do you mean,' said Adam, a sudden delirious hope rising in his heart, 'that you've still got my thousand?'

'Not so fast,' said the Major. 'I'm spinning this yarn. Well, on the day of the race I didn't know what to do. One half of me said, keep the thousand. The chap's bound to turn up some time, and it's his business to do his own punting – the other half said, put it on the favourite for him and give him a run for his money.'

'So you put it on the favourite?' Adam's heart felt like lead again.

'No, I didn't. In the end I said, well, the young chap must be frightfully rich. If he likes to throw away his money, it's none of my business, so I planked it all on Indian Runner for you.'

'You mean . . .'

'I mean I've got the nice little packet of thirty-five thou. waiting until you condescend to call for it.'

'Good heavens . . . look here, have a drink, won't you?'

'That's a thing I never refuse.'

'Archie, lend me some money until I get this fortune.'

'How much?'

'Enough to buy five bottles of champagne.'

'Yes, if you can get them.'

The barmaid had a case of champagne at the back of the tent. ('People often feel queer through watching the cars go by so fast – ladies especially,' she explained.) So they took a bottle each and sat on the side of the hill and drank to Adam's prosperity.

'Hullo, everybody,' said the loudspeaker. 'Car No. 28, the Italian Omega, driven by Captain Marino, has just completed the course in twelve minutes one second, lapping at an average speed of 78.3 miles per hour. This is the fastest time yet recorded.'

A burst of applause greeted this announcement, but Adam said, 'I've rather lost interest in this race.'

'Look here, old boy,' the Major said when they were well settled down, 'I'm rather in a hole. Makes me feel an awful ass, saying so, but the truth is I got my notecase pinched in the crowd. Of course, I've got plenty of small change to see me back to the hotel and they'll take a cheque of mine there, naturally, but the fact is I was keen to make a few bets with some chaps I hardly know. I wonder, old boy, could you possibly lend me a fiver? I can give it to you at the same time as I hand over the thirty-five thousand.'

'Why, of course,' said Adam. 'Archie, lend me a fiver, can you?'

'Awfully good of you,' said the Major, tucking the notes into his hip pocket. 'Would it be all the same if you made it a tenner while we're about it?'

'I'm sorry,' said Archie, with a touch of coldness. 'I've only just got enough to get home with.'

'That's all right, old boy, *I* understand. Not another word . . . Well, here's to us all.'

'I was on the course at the November Handicap,' said Adam. 'I thought I saw you.'

'It would have saved a lot of fuss if we'd met, wouldn't it? Still, all's well that ends well.'

'What an *angelic* man your Major is,' said Miss Runcible.

When they had finished their champagne, the Major – now indisputably drunk – rose to go.

'Look here, old boy,' he said. 'I must be toddling along now. Got to see some chaps. Thanks no end for the binge. So jolly having met you all again. Bye-bye, little lady.'

'When shall we meet again?' said Adam.

'Any time, old boy. Tickled to death to see you any time you care to drop in. Always a pew and a drink for old friends. So long everybody.'

'But couldn't I come and see you soon? About the money, you know.'

'Sooner the better, old boy. Though I don't know what you mean about money.'

'My thirty-five thousand.'

'Why, yes, to be sure. Fancy my forgetting that. I tell you what. You roll along to-night to the Imperial and I'll give it to you then. Jolly glad to get it off my chest. Seven o'clock at the American bar – or a little before.'

'Let's go back and look at the motor cars,' said Archie.

They went down the hill feeling buoyant and detached (as one should if one drinks a great deal before luncheon). When they reached the pits they decided they were hungry. It seemed too far to climb up to the dining tent, so they ate as much of the mechanic's lunch as Miss Runcible's cigarette had spared.

Then a mishap happened to No. 13. It drew into the side uncertainly, with the mechanic holding the steering-wheel. A spanner, he told them, thrown from Marino's car as they were passing him under the railway bridge, had hit Miles' friend on the shoulder. The mechanic helped him get out, and supported him to the Red Cross tent. 'May as well scratch,' he said. 'He won't be good for anything more this afternoon. It's asking for trouble having a No. 13.' Miles went to help his friend, leaving Miss Runcible and Adam and Archie staring rather stupidly at their motor car. Archie hiccoughed slightly as he ate the mechanic's apple.

Soon an official appeared.

'What happened here?' he said.

'Driver's just been murdered,' said Archie. 'Spanner under the railway bridge. Marino.'

'Well, are you going to scratch? Who's spare driver?'

'I don't know. Do you, Adam? I shouldn't be a bit surprised if they hadn't murdered the spare driver, too.'

'I'm spare driver,' said Miss Runcible. 'It's on my arm.'

'She's spare driver. Look, it's on her arm.'

'Well, do you want to scratch?'

'Don't you scratch, Agatha.'

'No, I don't want to scratch.'

'All right. What's your name?'

'Agatha. I'm the spare driver. It's on my arm.'

'I can see it is – all right, start off as soon as you like.'

'Agatha,' repeated Miss Runcible firmly as she climbed into the car. 'It's on my arm.'

'I say, Agatha,' said Adam. 'Are you sure you're all right?'

'It's on my arm,' said Miss Runcible severely.

'I mean, are you quite certain it's absolutely safe?'

'Not *absolutely* safe, Adam. Not if they throw spanners. But I'll go quite slowly at first until I'm used to it. Just you see. Coming too?'

'I'll stay and wave the flag,' said Adam.

'That's right. Good-bye . . . goodness, how too stiff-scaring . . .'

The car shot out into the middle of the road, missed a collision by a foot, swung round and disappeared with a roar up the road.

'I say, Archie, is it all right being tight in a car, if it's on a race course? They won't run her in or anything?'

'No, no, that's all right. All tight on the race course.'

'Sure?'

'Sure.'

'All of them?'

'Absolutely everyone – tight as houses.'

'That's all right then. Let's go and have a drink.'

So they went up the hill again, through the Boy Scouts, to the refreshment tent.

It was not long before Miss Runcible was in the news.

'Hullo, everybody,' said the loud speaker. 'No. 13, the English Plunket-Bowse, driven by Miss Agatha, came into collision at Headlong Corner with No. 28, the Italian Omega car, driven by Captain Marino. No. 13 righted itself and continued on the course. No. 28 overturned and has retired from the race.'

'Well done, Agatha,' said Archie.

A few minutes later:

'Hullo, everybody. No. 13, the English Plunket-Bowse, driven by Miss Agatha, has just completed the course in nine minutes forty-one seconds. This constitutes a record for the course.'

Patriotic cheers broke out on all sides, and Miss Runcible's health was widely drunk in the refreshment tent.

A few minutes later:

'Hullo, everybody; I have to contradict the announcement recently made that No. 13, the English Plunket-Bowse, driven by Miss Agatha, had established a record for the course. The stewards have now reported that No. 13 left the road just after the level crossing and cut across country for five miles, rejoining the track at the Red Lion corner. The lap has therefore been disallowed by the judges.'

*

A few minutes later:

'Hullo, everybody; No. 13, the English Plunket-Bowse car, driven by Miss Agatha, has retired from the race. It disappeared from the course some time ago, turning left instead of right at Church Corner, and was last seen proceeding south on the bye-road, apparently out of control.'

'My dear, that's lucky for me,' said Miles. 'A really good story my second day on the paper. This ought to do me good with the *Excess – very* rich-making,' and he hurried off to the post office tent – which was one of the amenities of the course – to despatch a long account of Miss Runcible's disaster.

Adam accompanied him and sent a wire to Nina: *Drunk Major in refreshment tent not bogus thirty-five thousand married to-morrow everything perfect Agatha lost love Adam.*

'That seems quite clear,' he said.

They went to the hospital tent after this – another amenity of the course – to see how Miles' friend was getting on. He seemed in some pain and showed anxiety about his car.

'I think it's very heartless of him,' said Adam. 'He ought to be worried about Agatha. It only shows . . .'

'Motor men *are* heartless,' said Miles, with a sigh.

Presently Captain Marino was borne in on a stretcher. He turned on his side with a deep groan and spat at Miles' friend as he went past him. He also spat at the doctor who came to bandage him and bit one of the V.A.D.'s.[35]

They said Captain Marino was no gentleman in the hospital tent.

There was no chance of leaving the course before the end of the race, Archie was told, and the race would not be over for at least two hours. Round and round went the stream of cars. At intervals the Boy Scouts posted a large red R against one or other of the numbers, as engine trouble or collision or Headlong Corner took its toll. A long queue stretched along the top of the hill from the door of the luncheon tent. Then it began to rain.

There was nothing for it but to go back to the bar.

At dusk the last car completed its course. The silver gilt trophy was presented to the winner. The loud speaker broadcast 'God

Save the King', and a cheerful 'Good-bye, everybody'. The tail of the queue outside the dining tent were respectfully informed that no more luncheons could be served. The barmaids in the refreshment tent said, 'All glasses, ladies and gentlemen, please.' The motor ambulances began a final round of the track to pick up survivors. Then Adam and Miles and Archie Schwert went to look for their car.

Darkness fell during the drive back. It took an hour to reach the town. Adam and Miles and Archie Schwert did not talk much. The effects of their drinks had now entered on that secondary stage, vividly described in temperance hand-books, when the momentary illusion of well-being and exhilaration gives place to melancholy, indigestion and moral decay. Adam tried to concentrate his thoughts upon his sudden wealth, but they seemed unable to adhere to this high pinnacle, and as often as he impelled them up, slithered back helplessly to his present physical discomfort.

The sluggish procession in which they were moving led them eventually to the centre of the town and the soberly illuminated front of the Imperial Hotel. A torrential flow of wet and hungry motor enthusiasts swept and eddied about the revolving doors.

'I shall die if I don't eat something soon,' said Miles. 'Let's leave Agatha until we've had a meal.'

But the manager of the 'Imperial' was unimpressed by numbers or necessity and manfully upheld the integrity of British hotel-keeping. Tea, he explained, was served daily in the Palm Court, with orchestra on Thursdays and Sundays, between the hours of four and six. A *table d'hôte* dinner was served in the dining-room from seven-thirty until nine o'clock. An *à la carte* dinner was also served in the grill-room at the same time. It was now twenty minutes past six. If the gentlemen cared to return in an hour and ten minutes he would do his best to accommodate them, but he could not promise to reserve a table. Things were busy that day. There had been motor races in the neighbourhood, he explained.

The commissionaire was more helpful, and told them that there was a tea-shop restaurant called the Café Royal a little way down the High Street, next to the Cinema. He seemed, however, to have given the same advice to all comers, for the Café Royal was crowded and overflowing. Everyone was being thoroughly cross, but only the most sarcastic and overbearing were given tables, and only the gross and outrageous were given food. Adam and Miles and Archie Schwert then tried two more tea-shops, one kept by 'ladies' and called 'The Honest Injun', a workmen's dining-room and a fried-fish shop. Eventually they bought a bag of mixed biscuits at a co-operative store, which they ate in the Palm Court of the 'Imperial', maintaining a moody silence.

It was now after seven, and Adam remembered his appointment in the American bar. There, too, inevitably, was a dense crowd. Some of the 'Speed Kings' themselves had appeared, pink from their baths, wearing dinner jackets and stiff white shirts, each in his circle of admirers. Adam struggled to the bar.

'Have you seen a drunk Major in here anywhere?' he asked.

The barmaid sniffed. 'I should think not, indeed,' she said. 'And I shouldn't serve him if he *did* come in. I don't have people of that description in *my* bar. *The very idea.*'

'Well, perhaps he's not drunk now. But have you seen a stout, red-faced man, with a single eyeglass and a turned-up moustache?'

'Well, there *was* someone like that not so long ago. Are you a friend of his?'

'I want to see him badly.'

'Well, all I can say is I wish you'd try and look after him and don't bring him in here again. Going on something awful he was. Broke two glasses and got very quarrelsome with the other gentlemen. He had three or four pound notes in his hand. Kept waving them about and saying, "D'you know what? I met a mutt to-day. I owe him thirty-five thousand pounds and he lent me a fiver." Well, that's not the way to talk before strangers, is it? He went out ten minutes ago. I was glad to see the back of him, I can tell you.'

'Did he say that – about having met a mutt?'

'Didn't stop saying it the whole time he was in here – most monotonous.'

But as Adam left the bar he saw the Major coming out of the

gentlemen's lavatory. He was walking very deliberately, and stared at Adam with a glazed and vacant eye.

'Hi!' cried Adam. 'Hi!'

'Cheerio,' said the drunk Major distantly.

'I say,' said Adam. 'What about my thirty-five thousand pounds?'

The drunk Major stopped and adjusted his monocle.

'Thirty-five thousand and five pounds,' he said. 'What about them?'

'Well, where are they?'

'They're safe enough. National and Provincial Union Bank of England, Limited. A perfectly sound and upright company. I'd trust them with more than that if I had it. I'd trust them with a million, old boy, honest I would. One of those fine old companies, you know. They don't make companies like that now. I'd trust that bank with my wife and kiddies . . . You mustn't think I'd put your money into anything that wasn't straight, old boy. You ought to know me well enough for that . . .'

'No, of course not. It's terribly kind of you to have looked after it – you said you'd give me a cheque this evening. Don't you remember?'

The drunk Major looked at him craftily. 'Ah,' he said. 'That's another matter. I told *someone* I'd give him a cheque. But how am I to know it was you? . . . I've got to be careful, you know. Suppose you were just a crook dressed up. I don't say you are, mind, but supposing. Where'd I be then? You have to look at both sides of a case like this.'

'Oh, God . . . I've got two friends here who'll swear to you I'm Adam Symes. Will that do?'

'Might be a gang. Besides *I* don't know that the name of the chap who gave me the thousand *was* Adam what-d'you-call-it at all. Only your word for it. I'll tell you what,' said the Major, sitting down in a deep armchair, 'I'll sleep on it. Just forty winks. I'll let you know my decision when I wake up. Don't think me suspicious, old boy, but I've got to be careful . . . other chap's money, you know . . .' And he fell asleep.

Adam struggled through the crowd to the Palm Court, where he had left Miles and Archie. News of No. 13 had just come through. The car had been found piled up on the market cross of a large village about fifteen miles away (doing irreparable damage to a monument already scheduled for preservation by the Office of Works). But there was no sign of Miss Runcible.

'I suppose we ought to do something about it,' said Miles. 'This is the most miserable day I ever spent. Did you get your fortune?'

'The Major was too drunk to recognize me. He's just gone to sleep.'

'*Well.*'

'We must go to this beastly village and look for Agatha.'

'I can't leave my Major. He'll probably wake up soon and give the fortune to the first person he sees.'

'Let's just go and shake him until he gives us the fortune now,' said Miles.

But this was impracticable, for when they reached the chair where Adam had left him, the drunk Major was gone.

The hall porter remembered him going out quite clearly. He had pressed a pound into his hand, saying, 'Met-a-mutt-to-day', and taken a taxi to the station.

'D'you know,' said Adam. 'I don't believe that I'm ever going to get that fortune.'

'Well, I don't see that you've very much to complain of,' said Archie. 'You're no worse off than you were. *I've* lost a fiver and five bottles of champagne.'

'That's true,' said Adam, a little consoled.

They got into the car and drove through the rain to the village where the Plunket-Bowse had been found. There it stood, still smoking and partially recognizable, surrounded by admiring villagers. A constable in a waterproof cape was doing his best to preserve it intact from the raids of souvenir hunters who were collecting the smaller fragments.

No one seemed to have witnessed the disaster. The younger members of the community were all at the races, while the elders were engaged in their afternoon naps. One thought he had heard a crash.

Inquiries at the railway station, however, disclosed that a young lady, much dishevelled in appearance, and wearing some kind of band on her arm, had appeared in the booking office early that afternoon and asked where she was. On being told, she said, well, she wished she wasn't, because someone had left an enormous stone spanner in the middle of the road. She admitted feeling rather odd. The stationmaster had asked her if she would like to come in and sit down and offered to get her some brandy. She said, 'No, no more brandy', and bought a first-class ticket to London. She had left on the 3.25 train.

'So that's all right,' said Archie.

Then they left the village and presently found an hotel on the Great North Road, where they dined and spent the night. They reached London by luncheon-time next day, and learned that Miss Runcible had been found early that morning staring fixedly at a model engine in the central hall at Euston Station. In answer to some gentle questions, she replied that to the best of her knowledge she had no name, pointing to the brassard on her arm, as if in confirmation of this fact. She had come in a motor car, she explained, which would not stop. It was full of bugs which she had tried to kill with drops of face lotion. One of them threw a spanner. There had been a stone thing in the way. They shouldn't put up symbols like that in the middle of the road, should they, or should they?

So they conveyed her to a nursing-home in Wimpole Street and kept her for some time in a darkened room.

Chapter Eleven

*

Adam rang up Nina.

'Darling, I've been so happy about your telegram. Is it really true?'

'No, I'm afraid not.'

'The Major *is* bogus?'

'Yes.'

'You haven't got any money?'

'No.'

'We aren't going to be married to-day?'

'No.'

'I see.'

'Well?'

'I said, I see.'

'Is that all?'

'Yes, that's all, Adam.'

'I'm sorry.'

'I'm sorry, too. Good-bye.'

'Good-bye, Nina.'

Later Nina rang up Adam.

'Darling, is that you? I've got something rather awful to tell you.'

'Yes?'

'You'll be furious.'

'Well?'

'I'm engaged to be married.'

'Who to?'

'I hardly think I can tell you.'

'Who?'

'Adam, you won't be beastly about it, will you?'

'Who is it?'

'Ginger.'

'I don't believe it.'

'Well, I am. That's all there is to it.'

'You're going to marry Ginger?'

'Yes.'

'I see.'

'Well?'

'I said, I see.'

'Is that all?'

'Yes, that's all, Nina.'

'When shall I see you?'

'I don't want ever to see you again.'

'I see.'

'Well?'

'I said, I see.'

'Well, good-bye.'

'Good-bye . . . I'm sorry, Adam.'[36]

Chapter Twelve

*

Ten days later Adam bought some flowers at the corner of Wigmore Street and went to call on Miss Runcible at her nursing-home. He was shown first into the Matron's room. She had numerous photographs in silver frames and a very nasty fox terrier. She smoked a cigarette in a greedy way, making slight sucking noises.

'Just taking a moment off in my den,' she explained. 'Down, Spot, down. But I can see you're fond of dogs,' she added, as Adam gave Spot a half-hearted pat on the head. 'So you want to see Miss Runcible? Well, I ought to warn you first that she must have no kind of excitement whatever. She's had a severe shock. Are you a relation, may I ask?'

'No, only a friend.'

'A very *special* friend, perhaps, eh?' said the Matron archly. 'Never mind, I'll spare your blushes. Just you run up and see her. But not more than five minutes, mind, or you'll have me on your tracks.'

There was a reek of ether on the stairs which reminded Adam of the times when, waiting to take her to luncheon, he had sat on Nina's bed while she did her face. (She invariably made him turn his back until it was over, having a keen sense of modesty about this one part of her toilet, in curious contrast to some girls, who would die rather than be seen in their underclothes, and yet openly flaunt unpainted faces in front of anyone.)

It hurt Adam deeply to think much about Nina.

Outside Miss Runcible's door hung a very interesting chart which showed the fluctuations of her temperature and pulse and many other curious details of her progress. He studied this with pleasure until a nurse, carrying a tray of highly polished surgical instruments, gave him such a look that he felt obliged to turn away.

Miss Runcible lay in a high, narrow bed in a darkened room.

A nurse was crocheting at her side when Adam entered. She rose, dropping a few odds and ends from her lap, and said, 'There's someone come to see you, dear. Now remember you aren't to talk much.' She took the flowers from Adam's hand, said, 'Look, what lovelies. Aren't you a lucky girl?' and left the room with them. She returned a moment later carrying them in a jug of water. 'There, the thirsties,' she said. 'Don't they love to get back to the nice cool water?'

Then she went out again.

'Darling,' said a faint voice from the bed, 'I can't really see who it is. Would it be awful to draw the curtains?'

Adam crossed the room and let in the light of the grey December afternoon.

'My dear, how blind-making. There are some cocktail things in the wardrobe. Do make a big one. The nurses love them so. It's such a nice nursing-home this, Adam, only all the nurses are starved, and there's a breathtaking young man next door who keeps putting his head in and asking how I am. *He* fell out of an *aeroplane*, which is rather grand, don't you think?'

'How are you feeling, Agatha?'

'Well, rather odd, to tell you the truth . . . How's Nina?'

'She's got engaged to be married – haven't you heard?'

'My dear, the nurses are interested in no one but Princess Elizabeth. Do tell me.'

'A young man called Ginger.'

'*Well?*'

'Don't you remember him? He came on with us after the airship party.'

'Not the one who was sick?'

'No, the other.'

'I don't remember . . . does Nina call him Ginger?'

'Yes.'

'Why?'

'He asked her to.'

'*Well!*'

'She used to play with him when they were children. So she's going to marry him.'

'My dear, isn't that rather sad-making for you?'

'I'm desperate about it. I'm thinking of committing suicide, like Simon.'

'Don't do that, darling . . . did Simon commit suicide?'

'My dear, you know he did. The night all those libel actions started.'

'Oh, *that* Simon. I thought you meant *Simon*.'

'Who's Simon?'

'The young man who fell out of the aeroplane. The nurses call him Simple Simon because it's affected his brains . . . but, Adam, I *am* sorry about Nina. I'll tell you what we'll do. As soon as I'm well again we'll make Mary Mouse give a lovely party to cheer you up.'

'Haven't you heard about Mary?'

'No, what?'

'She went off to Monte Carlo with the Maharajah of Pukkapore.'

'*My dear*, aren't the Mice furious?'

'She's just receiving religious instruction before her official reception as a royal concubine. Then they're going to India.'

'How people are *disappearing*, Adam. Did you get that money from the drunk Major?'

'No, he disappeared too.'

'D'you know, all that time when I was dotty I had the most awful dreams. I thought we were all driving round and round in a motor race and none of us could stop, and there was an enormous audience composed entirely of gossip writers and gate-crashers and Archie Schwert and people like that, all shouting to us at once to go faster, and car after car kept crashing until I was left all alone driving and driving – and then I used to crash and wake up.'

Then the door opened, and Miles came popping in.

'Agatha, Adam, my dears. The *time* I've had trying to get in. I can't tell you how bogus they were downstairs. First I said I was Lord Chasm, and that wasn't any good; and I said I was one of the doctors, and that wasn't any good; and I said I was your young man, and *that* wasn't any good; and I said I was a gossip writer, and they let me up at once and said I wasn't to excite you, but would I put a piece in my paper about their nursing-home. *How* are you, Aggie darling? I brought up some new records.'

'You are angelic. Do let's try them. There's a gramophone under the bed.'

'There's a whole lot more people coming to see you to-day. I saw them all at luncheon at Margot's. Johnny Hoop and Van and Archie Schwert. I wonder if they'll all manage to get in.'

They got in.

So soon there was quite a party, and Simon appeared from next door in a very gay dressing-gown, and they played the new records and Miss Runcible moved her bandaged limbs under the bed-clothes in negro rhythm.

Last of all, Nina came in looking quite lovely and very ill.

'Nina, I hear you're engaged.'

'Yes, it's very lucky. My papa has just put all his money into a cinema film and lost it all.'

'My dear, it doesn't matter at all. My papa lost all his twice. It doesn't make a bit of difference. That's just one of the things one has to learn about losing all one's money . . . Is it true that you really call him Ginger?'

'Well, yes, only, Agatha, please don't be unkind about it.'

And the gramophone was playing the song which the black man sang at the Café de la Paix.

Then the nurse came in.

'Well, you are noisy ones, and no mistake,' she said. 'I don't know what the Matron would say if she were here.'

'Have a chocolate, sister?'

'*Ooh, chocs!*'

Adam made another cocktail.

Miles sat on Miss Runcible's bed and took up the telephone and began dictating some paragraphs about the nursing-home.

'What it is to have a friend in the Press,' said the nurse.

Adam brought her a cocktail. 'Shall I?' she said. 'I hope you haven't made it too strong. Suppose it goes to my head? What would the patients think if their sister came in tiddly. Well, if you're *sure* it won't hurt me, thanks.'

*

'. . . *Yesterday I visited the Hon. Agatha Runcible comma Lord Chasm's lovely daughter comma at the Wimpole Street nursing-home where she is recovering from the effects of the motor accident recently described in this column stop Miss Runcible was entertaining quite a large party which included . . .*'

Adam, handing round cocktails, came to Nina.

'I thought we were never going to meet each other again.'

'We were obviously bound to, weren't we?'

'Agatha's looking better than I expected, isn't she? What an amusing nursing-home.'

'Nina, I must see you again. Come back to Lottie's this evening and have dinner with me.'

'No.'

'*Please.*'

'No. Ginger wouldn't like it.'

'Nina, you aren't in love with him?'

'No, I don't think so.'

'Are you in love with me?'

'I don't know . . . I was once.'

'Nina, I'm absolutely miserable not seeing you. Do come and dine with me to-night. What can be the harm in that?'

'My dear, I know exactly what it will mean.'

'Well, why not?'

'You see, Ginger's not like us really about that sort of thing. He'd be furious.'

'Well, what about me? Surely I have first claim?'

'Darling, don't *bully*. Besides, I used to play with Ginger as a child. His hair was a very pretty colour then.'

'. . . *Mr "Johnny" Hoop, whose memoirs are to be published next month, told me that he intends to devote his time to painting in future, and is going to Paris to study in the spring. He is to be taken into the studio of . . .*'

'For the last time, Nina . . .'

'Well, I suppose I must.'

'*Angel!*'

'I believe you knew I was going to.'

'. . . *Miss Nina Blount, whose engagement to Mr "Ginger" Littlejohn, the well-known polo player . . . Mr Schwert . . .*'

'If only you were as rich as Ginger, Adam, or only half as rich. Or if only you had any money at all.'

'Well,' said the Matron, appearing suddenly. 'Whoever heard of cocktails and a gramophone in a concussion case? Sister Briggs, pull down those curtains at once. Out you go, the whole lot of you. Why, I've known cases die with less.'

Indeed, Miss Runcible was already showing signs of strain. She was sitting bolt upright in bed, smiling deliriously, and bowing her bandaged head to imaginary visitors.

'*Darling,*' she said. 'How *too* divine . . . *how* are you? . . . and how are *you*? . . . how angelic of you all to come . . . only you must be careful not to fall out at the corners . . . ooh, just missed it. There goes that nasty Italian car . . . I wish I knew which thing was which in this car . . . darling, do try and drive more straight, my sweet, you were nearly into me then . . . Faster . . .'

'That's all right, Miss Runcible, that's all right. You mustn't get excited,' said the Matron. 'Sister Briggs, run for the ice-pack quickly.'

'All friends here,' said Miss Runcible, smiling radiantly. 'Faster . . . Faster . . . it'll stop all right when the time comes . . .'

That evening Miss Runcible's temperature went rocketing up the chart in a way which aroused great interest throughout the nursing-home. Sister Briggs, over her evening cup of cocoa, said she would be sorry to lose that case. Such a nice bright girl – but terribly excitable.

At Shepheard's Hotel Lottie said to Adam:

'That chap's been in here again after you.'

'What chap, Lottie?'

'How do I know what chap? Same chap as before.'

'You never told me about a chap.'

'Didn't I, dear? Well, I meant to.'

'What did he want?'

'I don't know – something about money. Dun,[37] I expect. Says he is coming back to-morrow.'

'Well, tell him I've gone to Manchester.'

'That's right, dear . . . What about a glass of wine?'

Later that evening Nina said: 'You don't seem to be enjoying yourself very much to-night.'

'Sorry, am I being a bore?'

'I think I shall go home.'

'Yes.'

'Adam, darling, what's the matter?'

'I don't know . . . Nina, do you ever feel that things simply can't go on much longer?'

'What d'you mean by things – us or everything?'

'Everything.'

'No – I wish I did.'

'I dare say you're right . . . what are you looking for?'

'Clothes.'

'Why?'

'Oh, Adam, what *do* you want . . . you're too impossible this evening.'

'Don't let's talk any more, Nina, d'you mind?'

Later he said: 'I'd give anything in the world for something different.'

'Different from me or different from everything?'

'Different from everything . . . only I've got nothing . . . what's the good of talking?'

'Oh, Adam, my dearest . . .'

'Yes?'

'Nothing.'

When Adam came down next morning Lottie was having her morning glass of champagne in the parlour.

'So your little bird's flown, has she? Sit down and have a glass of wine. That dun's been in again. I told him you was in Manchester.'

'Splendid.'

'Seemed rather shirty about it. Said he'd go and look for you.'

'Better still.'

Then something happened which Adam had been dreading for days. Lottie suddenly said:

'And that reminds me. What about *my* little bill?'

'Oh, yes,' said Adam, 'I've been meaning to ask for it. Have it made out and sent up to me some time, will you?'

'I've got it here. Bless you, what a lot you seem to have drunk.'

'Yes, I do, don't I? Are you sure some of this champagne wasn't the Judge's?'

'Well, it may have been,' admitted Lottie. 'We get a bit muddled with the books now and then.'

'Well, thank you so much, I'll send you down a cheque for this.'

'No, dear,' said Lottie. 'Suppose you write it down here. Here's the pen, here's the ink, and here's a blank cheque book.'

(Bills are delivered infrequently and irregularly at Lottie's, but when they come, there is no getting away from them.) Adam wrote out a cheque for seventy-eight pounds sixteen shillings.

'And twopence for the cheque,' said Lottie.

And twopence, Adam added.

'There's a dear,' said Lottie, blotting the cheque and locking it away in a drawer. 'Why, look who's turned up. If it isn't Mr Thingummy.'

It was Ginger.

'Good morning, Mrs Crump,' he said rather stiffly.

'Come and sit down and have a glass of wine, dear. Why, I knew you before you were born.'

'Hullo, Ginger,' said Adam.

'Look here, Symes,' said Ginger, looking in an embarrassed manner at the glass of champagne which had been put into his hand, 'I want to speak to you. Perhaps we can go somewhere where we shan't be disturbed.'

'Bless you, boys, I won't disturb you,' said Lottie. 'Just you have a nice talk. I've got lots to see to.'

She left the parlour, and soon her voice could be heard raised in anger against the Italian waiter.

'Well?' said Adam.

'Look here, Symes,' said Ginger, 'what I mean to say is what I'm going to say may sound damned unpleasant you know and all that but look here you know damn it I mean *the better man won* – not that I mean I'm the *better* man. Wouldn't say that for a minute. And anyway Nina's a damn sight too good for either of us. It's just that I've been lucky. Awful rough luck on you I mean and all that but still when you come to think of it after all well look here damn it I mean d'you see what I mean?'

'Not quite,' said Adam gently. 'Now tell me again. Is it something about Nina?'

'Yes, it is,' said Ginger in a rush. 'Nina and I are engaged, and I'm not going to have you butting in or there'll be hell to pay.' He paused, rather taken aback at his own eloquence.

'What makes you think I'm butting in?'

'Well, hang it all, she dined with you last night, didn't she, and stayed out jolly late, too.'

'How do you know how late she stayed out?'

'Well, as a matter of fact, you see I wanted to speak to her about something rather important, so I rang her up once or twice and didn't get an answer until three o'clock.'

'I suppose you rang her up about every ten minutes?'

'Oh no, damn it, not as often as that,' said Ginger. 'No, no, not as often as that. I know it sounds rather unsporting and all that, but you see I wanted to speak to her, and, anyway, when I did get through, she just said she had a pain and didn't want to talk: *well, I mean to say*. After all, I mean, one is a gentleman. It isn't as though you were just a sort of friend of the family, is it? I mean, you were more or less engaged to her yourself, weren't you, at one time? Well, what would you have thought if I'd come butting in? You must look at it like that, from my point of view, too, mustn't you, I mean?'

'Well, I think that's rather what did happen.'

'Oh no, look here, Symes, I mean, damn it; you mustn't say things like that. D'you know all the time I was out East I had Nina's photograph over my bed, honest I did. I expect you think that's sentimental and all that, but what I mean is I didn't stop

164

thinking of that girl once all the time I was away. Mind you, there were lots of other frightfully jolly girls out there, and I don't say I didn't sometimes get jolly pally with them, you know, tennis and gymkhana and all that sort of thing, I mean, and dancing in the evenings, but never anything serious, you know. Nina was the only girl I really thought of, and I'd sort of made up my mind when I came home to look her up, and if she'd have me . . . see what I mean? So you see it's awfully rough luck on me when someone comes butting in. You must see that, don't you?'

'Yes,' said Adam.

'And there's another thing, you know, sentiment and all that apart. I mean Nina's a girl who likes nice clothes and things, you know, comfort and all that. Well, I mean to say, of course, her father's a topping old boy, absolutely one of the best, but he's rather an ass about money, if you know what I mean. What I mean, Nina's going to be frightfully hard up, and all that, and I mean you haven't got an awful lot of money, have you?'

'I haven't any at all.'

'No, I mean, that's what I mean. *Awfully rough on you.* No one thinks the worse of you, respects you for it, I mean earning a living and all that. Heaps of fellows haven't any money nowadays. I could give you the names of dozens of stout fellows, absolute toppers, who simply haven't a bean. No, all I mean is, when it comes to marrying, then that does make a difference, doesn't it?'

'What you've been trying to say all this time is that you're not sure of Nina?'

'Oh, rot, my dear fellow, absolute bilge. Damn it, I'd trust Nina anywhere, of course I would. After all, damn it, what does being in love mean if you can't trust a person?'

('What, indeed?' thought Adam), and he said, 'Now, Ginger, tell the truth. What's Nina worth to you?'

'Good Lord, why what an extraordinary thing to ask; everything in the world of course. I'd go through fire and water for that girl.'

'Well, I'll sell her to you.'

'No, why, look here, good God, damn it, I mean . . .'

'I'll sell my share in her for a hundred pounds.'

'You pretend to be fond of Nina and you talk about her like that! Why, hang it, it's not decent. Besides, a hundred pounds is the deuce of a lot. I mean, getting married is a damned expensive business, don't you know. And I'm just getting a couple of polo ponies over from Ireland. That's going to cost a hell of a lot, what with one thing and another.'

'A hundred down, and I leave Nina to you. I think it's cheap.'

'Fifty.'

'A hundred.'

'Seventy-five.'

'A hundred.'

'I'm damned if I'll pay more than seventy-five.'

'I'll take seventy-eight pounds sixteen and twopence. I can't go lower than that.'

'All right, I'll pay that. *You really will go away?*'

'I'll try, Ginger. Have a drink.'

'No, thank you . . . this only shows what an escape Nina's had – poor little girl.'

'Good-bye, Ginger.'

'Good-bye, Symes.'

'Young Thingummy going?' said Lottie, appearing in the door. 'I was just thinking about a little drink.'

Adam went to the telephone-box . . . 'Hullo, is that Nina?'

'Who's speaking, please? I don't think Miss Blount is in.'

'Mr Fenwick-Symes.'

'Oh, Adam. I was afraid it was Ginger. I woke up feeling I just couldn't bear him. He rang up last night just as I got in.'

'I know. Nina, darling, something awful's happened.'

'What?'

'Lottie presented me with her bill.'

'Darling, what *did* you do?'

'Well, I did something rather extraordinary . . . My dear, I sold *you*.'

'Darling . . . *who to?*'

'Ginger. You fetched seventy-eight pounds sixteen and twopence.'

'*Well?*'

'And now I never am going to see you again.'

'Oh, but Adam, I think this is beastly of you; I don't want not to see you again.'

'I'm sorry . . . Good-bye, Nina, darling.'

'Good-bye, Adam, my sweet. But I think you're rather a cad.'

Next day Lottie said to Adam, 'You know that chap I said came here asking for you?'

'The dun?'

'Well, he wasn't a dun. I've just remembered. He's a chap who used to come here quite a lot until he had a fight with a Canadian. He was here the night that silly Flossie killed herself on the chandelier.'

'Not the drunk Major.'

'He wasn't drunk yesterday. Not so as you'd notice anyway. Red-faced chap with an eyeglass. You ought to remember him, dear. He was the one made that bet for you on the November Handicap.'

'But I must get hold of him at once. What's his name?'

'Ah, that I couldn't tell you. I *did* know, but it's slipped my memory. He's gone to Manchester to look for you. Pity your missing him!'

Then Adam rang up Nina. 'Listen,' he said. 'Don't do anything sudden about Ginger. I may be able to buy you back. The drunk Major has turned up again.'

'But, darling, it's too late. Ginger and I got married this morning. I'm just packing for our honeymoon. We're going in an aeroplane.'

'Ginger wasn't taking any chances, was he? Darling, don't go.'

'No, I must. Ginger says he knows a "tophole little spot not far from Monte with a very decent nine-hole golf course".'

'*Well?*'

'*Yes, I know* . . . we shall only be away a few days. We're coming back to spend Christmas with Papa. Perhaps we shall be able to arrange something when we get back. I do hope so.'

'Good-bye.'

'Good-bye.'

Ginger looked out of the aeroplane: 'I say, Nina,' he shouted, 'when you were young did you ever have to learn a thing out of a poetry book about: *"This sceptre'd isle, this earth of majesty, this something or other Eden"*? D'you know what I mean? – *"this happy breed of men, this little world, this precious stone set in the silver sea . . .*

This blessed plot,[38] *this earth, this realm, this England*

This nurse, this teeming womb of royal kings

Feared by their breed and famous by their birth . . ."

I forget how it goes on. Something about a stubborn Jew. But you know the thing I mean?'

'It comes in a play.'

'No, a blue poetry book.'

'I acted in it.'

'Well, they may have put it into a play since. It was in a blue poetry book when I learned it. Anyway, you know what I mean?'

'Yes, why?'

'Well, I mean to say, don't you feel somehow, up in the air like this and looking down and seeing everything underneath. I mean, don't you have a sort of feeling rather like that, if you see what I mean?'

Nina looked down and saw inclined at an odd angle a horizon of straggling red suburb; arterial roads dotted with little cars; factories, some of them working, others empty and decaying; a disused canal; some distant hills sown with bungalows; wireless masts and overhead power cables; men and women were indiscernible except as tiny spots; they were marrying and shopping and making money and having children. The scene lurched and tilted again as the aeroplane struck a current of air.

'I think I'm going to be sick,' said Nina.

'Poor little girl,' said Ginger. 'That's what the paper bags are for.'

There was rarely more than a quarter of a mile of the black road to be seen at one time. It unrolled like a length of cinema film. At the edges was confusion; a fog spinning past: *'Faster, faster,'* they shouted above the roar of the engine. The road rose suddenly and the white car soared up the sharp ascent without slackening speed. At the summit of the hill there was a corner. Two cars had crept up, one on each side, and were closing in. 'Faster,' cried Miss Runcible, 'faster.'

'Quietly, dear, quietly. You're disturbing everyone. You must lie quiet or you'll never get well. Everything's quite all right. There's nothing to worry about. Nothing at all.'

They were trying to make her lie down. How could one drive properly lying down?

Another frightful corner. The car leant over on two wheels, tugging outwards; it was drawn across the road until it was within a few inches of the bank. One ought to brake down at the corners, but one couldn't see them coming lying flat on one's back like this. The back wheels wouldn't hold the road at this speed. Skidding all over the place.

'*Faster. Faster.*'

The stab of a hypodermic needle.

'There's nothing to worry about, dear ... *nothing at all ... nothing.*'

Chapter Thirteen

*

The film had been finished, and everyone had gone away; Wesley and Whitefield, Bishop Philpotts and Miss La Touche, Mr Isaacs, and all his pupils from the National Academy of Cinematographic Art. The park lay deep in snow, a clean expanse of white, shadowless and unspotted save for tiny broad arrows stamped by the hungry birds. The bellringers were having their final practice, and the air was alive with pealing bells.

Inside the dining-room Florin and Mrs Florin and Ada, the fifteen-year-old housemaid, were arranging branches of holly above the frames of the family portraits. Florin held the basket, Mrs Florin held the steps and Ada put the decorations in their places. Colonel Blount was having his afternoon nap upstairs.

Florin had a secret. It was a white calico banner of great age lettered in red ribbon with the words 'WELCOME HOME'. He had always known where it was, just where to put his hand on it, at the top of the black trunk in the far attic behind the two hip baths and the 'cello case.

'The Colonel's mother made it,' he explained, 'when he first went away to school, and it was always hung out in the hall whenever he and Mister Eric came back for the holidays. It used to be the first thing he'd look for when he came into the house – even when he was a grown man home on leave. "Where's my banner?" he'd say. We'll have it up for Miss Nina – Mrs Littlejohn, I should say.'

Ada said should they put some holly in Captain and Mrs Littlejohn's bedroom.

Mrs Florin said, whoever heard of holly in a bedroom, and she wasn't sure but that it was unlucky to take it upstairs.

Ada said, 'Well, perhaps just a bit of mistletoe over the bed.'

Mrs Florin said Ada was too young to think about things like that, and she ought to be ashamed of herself.

Florin said would Ada stop arguing and answering back and come into the hall to put up the banner. One string went on the nose of the rhinoceros, he explained, the other round the giraffe.

Presently Colonel Blount came down.

'Should I light the fires in the big drawing-room?' asked Mrs Florin.

'Fires in the big drawing-room? No, why should you want to do that, Mrs Florin?'

'Because of Captain and Mrs Littlejohn – you haven't forgotten, have you, sir, that they're coming to stay this afternoon?'

'Captain and Mrs Fiddlesticks. Never heard of them. Who asked them to stay I should like to know? *I* didn't. Don't know who they are. Don't want them . . . Besides, now I come to think of it, Miss Nina and her husband said they were coming down. I can't have the whole house turned into an hotel. If these people come, Florin, whoever they are, you tell them to go away. You understand? I won't have them, and I think it's very presumptuous of whoever asked them. It is not their place to invite guests here without consulting me.'

'Should I be lighting the fires in the big drawing-room for Miss Nina and her young gentleman, sir?'

'Yes, yes, certainly . . . and a fire in their bedroom, of course. And, Florin, I want you to come down to the cellar with me to look out some port . . . I've got the keys here . . . I have a feeling I'm going to like Miss Nina's husband,' he confided on their way to the cellar. 'I hear very good reports of him – a decent, steady young fellow, and not at all badly off. Miss Nina said in her letter that he used to come over here as a little boy. D'you remember him, Florin? Blest if I do . . . What's the name again?'

'Littlejohn, sir.'

'Yes. Littlejohn, to be sure. I had the name on the tip of my tongue only a minute ago. *Littlejohn.* I must remember that.'

'His father used to live over at Oakshott, sir. A very wealthy gentleman. Shipowners, I think they were. Young Mr Littlejohn used to go riding with Miss Nina, sir. Regular little monkey he was, sir, red-headed . . . a terrible one for cats.'

'Well, well, I dare say he's grown out of that. Mind the step,

Florin, it's all broken away. Hold the lamp higher, can't you, man. Now, what did we come for? Port, yes, port. Now, there's some '96 somewhere, only a few bottles left. What does it say on this bin? I can't read. Bring the light over here.'

'We drank up the last of the '96, sir, when the film-acting gentlemen was here.'

'Did we, Florin, did we? We shouldn't have done that, you know.'

'Very particular about his wine, Mr Isaacs was. My instructions was to give them whatever they wanted.'

'Yes, but '96 port . . . Well, well. Take up two bottles of the '04. Now, what else do we want? Claret – yes, *claret*. Claret, claret, claret, claret. Where do I keep the claret, Florin?'

Colonel Blount was just having tea – he had finished a brown boiled egg and was spreading a crumpet with honey – when Florin opened the library door and announced 'Captain and Mrs Littlejohn, sir.'

And Adam and Nina came in.

Colonel Blount put down his crumpet and rose to greet them.

'Well, Nina, it's a long time since you came to see your old father. So this is my son-in-law, eh? How do you do, my boy. Come and sit down, both of you. Florin will bring some more cups directly . . . Well,' he said, giving Adam a searching glance, 'I can't say I should have recognized you. I used to know your father very well indeed at one time. Used to be a neighbour of mine over at where-was-it. I expect you've forgotten those days. You used to come over here to ride with Nina. You can't have been more than ten or eleven . . . Funny, something gave me an idea you had red hair . . .'

'I expect you'd heard him called "Ginger",' said Nina, 'and that made you think of it.'

'Something of the kind, I dare say . . . extraordinary thing to call him "Ginger" when he's got ordinary fair hair . . . anyway, I'm very glad to see you, very glad. I'm afraid it'll be a very quiet week-end. We don't see many people here now. Florin says he's asked a Captain and Mrs Something-or-other to come and stay, damn his impudence, but I said I wouldn't see them. Why should I entertain Florin's friends? Servants seem to think after they've been with you some time they can do anything they like. There was poor old Lady Graybridge, now – they only found out after her death that her man had been letting lodgings all the time in the North Wing. She never could understand why none of the fruit ever came into the dining-room – the butler and his boarders were eating it all in the servants' hall. And after she was ill, and couldn't leave her room, he laid out a golf links in the park ... shocking state of affairs. I don't believe Florin would do a thing like that – still, you never know. It's the thin edge of the wedge asking people down for the week-end.'

In the kitchen Florin said: '*That's* not the Mr Littlejohn I used to know.'

Mrs Florin said, 'It's the young gentleman that came here to luncheon last month.'

Ada said, 'He's very nice looking.'

Florin and Mrs Florin said, 'You be quiet, Ada. Have you taken the hot water up to their bedroom yet? Have you taken up their suitcases? Have you unpacked them? Did you brush the Colonel's evening suit? Do you expect Mr Florin and Mrs Florin to do *all* the work of the house? And look at your apron again, you wretched girl, if it isn't the second you've dirtied to-day.'

Florin added, 'Anyway, Miss Nina noticed the banner.'

In the library Colonel Blount said, 'I've got a treat for you to-night, anyway. The last two reels of my cinema film have just come back from being developed. I thought we'd run through it to-night. We shall have to go across to the Rectory, because the Rector's got electric light, the lucky fellow. I told him to expect us. He didn't seem very pleased about it. Said he had to preach three sermons to-morrow, and be up at six for early service. That's not the Christmas spirit. Didn't want to bring the car round to fetch us either. It's only a matter of a quarter of a mile, no trouble to *him*, and how can we walk in the snow carrying all the apparatus? I said to him, "If you practised a little more Christianity yourself we might be more willing to subscribe to your foreign missions and the Boy Scouts and organ funds." Had him there. Dammit, I put the man in his job myself – if I haven't a right to his car, who has?'

When they went up to change for dinner Nina said to Adam, 'I knew papa would never recognize you.'

Adam said, 'Look, someone's put mistletoe over our bed.'

'I think you gave the Florins rather a surprise.'

'My dear, what will the Rector say? He drove me to the station the first time I came. He thought I was mad.'

'. . . Poor Ginger. I wonder, are we treating him terribly badly? . . . It seemed a direct act of fate that he should have been called up to join his regiment just at this moment.'

'I left him a cheque to pay for you.'

'Darling, you know it's a bad one.'

'No cheque is bad until it's refused by the bank. Tomorrow's Christmas, then Boxing Day, then Sunday. He can't pay it in until Monday, and anything may have happened by then. The drunk Major may have turned up. If the worst comes to the worst I can always send you back to him.'

'I expect it will end with that . . . Darling, the honeymoon *was* hell . . . frightfully cold, and Ginger insisted on walking about on a terrace after dinner to see the moon on the Mediterranean – he played golf all day, and made friends with the other English people in the hotel. I can't tell you what it was like . . . too spirit-crushing, as poor Agatha used to say.'

'Did I tell you I went to Agatha's funeral? There was practically no one there except the Chasms and some aunts. I went with Van, rather tight, and got stared at. I think they felt I was partly responsible for the accident . . .'

'What about Miles?'

'He's had to leave the country, didn't you know?'

'Darling, I only came back from my honeymoon to-day. I haven't heard anything . . . You know there seems to be none of us left now except you and me.'

'And Ginger.'

'Yes, and Ginger.'

The cinematograph exhibition that evening was not really a success.

The Rector arrived while they were finishing dinner, and was shown into the dining-room shaking the snow from the shoulders of his overcoat.

'Come in, Rector, come in. We shan't be many minutes now. Take a glass of port and sit down. You've met my daughter, haven't you? And this is my new son-in-law.'

'I think I've had the pleasure of meeting him before too.'

'Nonsense, first time he's been here since he was so high – long before your time.'

The Rector sipped his port and kept eyeing Adam over the top of his glass in a way which made Nina giggle. Then Adam giggled too, and the Rector's suspicions were confirmed. In this way relations were already on an uneasy basis before they reached the Rectory. The Colonel, however, was far too intent over the transport of his apparatus to notice anything.

'This is your first visit here?' said the Rector as he drove through the snow.

'I lived near here as a boy, you know,' said Adam.

'Ah . . . but you were down here the other day, were you not? The Colonel often forgets things . . .'

'No, no. I haven't been here for fifteen years.'

'I *see*,' said the Rector with sinister emphasis, and murmured under his breath, 'Remarkable . . . very sad and remarkable.'

The Rector's wife was disposed to make rather a party of it, and had arranged some coffee and chocolate biscuits in the drawing-room, but the Colonel soon put an end to any frivolity of this kind by plunging them all in darkness.

He took out the bulbs of their electric lights and fitted in the plug of his lantern. A bright beam shot across the drawing-room like a searchlight, picking out the Rector, who was whispering in his wife's ear the news of his discovery.

'. . . the same young man I told you of,' he was saying. 'Quite off his head, poor boy. He didn't even remember coming here before.

One expects that sort of thing in a man of the Colonel's age, but for a young man like that . . . a very bad look-out for the next generation . . .'

The Colonel paused in his preparation.

'I say, Rector, I've just thought of something. I wish old Florin were here. He was in bed half the time they were taking the film. I know he'd love to see it. Could you be a good chap and run up in the car and fetch him?'

'No, really, Colonel, I hardly think that's necessary. I've just put the car away.'

'I won't start before you come back, if that's what you're thinking of. It'll take me some time to get everything fixed up. We'll wait for you. I promise you that.'

'My dear Colonel, it's snowing heavily – practically a blizzard. Surely it would be a mistaken kindness to drag an elderly man out of doors on a night like this in order to see a film which, I have no doubt, will soon be on view all over the country?'

'All right, Rector, just as you think best. I only thought after all it is Christmas . . . damn the thing; I got a nasty shock then.'

Adam and Nina and the Rector and his wife sat in the dark patiently. After a time the Colonel unrolled a silvered screen.

'Just help me take all these things off the chimney-piece, some-one,' he said.

The Rector's wife scuttered to the preservation of her ornaments.

'Will it bear, do you think?' asked the Colonel, mounting precariously on the top of the piano, and exhibiting in his excitement an astonishing fund of latent vitality. 'Now hand up the screen to me, will you? That's splendid. You don't mind a couple of screws in your wall, do you, Rector? Quite small ones.'

Presently the screen was fixed and the lens directed so that it threw on to it a small square of light.

The audience sat down expectantly.

'*Now*,' said the Colonel, and set the machine in motion.

There was a whirring sound, and suddenly there appeared on the screen the spectacle of four uniformed horsemen galloping backwards down the drive.

'Hullo,' said the Colonel. 'Something wrong there . . . that's funny. I must have forgotten to rewind it.'

The horsemen disappeared, and there was a fresh whirring as the film was transferred to another spool.

'Now,' said the Colonel, and sure enough there appeared in small and clear letters the notice, 'THE WONDERFILM COMPANY OF GREAT BRITAIN PRESENTS'. This legend, vibrating a good deal, but without other variation, filled the screen for some time – ('Of course, I shall cut the captions a bit before it's shown commercially,' explained the Colonel) – until its place was taken by 'EFFIE LA TOUCHE IN'. This announcement was displayed for practically no time at all; indeed, they had scarcely had time to read it before it was whisked away obliquely. ('Damn,' said the Colonel. 'Skidded.') There followed another long pause, and then:

'A BRAND FROM THE BURNING, A FILM BASED ON THE LIFE OF JOHN WESLEY.'

('*There*,' said the Colonel.)

'EIGHTEENTH-CENTURY ENGLAND.'

There came in breathless succession four bewigged men in fancy costume, sitting round a card table. There were glasses, heaps of money and candles on the table. They were clearly gambling feverishly and drinking a lot. ('There's a song there, really,' said the Colonel, 'only I'm afraid I haven't got a talkie apparatus yet.') Then a highwayman holding up the coach which Adam had seen; then some beggars starving outside Doubting Church; then some ladies in fancy costume dancing a minuet. Sometimes the heads of the dancers would disappear above the top of the pictures; sometimes they would sink waist-deep as though in a quicksand; once Mr Isaacs appeared at the side in shirt-sleeves, waving them on. ('I'll have him out,' said the Colonel.)

'EPWORTH RECTORY, LINCOLNSHIRE (ENG.)'

('That's in case it's taken up in the States,' said the Colonel. 'I don't believe there is a Lincolnshire over there, but it's always courteous to put that in case.')

A corner of Doubting Hall appeared with clouds of smoke billowing from the windows. A clergyman was seen handing out a succession of children with feverish rapidity of action. ('It's on fire, you see,' said the Colonel. 'We did that quite simply, by burning some stuff Isaacs had. It did make a smell.')

So the film went on eventfully for about half an hour. One of its peculiarities was that whenever the story reached a point of dramatic and significant action, the film seemed to get faster and faster. Villagers trotted to church as though galvanized; lovers shot in and out of windows; horses flashed past like motor cars; riots happened so quickly that they were hardly noticed. On the other hand, any scene of repose or inaction, a conversation in a garden between two clergymen, Mrs Wesley at her prayers, Lady Huntingdon asleep, etc., seemed prolonged almost unendurably. Even Colonel Blount suspected this imperfection.

'I think I might cut a bit there,' he said, after Wesley had sat uninterruptedly composing a pamphlet for four and a half minutes.

When the reel came to an end everyone stirred luxuriously.

'Well, that was very nice,' said the Rector's wife, 'very nice and instructive.'

'I really must congratulate you, Colonel. A production of absorbing interest. I had no idea Wesley's life was so full of adventure. I see I must read up my Lecky.'

'Too divine, Papa.'

'Thank you so much, sir, I enjoyed that immensely.'

'But, bless you, that isn't the end,' said the Colonel. 'There are four more reels yet.'

'Oh, that's good.' 'But how delightful.' 'Splendid.' 'Oh.'

But the full story was never shown. Just at the beginning of the second part – when Wesley in America was being rescued from Red Indians by Lady Huntingdon disguised as a cowboy – there occurred one of the mishaps from which the largest super-cinemas are not absolutely immune. There was a sudden crackling sound, a long blue spark, and the light was extinguished.

'Oh, dear,' said the Colonel, 'I wonder what's happened now. We were just getting to such an exciting place.' He bent all his energies on the apparatus, recklessly burning his fingers, while his audience sat in darkness. Presently the door opened and a house-maid appeared carrying a candle.

'If you please, mum,' she said, 'the light's gone out all over the house.'

The Rector hurried across to the door and tried the switch in the passage. He clicked it up and down several times; he tapped it like a barometer and shook it slightly.

'It looks as though the wires were fused,' he said.

'Really, Rector, how very inconvenient,' said the Colonel crossly. 'I can't possibly show the film without electric current. Surely there must be something you can do?'

'I am afraid it will be a job for an electrician; it will be scarcely possible to get one before Monday,' said the Rector with scarcely Christian calm. 'In fact it is clear to me that my wife and myself and my whole household will have to spend the entire Christmas week-end in darkness.'

'Well,' said the Colonel. 'I never expected this to happen. Of course, I know it's just as disappointing for you as it is for me. All the same . . .'

The housemaid brought in some candles and a bicycle lamp.

'There's only these in the house, sir,' she said, 'and the shops don't open till Monday.'

'I don't think in the circumstances my hospitality can be of much more use to you, can it, Colonel? Perhaps you would like me to ring up and get a taxi out from Aylesbury.'

'What's that? *Taxi?* Why, it's ridiculous to get a taxi out from Aylesbury to go a quarter of a mile!'

'I'm sure Mrs Littlejohn wouldn't like to walk all the way on a night like this?'

'Perhaps a taxi would be a good idea, Papa.'

'Of course, if you'd care to take shelter here . . . it may clear up a little. But I think you'd find it very wretched, sitting here in the dark?'

'No, no, of course, order a taxi,' said the Colonel.

On the way back to the house he said, 'I'd half made up my mind to lend him some of our lamps for the week-end. I certainly shan't now. Fancy hiring a taxi seven miles to drive us a few hundred yards. On Christmas Eve, too. No wonder they find it hard to fill their churches when that's their idea of Christian fellowship. Just when I'd brought my film all that way to show them . . .'

Next morning Adam and Nina woke up under Ada's sprig of mistletoe to hear the bells ringing for Christmas across the snow. 'Come all to church, good people; good people come to church.' They had each hung up a stocking the evening before, and Adam had put a bottle of scent and a scent spray into Nina's, and she had put two ties and a new kind of safety-razor into his. Ada brought them their tea and wished them a happy Christmas. Nina had remembered to get a present for each of the Florins, but had forgotten Ada, so she gave her the bottle of scent.

'Darling,' said Adam, 'it cost twenty-five shillings – on Archie Schwert's account at Asprey.'

Later they put some crumbs of their bread and butter on the windowsill and a robin redbreast came to eat them. The whole day was like that.

Adam and Nina breakfasted alone in the dining-room. There was a row of silver plates kept hot by spirit lamps which held an omelette and devilled partridges and kedgeree and kidneys and sole and some rolls; there was also a ham and a tongue and some brawn and a dish of pickled herrings. Nina ate an apple and Adam ate some toast.

Colonel Blount came down at eleven wearing a grey tail coat. He wished them a very good morning and they exchanged gifts. Adam gave him a box of cigars; Nina gave him a large illustrated book about modern cinema production; he gave Nina a seed pearl brooch which had belonged to her mother, and he gave Adam a calendar with a coloured picture of a bulldog smoking a clay pipe and a thought from Longfellow for each day in the year.

At half-past eleven they all went to Matins.

'It will be a lesson to him in true Christian forgiveness,' said the Colonel (but he ostentatiously read his Bible throughout the sermon). After church they called in at two or three cottages.

Florin had been round the day before distributing parcels of grocery. They were all pleased and interested to meet Miss Nina's husband. Many of them remembered him as a little boy, and remarked that he had grown out of all recognition. They reminded him with relish of many embarrassing episodes in Ginger's childhood, chiefly acts of destruction and cruelty to cats.

After luncheon they went down to see all the decorations in the servants' hall.

This was a yearly custom of some antiquity, and the Florins had prepared for it by hanging paper streamers from the gas brackets. Ada was having middle-day dinner with her parents who lived among the petrol pumps at Doubting village, so the Florins ate their turkey and plum pudding alone.

'I've seen as many as twenty-five sitting down to Christmas dinner at this table,' said Florin. 'Regular parties they used to have when the Colonel and Mr Eric were boys. Theatricals and all the house turned topsy-turvy, and every gentleman with his own valet.'

'Ah,' said Mrs Florin.

'Times is changed,' said Florin, picking a tooth.

'Ah,' said Mrs Florin.

Then the family came in from the dining-room.

The Colonel knocked on the door and said, 'May we come in, Mrs Florin?'

'That you may, sir, and welcome,' said Mrs Florin.

Then Adam and Nina and the Colonel admired the decorations and handed over their presents wrapped in tissue paper. Then the Colonel said, 'I think we should take a glass of wine together.'

Florin opened a bottle of sherry which he had brought up that morning and poured out the glasses, handing one first to Nina, then to Mrs Florin, then to the Colonel, then to Adam, and, finally, taking one for himself.

'My very best wishes to you, Mrs Florin,' said the Colonel, raising his glass, 'and to you, Florin. The years go by, and we none of us get any younger, but I hope and trust that there are many

Christmases in store for us yet. Mrs Florin certainly doesn't look a day older than when she first came here. My best wishes to you both for another year of health and happiness.'

Mrs Florin said, 'Best respects, sir, and thank you, sir, and the same to you.'

Florin said, 'And a great pleasure it is to see Miss Nina – Mrs Littlejohn, I should say – with us once more at her old home, and her husband too, and I'm sure Mrs Florin and me wish them every happiness and prosperity in their married life together, and all I can say, if they can be as happy together as me and Mrs Florin has been, well, that's the best I can wish them.'

Then the family went away, and the house settled down to its afternoon nap.

After dinner that night Adam and the Colonel filled up their port glasses and turned their chairs towards the fire. Nina had gone into the drawing-room to smoke.

'You know,' said the Colonel, poking back a log with his foot, 'I'm very glad that Nina has married you, my boy. I've liked you from the moment I saw you. She's a headstrong girl – always was – but I knew that she'd make a sensible choice in the end. I foresee a very agreeable life ahead of you two young people.'

'I hope so, sir.'

'I'm sure of it, my boy. She's very nearly made several mistakes. There was an ass of a fellow here the other day wanting to marry her. A journalist. Awful silly fellow. He told me my old friend Canon Chatterbox was working on his paper. Well, I didn't like to contradict him – he ought to have known, after all – but I thought it was funny at the time, and then, d'you know, after he'd gone I was going through some old papers upstairs and I came on a cutting from the *Worcester Herald* describing his funeral. He died in 1912. Well, he must have been a muddle-headed sort of fellow to make a mistake like that, mustn't he? . . . Have some port?'

'Thank you.'

'Then there was another chap. Came here selling vacuum cleaners, if you please, and asked me to give him a thousand pounds! Impudent young cub. I soon sent him about his business ... But you're different, Littlejohn. Just the sort of son-in-law I'd have chosen for myself. Your marriage has been a great happiness to me, my boy.'

At this moment Nina came in to say that there were carol singers outside the drawing-room window.

'Bring 'em in,' said the Colonel. 'Bring 'em in. They come every year. And tell Florin to bring up the punch.'

Florin brought up the punch in a huge silver punch bowl and Nina brought in the waits. They stood against the sideboard, caps in hand, blinking in the gaslight, and very red about the nose and cheeks with the sudden warmth.

'Oh, tidings of comfort and joy,' they sang, *'comfort and joy,*
Oh, tidings of comfort and joy.'

They sang *Good King Wenceslas*, and *The First Noël*, and *Adeste Fideles*, and *While Shepherds Watched Their Flocks*. Then Florin ladled out the punch, seeing that the younger ones did not get the glasses intended for their elders, but that each, according to his capacity, got a little more, but not much more, than was good for him.

The Colonel tasted the punch and pronounced it excellent. He then asked the carol singers their names and where they came from, and finally gave their leader five shillings and sent them off into the snow.

'It's been just like this every year, as long as I can remember,' said the Colonel. 'We always had a party at Christmas when we were boys ... acted some very amusing charades too ... always a glass of sherry after luncheon in the servants' hall and carol singers in the evening ... Tell me,' he said, suddenly changing the subject, 'did you *really* like what you saw of the film yesterday?'

'It was the most divine film I ever saw, Papa.'

'I enjoyed it enormously, sir, really I did.'

'Did you? Did you? Well, I'm glad to hear that. I don't believe the Rector did – not properly. Of course, you only saw a bit of it, most disappointing. I didn't like to say so at the time, but I thought it most negligent of him to have his electric light in that sort of condition so that it wouldn't last out for one evening. Most inconsiderate to anyone who wants to show a film. But it's a glorious film, isn't it? You did think so?'

'I never enjoyed a film so much, honestly.'

'It makes a stepping stone in the development of the British film industry,' said the Colonel dreamily. 'It is the most important all-talkie super-religious film to be produced solely in this country by British artists and management and by British capital. It has been directed throughout regardless of difficulty and expense, and supervised by a staff of expert historians and theologians. Nothing has been omitted that would contribute to the meticulous accuracy of every detail. The life of that great social and religious reformer John Wesley is for the first time portrayed to a British public in all its humanity and tragedy . . . I'm glad you realized all that, my boy, because, as a matter of fact, I had a proposal to make to you about it. I'm getting an old man and can't do everything, and I feel my services should be better spent in future as an actor and producer, rather than on the commercial side. One needs someone young to manage that. Now what I thought was, that perhaps you would care to come in with me as business partner. I bought the whole thing from Isaacs and, as you're one of the family, I shouldn't mind selling you a half-share for, say, two thousand pounds. I know that that isn't much to you, and you'd be humanly certain to double your money in a few months. What do you say to it?'

'*Well* . . .' said Adam.

But he was never called upon to answer, for just at that moment the door of the dining-room opened and the Rector came in.

'Hullo, Rector, come in. This is very neighbourly of you to come and call at this time of night. A happy Christmas to you.'

'Colonel Blount, I've got very terrible news. I had to come over and tell you . . .'

'I say, I am sorry. Nothing wrong at the Rectory, I hope?'

'Worse, far worse. My wife and I were sitting over the fire after dinner, and as we couldn't read – not having any light – we put on the wireless. They were having a very pretty carol service. Suddenly they stopped in the middle and a special news bulletin was read . . . Colonel, the most terrible and unexpected thing – *War has been declared*.'

Happy Ending

*

On a splintered tree stump in the biggest battlefield in the history of the world, Adam sat down and read a letter from Nina. It had arrived early the day before, but in the intensive fighting which followed he had not had a spare minute in which to open it.

Doubting Hall,
Aylesbury.

Dearest Adam – I wonder how you are. It is difficult to know what is happening quite because the papers say such odd things. Van has got a divine job making up all the war news and he invented a lovely story about you the other day how you'd saved hundreds of people's lives and there's what they call a popular agitation saying why haven't you got the V.C. so probably you will have by now isn't it amusing

Ginger and I are very well. Ginger has a job in an office in Whitehall and wears a very grand sort of uniform and my dear I'm going to have a baby isn't it too awful but Ginger has quite made up his mind it's his and is as pleased as anything so that's all right. He's quite forgiven you about last Christmas and says anyway you're doing your bit now and in war time one lets bygones be bygones.

Doubting is a hospital did you know. Papa shows his film to the wounded and they adore it. I saw Mr Benfleet and he said how awful it was when one had given all one's life in the cause of culture to see everything one's stood for swept away but he's doing very well with his 'Sword Unsheathed' series of war poets.

There's a new Government order that we have to sleep in gas masks because of the bombs but no one does. They've put Archie in prison as an undesirable alien Ginger saw to that he's terrific about spies. I'm sick such a lot because of this baby but everyone says it's patriotic to have babies in war time why?

Lots of love my angel take care of your dear self.

N.

He put it back in its envelope and buttoned it into his breast-pocket. Then he took out a pipe, filled it and began to smoke. The scene all round him was one of unrelieved desolation; a great expanse of mud in which every visible object was burnt or broken. Sounds of firing thundered from beyond the horizon, and somewhere above the grey clouds there were aeroplanes. He had had no sleep for thirty-six hours. It was growing dark.

Presently he became aware of a figure approaching, painfully picking his way among the strands of barbed wire which strayed across the ground like drifting cobweb; a soldier clearly. As he came nearer Adam saw that he was levelling towards him a liquid-fire projector. Adam tightened his fingers about his Huxdane-Halley bomb[39] (for the dissemination of leprosy germs), and in this posture of mutual suspicion they met. Through the dusk Adam recognized the uniform of an English staff officer. He put the bomb back in his pocket and saluted.

The newcomer lowered his liquid-fire projector and raised his gas mask. 'You're English, are you?' he said. 'Can't see a thing. Broken my damned monocle.'

'Why,' said Adam. 'You're the drunk Major.'

'I'm not drunk, damn you, sir,' said the drunk Major, 'and, what's more, I'm a General. What the deuce are *you* doing here?'

'Well,' said Adam. 'I've lost my platoon.'

'Lost your platoon . . . I've lost my whole bloody division!'

'Is the battle over, sir?'

'I don't know, can't see a thing. It was going on all right last time I heard of it. My car's broken down somewhere over there. My driver went out to try and find someone to help and got lost, and I went out to look for him, and now I've lost the car too. Damn difficult country to find one's way about in. No landmarks . . . Funny meeting you. I owe you some money.'

'Thirty-five thousand pounds.'

'Thirty-five thousand and five. Looked for you everywhere before this scrap started. I can give you the money now if you like.'

'The pound's not worth much nowadays, is it?'

'About nothing. Still, I may as well give you a cheque. It'll buy you a couple of drinks and a newspaper. Talking of drinks, I've got a case of bubbly in the car if we could only find it. Salvaged it out of an R.A.F. mess that got bombed back at H.Q. Wish I could find that car.'

Eventually they did find it. A Daimler limousine sunk to the axles in mud.

'Get in and sit down,' said the General hospitably. 'I'll turn the light on in a second.'

Adam climbed in and found that it was not empty. In the corner, crumpled up in a French military greatcoat, was a young woman fast asleep.

'*Hullo*, I'd forgotten all about you,' said the General. 'I picked up this little lady on the road. I can't introduce you, because I don't know her name. Wake up, mademoiselle.'

The girl gave a little cry and opened two startled eyes.

'That's all right, little lady, nothing to be scared about – all friends here. *Parlez anglais?*'

'Sure,' said the girl.

'Well, what about a spot?' said the General, peeling the tinfoil from the top of a bottle. 'You'll find some glasses in the locker.'

The woebegone fragment of womanhood in the corner looked a little less terrified when she saw the wine. She recognized it as the symbol of international goodwill.

'Now perhaps our fair visitor will tell us her name,' said the General.

'I dunno,' she said.

'Oh, come, little one, you mustn't be shy.'

'I dunno. I been called a lot of things. I was called Chastity once. Then there was a lady at a party and she sent me to Buenos Aires and then when the war came she brought me back again and I was with the soldiers training at Salisbury Plain. That was swell. They called me Bunny – I don't know why. Then they sent me over here and I was with the Canadians what they called me wasn't nice and then they left me behind when they retreated and I took up with some foreigners. They were nice too though they *were* fighting against the English. Then *they* ran away and the lorry I was in got stuck in the ditch so I got in with some other foreigners who were on the same side as the English and they were beasts but

I met an American doctor who had white hair and he called me Emily because he said I reminded him of his daughter back home so he took me to Paris and we had a lovely week till he took up with another girl in a night club so he left me behind in Paris when he went back to the front and I hadn't no money and they made a fuss about my passport so they called me *numéro mille soixante dix-huit* and they sent me and a lot of other girls off to the East to be with the soldiers there. At least they would have done only the ship got blown up so I was rescued and the French sent me up here in a train with some different girls who were very unrefined. Then I was in a tin hut with the girls and then yesterday they had friends and I was alone so I went for a walk and when I came back the hut was gone and the girls were gone and there didn't seem anyone anywhere until you came in your car and now I don't rightly know where I am. *My*, isn't war awful?'

The General opened another bottle of champagne.

'Well, you're as right as rain now, little lady,' he said, 'so let's see you smile and look happy. You mustn't sit there scowling, you know – far too pretty a little mouth for that. Let me take off that heavy coat. Look, I'll wrap it round your knees. There, now, isn't that better? . . . Fine, strong little legs, eh? . . .'

Adam did not embarrass them. The wine and the deep cushions and the accumulated fatigue of two days' fighting drew him away from them and, oblivious to all the happy emotion pulsing near him, he sank into sleep.

The windows of the stranded motor car shone over the wasted expanse of the battlefield. Then the General pulled down the blinds, shutting out that sad scene.

'Cosier now, eh?' he said.

And Chastity in the prettiest way possible fingered the decorations on his uniform and asked him all about them.

And presently, like a circling typhoon, the sounds of battle began to return.

THE END

APPENDIX

The 1965 Preface and the 1932 Play

Waugh wrote the Preface below for the Uniform Edition of his novels. It has been referred to in the Introduction as one place where Waugh wrote disparagingly about the novel. He also spoke disparagingly about it, notably in a 1962 interview for the *Paris Review*, accusing it specifically of overlong individual scenes, ill-construction and cribbing material from Firbank. None of these charges bears much examination.

This preface refers to a play version of the novel. There were two, the first of which failed to win the approval (then, of course, necessary) for public performing from the Lord Chamberlain.[1] The rewritten version by Dennis Bradley secured the licence, opened at the Vaudeville Theatre in April 1932, and closed six weeks later. It makes for dispiriting reading, overegging as it does the delicacies of the novel's language and suggestiveness. The scene at Lottie's in Chapter 3 is described in one of the play's typical stage directions as an 'orgy';[2] Agatha titillatingly part-strips in the Customs scene;[3] jokes are pushed to the grotesquely embarrassing: 'I'm sorry. I'm afraid I must have appeared discourteous. I thought you were a vacuum cleaner'.[4] A chorus of draped figures lamented between the Acts, which does at least suggest a recognition of a mixture of tonal possibilities in the original.

Preface

This was a totally unplanned novel. I had the facility at the age of twenty-five to sit down at my table, set a few characters on the

1. See Stannard, p. 286.
2. *Vile Bodies, a Play*, p. 41.
3. ibid., p. 29.
4. ibid., p. 68.

move, write 3,000 words a day, and note with surprise what happened. The composition of *Vile Bodies* was interrupted by a sharp disturbance in my private life and was finished in a very different mood from that in which it was begun. The reader may, perhaps, notice the transition from gaiety to bitterness.

It was the first of my books to be a popular success. *Decline and Fall* had been well reviewed but its sales in its first year were small, fewer than 3,000 copies if I remember rightly. *Vile Bodies* caught the public fancy for extraneous reasons. 'The Bright Young People' with whom it deals, and of whom I was a member rather on the fringe than in the centre, were one of the newspaper topics of the time. They were totally unlike the various, publicized groups of modern youth, being mostly of good family and education and sharp intelligence, but they were equally anarchic and short-lived. The jargon most of us spoke came new to the novel reader and so captivated one prominent dramatic critic that for weeks he introduced into articles week after week: ' "Too sick-making", as Mr Waugh would say.' There was also a pretty accurate description of Mrs Rosa Lewis and her Cavendish Hotel, just on the brink of their decline but still famous. I think I can claim that this was the first English novel in which dialogue on the telephone plays a large part. For reasons of novelty the many gross faults were overlooked. There were not many comic writers at that time and I filled a gap. I began under the brief influence of Ronald Firbank but struck out for myself. It is not a book I enjoy re-reading but there are one or two funny scenes which redeem it from banality. I like Colonel Blount, though he is a figure from conventional farce. He was brilliantly played by Athol Stewart in a very poor dramatic version. I may add that at the time I invented 'Father Rothschild' I had never met a Jesuit.

Combe Florey 1964   E.W.

NOTES

1. 'last week's Prime Minister': Ramsay MacDonald's second Labour government was formed in June 1929 (his first was 1923–4). It replaced Baldwin's second Conservative administration (1924–9).

2. 'the Home Secretary': Baldwin's Home Secretary, Sir William Joynson Hicks ('Jix'), a figure of high comedy to the young, none the less exercised considerable power in his crusade against immorality – main targets being literary 'obscenities' and drinking in nightclubs after hours.

3. 'The way they looked': the variants here are discussed in the Note on the Text. The word 'delved', inked on to the typescript, gets incidental support from being used in Waugh's 1930 *Daily Mail* article about, among other things, Miss Runcible, where writing novels is defined as 'scraping and delving until one finds a few discarded valuables' (*Essays, Articles and Reviews*, p. 73).

4. '*tapette*': French slang: pansy, effeminate male homosexual (this is the earliest citation in the *OED*).

5. 'strawberry leaves': as ornamentation on a Duke's coronet. Thus old landed aristocracy.

6. 'the Liberal Party': from the summer of 1927 the Liberals' fortunes revived in by-election successes, and Lloyd George, with the help of radical thinkers like Keynes, published far-reaching pamphlets on, for instance, unemployment; so the May 1929 general election result was a sharp disappointment. Although winning more than 5 million votes they only secured 59 seats. (Labour: *c.* 9 million votes, 288 seats; Conservatives: *c.* 8 million votes, 260 seats.)

7. 'five-hundred-pound note': then available as legal currency. Prices have multiplied by a factor of about 40 since the late

Twenties. Waugh's income of £2,500 after the success of *Vile Bodies* was between double and triple an Oxford professorial salary. Average male salaries in 1931 were under £150. By the end of the Twenties fashionable cabarets were bringing in £1,000 a week, the Mayfair Hotel was paying £10,000 a year to its dance-band Music Director, and Americans were paying more than £7,000 for three months' grouse shooting in Scotland. The young man here who had planned to buy a new car could have bought an Austin 7 in 1931 for about £110.

8. 'definitely'. Waugh wrote 'definitively', the typist made it 'definitely', Waugh carefully inked over that on the typescript with 'definitively', and here's 'definitely' back again. A change of heart in later correcting is, shall we say, rather less likely than another third-party error.

9. 'gossip writers': as was Patrick Balfour, Lord Kinross. Balfour's *Society Racket* (1933) has very valuable material on the evolution of the gossip columns. Before the Twenties 'social columnists were all outside ... Society's ranks', which effectively isolated the behaviour of the rich from the public. The first signed social columns came in the later Twenties and were the work of society people themselves (like Balfour) 'recording each other's doings in the Press'. Parties consequently changed from being 'a dispensation of hospitality with its consequent obligations' to being 'a sort of public spectacle' (pp. 95–7). Balfour also quotes *Harpers Bazaar* in 1929 on the surprising jobs held down by peers, including one selling underclothes in a large store (p. 79). (See note on The Bright Young Things and Their Parties.)

10. footnote: Brian Howard's 'Great Urban Dionysia Party', for his twenty-fourth birthday, had an invitation bordered by lists headed 'J'Accuse' and 'J'Adore' (see Carpenter, p. 168). The former included 'The Bright Young People'; the latter included 'Havelock Ellis' (the reforming sexologist whose book was also a favourite, along with *Wind in the Willows*, of the young Peter Beste-Chetwynde in *Decline and Fall*). The manuscript's first version of this footnote contains one of a number of examples of uncertain slippage between narrative history and documentary reportage: for 'were at this time', Waugh first tried 'are . . . invitation cards nowadays'.

11. 'brewing families': a joke for Bryan and Diana Guinness, later Lord Moyne and Diana Mosley, the novel's dedicatees.

12. 'Independent Labour Party': founded in the 1890s as a radical-socialist party, technically separate from but in practice more like a pressure group within the main party. By 1929 its influence had considerably waned. It's characteristic of Miss Runcible not to have heard of it.

13. '*cachet Faivre*': presumably a hangover cure of French manu-facture (powder in capsule form?). Compare a 1927 diary entry: 'I said to Mrs H. that Inez was so ill last time I saw her and living on cachets de faivre. Mrs H: "I don't think I know the de Faivres"' (p. 291).

14. 'Greta Garbo': she arrived in the last years of the silent movie and the first talkies arrived just as *Vile Bodies* was being written. Cinemas had already spread to every community in the country (3,300 of them by 1929) and they were filled nightly.

15. 'an altercation in progress': Balfour describes earning the an-tagonism of a Lord Halsbury who summoned and accused him 'of writing that his daughter had been seen at a private dance unchaperoned' (p. 94).

16. 'smoking a pipe': 1 July 1927 diary entry extracts: 'I went up to London for Alec's farewell cocktail party and decided to accom-pany him to Nimes. Beastly party. Gave E.G. a pipe . . . Worst crossing in the world' (p. 285).

17. 'brougham': small electric carriage. But earlier (p. 46) they 'all' fitted into two taxicabs.

18. 'gate-crashers': in 1928 newspaper readers were much exer-cised by press coverage of the 'Ellesmere Gate-Crashing Scandal'. At an old-fashioned ball hosted by Lady Ellesmere 'there were 300 guests whom she did not recognize'. Four were asked to leave and their names publicized as a deterrent; but public opinion sided with the gate-crashers for their quite proper attempt to bring modernity (the more the merrier; bring a friend) into dowager society (see Balfour, p. 128).

19. 'Hullo': the manuscript has two earlier and more elaborate attempts at this dialogue which together show the plot in danger of momentary, surprising disarray. Both pre-emptively reveal the outcome of the horse race; one (none the less) has Nina saying 'I'm not terribly keen on our getting married just at the moment' and telling Adam that she has accepted a proposal of marriage from Archie Schwert. It might be noted that these passages were cancelled and replaced by the present text before the point at which Stannard argues the manuscript breaks off, at the end of Chapter 6, for the period during which Waugh's marriage broke down (see Stannard, p. 206).

20. 'Tecla': proprietary name of a make of artificial pearls.

21. 'chub fuddler': a joke singled out for approval by one reviewer (*Critical Heritage*, p. 105), but beyond the *OED*, so perhaps the joke is about what funnily-named jobs working people have and how one can't expect bright young novelists to get them right.

22. 'Titled Eccentrics': compare: 'My reference on this page to the skill of Lord Knutsford in designing his own shirts has brought me a number of letters ... Lord Ancaster ... is said to be the best knitter in the peerage and makes his own socks'; 'one eminent peer, a former Viceroy of Ireland, is called upon again and again to give his realistic imitation of a train. To perform this feat he vanishes behind a screen, and a succession of puffings, screech-ings, and whistlings are heard, indicating the start, journey, and slowing down of the train' (from the 'Dragoman' column in the *Daily Express*, quoted in Balfour, p. 102).

23. 'to dye the carnation': the most muted of the novel's homo-sexual jokes. The Oscar Wilde set wore green carnations as a badge of mutual recognition. Waugh many years later wrote about being 'in New York on St Patrick's Day, among the green carnations first invented by the Irishman, Oscar Wilde, for quite another significance' (*Essays, Articles and Reviews*, p. 384).

24. 'I don't say that there ain't any such thing as a green bowler': the manuscript's 'I don't say that there ain't such as a green bowler' is funnier and more idiomatic: included here as one example of presumed editorial regularizing (see Note on the Text).

25. 'Almanak de Gotha': French-language publication listing European royalty, nobility and diplomats.

26. 'I don't know if . . . before Christmas!': the two exclamation marks after 'marriage' and 'Christmas' in this passage may strike readers as uncharacteristically high-pitched for Waugh's tone. They are not in the manuscript. (Nor is the italicizing of 'go on'.) It looks as if Waugh, when revising, was overcompensating against possibly difficult feelings.

27. '*queer*': the slang use of the adjective was slower to enter the language than the noun. It hasn't entered Ginger's. This joke was added after the manuscript.

28. 'mother': in the manuscript it is 'mama'. This interesting variant (nobody but Waugh would bother changing it) suggests a need to avoid any suggestions of the infantile about Peter, in sharp contrast with his presentation in *Decline and Fall*. Correspondingly, his mother Margot seems a radically hardened adult compared with in the earlier novel. The young things are, perhaps, therefore yet more isolated.

29. 'flageolet': small flute, blown at its end.

30. 'Wesley': Waugh started on a biography of Wesley in the first weeks of marriage. Davie says that Waugh was put off the project after discovering that his new mother-in-law 'knew more about Wesley than he did' (*Diaries*, p. 296n).

31. 'paddled': 'padded', in the manuscript, is, despite the canal, surely right. Contrast 'paddling' on p. 100.

32. 'scrutineered': to inspect a car to ensure its compliance with regulations (this is the earliest citation in the *OED*). Waugh was very close to the Plunket Greene family (Richard was an amateur racing driver) and he went motor-racing with them in Belfast after the marriage break-up. See p. 147 onwards for the name of car 13.

33. 'dicky': spare seat at the back of a two-seater car, which can be closed down if not in use.

34. 'perfect joke': the manuscript has 'perfectly perfect joke', an example (from many) of a reading that it's difficult to believe Waugh wouldn't have preferred, included here for its play on doubling.

35. 'V.A.D.'s': Voluntary Aid Detachment.

36. 'I'm sorry, Adam': the manuscript is, by accident, poignantly expressive here. On a separate sheet, a first attempt at the last nine lines of the dialogue ends as if the order of speaking has been somewhere inverted. Thus the last two lines were: 'Goodbye. I'm sorry' / 'Goodbye, Nina'. The page is scored through by an extraordinarily elaborate single stroke of the pen, a design as much as a cancellation.

37. 'Dun': debt-collector. This failure of Adam's to recognize who his visitor might have been is perhaps the only awkward blip in the plotting.

38. 'plot': 'spot' in the manuscript. Ginger's misquotation of *Richard II*? Or Waugh's?

39. 'Huxdane-Halley bomb': the names Huxley and Haldane are suggested. The latter might be the biologist (d. 1964) or the earlier Liberal war minister (d. 1928); the former either the evolutionist (d. 1895), who coined the word 'agnostic', or the novelist Aldous, whose *Brave New World* was published two years later – or, in both cases, both.

THE BRIGHT YOUNG THINGS
AND THEIR PARTIES

Much has been written about the young things' parties in the period from the middle Twenties when they attracted the most attention, in the gossip columns and elsewhere. Books already mentioned, by Martin Stannard, Humphrey Carpenter and Martin Green, are good sources of material for the reader of Waugh's early novels, as, of course, are Waugh's own diaries and letters and those of his contemporaries. Evidence from newspapers and from magazines like *Vogue* is also invaluable (the 1975 retrospective history *In Vogue* has a useful survey and many fashion photographs). But perhaps most important is *Society Racket* (1933) by Patrick Balfour, a gossip columnist and party-goer himself; this 'critical survey of modern social life' provides much of the material used below.

From his perspective, so soon after the event, the party generation were marked by a sense of inconsequence – 'there was no particular object in anything that we did, but we were sensible of its full flavour as we did it'[1] – and that itself was due to post-war uncertainty, the young being 'dazed, and undecided what to believe, now that so much of what they had been taught to believe was meaningless'. The young were 'arrested' in growth; 'too fastidious for the new world, their roots were yet no longer implanted in the old. They were intermediates, like the creatures in Barrie's Never-Never Land who did not quite know what they were'.[2] And towards the end of the book Balfour identifies the 'charm' of the Twenties as an epoch in which 'we were never yet quite hard-boiled'.[3]

Probably the earliest publicly identified sighting of a set of bright young things was of a small group led by young women,

1. Balfour, p. 65.
2. ibid., p. 160.
3. ibid., p. 244.

including Lady Eleanor Smith and the Jungman sisters, who dressed up, played hoaxes (notably masquerading as foreign dignitaries), and attracted press attention with their organized treasure hunts. The *Daily Mail* of 26 July 1924 has (in capitals) 'Chasing Clues, New Society Game. Midnight Chase in London, 50 Motor Cars, The Bright Young People'. The report goes on to talk of a 'society', a 'nebulous body', a 'movement which has captured all smart London'. But it was more nebulous than a movement.

The treasure hunts and hoaxes led to the 'freak' parties. Many writers have chronicled these. Carpenter quotes a regular attender as observing that 'the actual party was often a bit of an anticlimax'[4] (the fun being in the preparation: a larger social issue could be made of that). Balfour makes the point that the most successful were ones organized by gifted socialites like David Tennant and Brian Howard. Typical of these was a Russian party 'for which an entire studio had been re-decorated for a single night to represent a Russian cabaret'.[5] Fancy-dress parties were the norm. 'Bottle-parties' attracted disapproval; Tennant's 'pyjama-and-bottle' party doubly so; most notorious was the 'bottle-and-bath' swimming-pool party co-hosted by, among others, Howard and Elizabeth Ponsonby at the St George's Baths in July 1928 (Waugh was just married; the diaries make no mention of this party). Tom Driberg wrote it up enthusiastically for the *Daily Express*;[6] the *Sunday Chronicle* struck a different note: 'Indignation is being expressed in London over the revelation that in the early hours of yesterday morning a large number of Society women danced in bathing dresses to the music of a negro band at a "swim-and-dance" gathering organized by some of Mayfair's Bright Young People'; it goes on to quote a 'well-known Society hostess' as saying that it is 'wholly wrong to introduce a coloured element to a scene where white men and women . . . are not appearing in the most dignified role'.

Balfour argues that these exploits (including, memorably, setting the Thames on fire at Henley) were a 'public demonstration

4. Carpenter, p. 168.
5. Balfour, p. 170.
6. See Carpenter, p. 167.

against the dulness of social life as exemplified still by the conventional entertainments of the dowagers';[7] none the less the continuing attentions of a disapproving or vicariously fascinated public, fed by the press coverage, turned 'what had once been a sub-conscious impulse' into a 'self-conscious crusade'. They 'grew defiant' and eventually 'destroyed themselves, degenerating into a slough of dope and other excesses'.[8]

A difficulty, addressed in the Introduction, is assessing exactly how the *Vile Bodies* parties are to be read, from what narrative perspective and distance, from what historical vantage point. Balfour calls it a matter of 'true satire' of their 'later and viler manifestations'[9] but I have tried to suggest something more multiple and unstable.

7. Balfour, p. 164.
8. ibid., p. 172.
9. ibid., p. 161.

NOTE ON NAMES

Many of the names in *Vile Bodies* are expressive, some (Malpractice, Titchcock) more easily decoded than, perhaps, others (Skimp, Crump). Occasionally they play topical jokes. The two named commercial travellers in Chapter 1 are Arthur and Mr Henderson. Arthur Henderson was Home Secretary in MacDonald's first Labour government (1923–4) and Foreign Secretary in the second (1929–31). Some names have intriguing histories or antecedents in the manuscript. Brief comments on a few are placed together here as a sample.

Adam Fenwick-Symes. The Introduction comments on the double-barrelled name (hardly ever used in the book) and on Adam's father, in its discussion of doubles and fathers. In Arlen's *The Green Hat*, Boy Fenwick is Iris Storm's first husband; he kills himself because of his wife's scandalous behaviour.

Ginger (Eddy) Littlejohn. He was originally going to be 'Mr Broughton' (a not very sly hint at sexual excitability); then the manuscript tries 'Eddy Saxon' (which suggests some cultural anxieties on Waugh's part). 'Littlejohn' makes Adam, by analogy, Robin Hood.

Agatha Runcible. This derives ultimately from an Oxford friend, Richard Pares, who proposed that Edward Lear's use of the word runcible meant 'about to crash' or 'liable to crash'.[1] Rouncy, dunce, gullible are all perhaps suggested.

Lord Monomark. Until a late stage in the manuscript he is 'Lord Ottercove' (which connects him rather easily to the powerful newspaper proprietor Lord Beaverbrook). 'Monomark' nicely combines suggestions of megalomania and illiteracy.

1. See Stannard, p. 202.

Johnny and Mrs Hoop. 'Hatte' in most of the manuscript which, as discussed in the Introduction, suggests the shadowy presence of Brian Howard. Martin Green's *Children of the Sun* has much to say about Howard. 'Hoop' suggests circus animals.

Father Rothschild S. J.[2] The Rothschilds, then as now, were powerful international bankers; Jesuits were conventionally assumed to be the wiliest of Catholics. As the first father in the novel he is also figuratively the Old Testament God of 'wrath', supervising this 'bad crossing' of transubstantiating souls (including an Adam, and angels led by an ape), and/or a Noah surveying the embarkation. Lottie Crump's head waiter is said to have often dandled the young Rothschild on his knee: his name is Doge, and Doges were the chief magistrates in Venice.

Lottie Crump. This magnificently realized character is more or less alone in the novel (but Mrs Melrose Ape is intended to suggest Aimée Semple MacPherson) in being firmly based on a clearly identifiable model (as Waugh admits in the 1965 Preface – though he denied it in the 1930 newspaper article mentioned in the Introduction).[3] Much written about, Rosa Lewis of the Cavendish Hotel (the 'Duchess of Duke Street' as later depicted on television) was sufficiently annoyed by the novel to ban Waugh from the premises. But it's worth noting that the real woman seems to have been more knowingly malicious than the Carroll-like figure in the novel, a characteristic blurring of satire and fantasy.[4] Crump perhaps suggests the easy availability at Shepheard's of sexual partners for single men.

2. S. J. stands for Society of Jesus, i.e. he is a Jesuit priest. He is discussed further in the Introduction.
3. *Essays, Articles and Reviews*, p. 73.
4. See Carpenter, pp. 169–74.

READ MORE IN PENGUIN

In every corner of the world, on every subject under the sun, Penguin represents quality and variety – the very best in publishing today.

For complete information about books available from Penguin – including Puffins, Penguin Classics and Arkana – and how to order them, write to us at the appropriate address below. Please note that for copyright reasons the selection of books varies from country to country.

In the United Kingdom: Please write to *Dept. EP, Penguin Books Ltd, Bath Road, Harmondsworth, West Drayton, Middlesex UB7 0DA*

In the United States: Please write to *Consumer Sales, Penguin USA, P.O. Box 999, Dept. 17109, Bergenfield, New Jersey 07621-0120.* VISA and MasterCard holders call 1-800-253-6476 to order Penguin titles

In Canada: Please write to *Penguin Books Canada Ltd, 10 Alcorn Avenue, Suite 300, Toronto, Ontario M4V 3B2*

In Australia: Please write to *Penguin Books Australia Ltd, P.O. Box 257, Ringwood, Victoria 3134*

In New Zealand: Please write to *Penguin Books (NZ) Ltd, Private Bag 102902, North Shore Mail Centre, Auckland 10*

In India: Please write to *Penguin Books India Pvt Ltd, 706 Eros Apartments, 56 Nehru Place, New Delhi 110 019*

In the Netherlands: Please write to *Penguin Books Netherlands bv, Postbus 3507, NL-1001 AH Amsterdam*

In Germany: Please write to *Penguin Books Deutschland GmbH, Metzlerstrasse 26, 60594 Frankfurt am Main*

In Spain: Please write to *Penguin Books S. A., Bravo Murillo 19, 1° B, 28015 Madrid*

In Italy: Please write to *Penguin Italia s.r.l., Via Felice Casati 20, I–20124 Milano*

In France: Please write to *Penguin France S. A., 17 rue Lejeune, F–31000 Toulouse*

In Japan: Please write to *Penguin Books Japan, Ishikiribashi Building, 2–5–4, Suido, Bunkyo-ku, Tokyo 112*

In Greece: Please write to *Penguin Hellas Ltd, Dimocritou 3, GR–106 71 Athens*

In South Africa: Please write to *Longman Penguin Southern Africa (Pty) Ltd, Private Bag X08, Bertsham 2013*

READ MORE IN PENGUIN

Penguin Twentieth-Century Classics offer a selection of the finest works of literature published this century. Spanning the globe from Argentina to America, from France to India, the masters of prose and poetry are represented in by the Penguin.

If you would like a catalogue of the Twentieth-Century Classics library, please write to:

Penguin Marketing, 27 Wrights Lane, London W8 5TZ

(Available while stocks last)

PENGUIN AUDIOBOOKS

A Quality of Writing that Speaks for Itself

Penguin Books has always led the field in quality publishing. Now you can listen at leisure to your favourite books, read to you by familiar voices from radio, stage and screen. Penguin Audiobooks are ideal as gifts, for when you are travelling or simply to enjoy at home. They are produced to an excellent standard, and abridgements are always faithful to the original texts. From thrillers to classic literature, biography to humour, with a wealth of titles in between, Penguin Audiobooks offer you quality, entertainment and the chance to rediscover the pleasure of listening.

You can order Penguin Audiobooks through Penguin Direct by telephoning (0181) 899 4036. The lines are open 24 hours every day. Ask for Penguin Direct, quoting your credit card details.

Published or forthcoming:

Emma by Jane Austen, read by Fiona Shaw

Persuasion by Jane Austen, read by Joanna David

Pride and Prejudice by Jane Austen, read by Geraldine McEwan

The Tenant of Wildfell Hall by Anne Brontë, read by Juliet Stevenson

Jane Eyre by Charlotte Brontë, read by Juliet Stevenson

Villette by Charlotte Brontë, read by Juliet Stevenson

Wuthering Heights by Emily Brontë, read by Juliet Stevenson

The Woman in White by Wilkie Collins, read by Nigel Anthony and Susan Jameson

Heart of Darkness by Joseph Conrad, read by David Threlfall

Tales from the One Thousand and One Nights, read by Souad Faress and Raad Rawi

Moll Flanders by Daniel Defoe, read by Frances Barber

Great Expectations by Charles Dickens, read by Hugh Laurie

Hard Times by Charles Dickens, read by Michael Pennington

Martin Chuzzlewit by Charles Dickens, read by John Wells

The Old Curiosity Shop by Charles Dickens, read by Alec McCowen

PENGUIN AUDIOBOOKS

Crime and Punishment by Fyodor Dostoyevsky, read by Alex Jennings

Middlemarch by George Eliot, read by Harriet Walter

Silas Marner by George Eliot, read by Tim Pigott-Smith

The Great Gatsby by F. Scott Fitzgerald, read by Marcus D'Amico

Madame Bovary by Gustave Flaubert, read by Claire Bloom

Jude the Obscure by Thomas Hardy, read by Samuel West

The Return of the Native by Thomas Hardy, read by Steven Pacey

Tess of the D'Urbervilles by Thomas Hardy, read by Eleanor Bron

The Iliad by Homer, read by Derek Jacobi

Dubliners by James Joyce, read by Gerard McSorley

The Dead and Other Stories by James Joyce, read by Gerard McSorley

On the Road by Jack Kerouac, read by David Carradine

Sons and Lovers by D. H. Lawrence, read by Paul Copley

The Fall of the House of Usher by Edgar Allan Poe, read by Andrew Sachs

Wide Sargasso Sea by Jean Rhys, read by Jane Lapotaire and Michael Kitchen

The Little Prince by Antoine de Saint-Exupéry, read by Michael Maloney

Frankenstein by Mary Shelley, read by Richard Pasco

Of Mice and Men by John Steinbeck, read by Gary Sinise

Travels with Charley by John Steinbeck, read by Gary Sinise

The Pearl by John Steinbeck, read by Hector Elizondo

Dr Jekyll and Mr Hyde by Robert Louis Stevenson, read by Jonathan Hyde

Kidnapped by Robert Louis Stevenson, read by Robbie Coltrane

The Age of Innocence by Edith Wharton, read by Kerry Shale

The Buccaneers by Edith Wharton, read by Dana Ivey

Mrs Dalloway by Virginia Woolf, read by Eileen Atkins

READ MORE IN PENGUIN

A CHOICE OF TWENTIETH-CENTURY CLASSICS

Ulysses James Joyce

Ulysses is unquestionably one of the supreme masterpieces, in any artistic form, of the twentieth century. A modernist classic, its ceaseless verbal inventiveness and astonishingly wide-ranging allusions confirm its standing as an imperishable monument to the human condition. 'It is the book to which we are all indebted and from which none of us can escape' – T. S. Eliot

The Heart of the Matter Graham Greene

Scobie is a highly principled police officer in a war-torn West African state. When he is passed over for promotion he is forced to borrow money to send his despairing wife on holiday. With a duty to repay his debts and an inability to distinguish between love, pity and responsibility to others and to God, Scobie moves inexorably towards his final damnation.

The Age of Innocence Edith Wharton

Into the world of propriety which composed the rigid world of Old New York society returns the Countess Olenska. Separated from her European husband and bearing with her an independence and impulsive awareness of life, she stirs the educated sensitivity of Newland Archer, who is engaged to be married to young May Welland.

The Worm Forgives the Plough John Stewart Collis

'The precise nature of an ancient country task and its tools, the characters of different trees and undergrowths, the solitudes and silences, the whole experience can seldom have been better or more lovingly described' – John Fowles

The End of the Chapter John Galsworthy

Here Galsworthy writes about the lives and loves of the Cherrells, cousins of the Forsytes. Galsworthy's grasp of political and social change and its effect on a family, as well as his incisive sense of character, make this a fine trilogy with which to end *The Forsyte Saga*.

READ MORE IN PENGUIN

A CHOICE OF TWENTIETH-CENTURY CLASSICS

Orlando Virginia Woolf

Sliding in and out of three centuries, and slipping between genders, Orlando is a sparkling incarnation of the personality of Vita Sackville-West as Virginia Woolf saw it.

Moravagine Blaise Cendrars

In *Moravagine* a young French doctor, specialist in nervous diseases, releases a murderer from a lunatic asylum and joins him in his travels through Europe. With Max Jacob and Apollinaire, Cendrars was at the forefront of the modern movement, a poet, film-maker, nomad and novelist whose finest novel is a fiercely iconoclastic and original masterpiece.

The Living and the Dead Patrick White

To hesitate on the edge of life or to plunge in and risk change – this is the dilemma explored in *The Living and the Dead*. 'Scene after scene is worked out with an exactness and subtlety which no second-string novelist can scent, far less nail to paper' – *Time*. 'He is, in the finest sense, a world novelist' – *Guardian*

Tell Me How Long the Train's Been Gone James Baldwin

Leo Proudhammer, a successful Broadway actor, is recovering from a near-fatal heart attack. Talent, luck and ambition have brought him a long way from the Harlem ghetto of his childhood. With Barbara, a white woman who has the courage to love the wrong man, and Christopher, a charismatic black revolutionary, Leo faces a turning-point in his life.

Memories of a Catholic Girlhood Mary McCarthy

Blending memories and family myths, Mary McCarthy takes us back to the twenties, when she was orphaned in a world of relations as colourful, potent and mysterious as the Catholic religion. 'Superb ... so heartbreaking that in comparison Jane Eyre seems to have got off lightly' – Anita Brookner

READ MORE IN PENGUIN

A CHOICE OF TWENTIETH-CENTURY CLASSICS

The Sea of Fertility   Yukio Mishima

'Mishima's thrilling storytelling is unique; there is nothing like it. His flashing style is perfect for his dark motives and there are times when his words are so splendid, and his concepts so tragic, that reading him becomes a profound experience' – *Sunday Times*

Nineteen Eighty-Four   George Orwell

'It is a volley against the authoritarian in every personality, a polemic against every orthodoxy, an anarchistic blast against every unquestioning conformist ... *Nineteen Eighty-Four* is a great novel and a great tract because of the clarity of its call, and it will endure because its message is a permanent one: erroneous thought is the stuff of freedom' – Ben Pimlott

The Little Demon   Fyodor Sologub

Peredonov, a schoolmaster, is exercised first by the idea of marrying to gain promotion, later by arson, torture and murder. His descent into paranoia and sexual perversion mirrors the obsessions of a petty provincial society, tyrannized by triviality and senseless bureaucracy.

A First Omnibus   Ivy Compton-Burnett
A Family and a Fortune • Parents and Children • A God and His Gifts

'Ivy Compton-Burnett is one of the most original, artful and elegant writers of our century ... She invented her own way of writing a novel; form and content (unlike her characters) make the happiest of marriages' – Hilary Mantel

Selected Short Stories   Rabindranath Tagore

Rabindranath Tagore (1861–1941) was the grand master of Bengali culture, and in the 1890s he concentrated on creating a new form, the short story. His work has been acclaimed for its vivid portrayal of Bengali life and landscapes, brilliantly polemical in its depiction of peasantry and gentry, the caste system, corrupt officialdom and dehumanizing poverty.

READ MORE IN PENGUIN

A CHOICE OF TWENTIETH-CENTURY CLASSICS

The Grand Babylon Hotel   Arnold Bennett

Focusing on Theodore Racksole's discovery of the world inside the luxury hotel he purchased on a whim, Arnold Bennett's witty and grandiose serial records the mysterious comings and goings of the eccentric aristocrats, stealthy conspirators and great nobles who grace the corridors of the Grand Babylon.

Mrs Dalloway   Virginia Woolf

Into *Mrs Dalloway* Virginia Woolf poured all her passionate sense of how other people live, remember and love as well as hate, and in prose of astonishing beauty she struggled to catch, impression by impression and minute by minute, the feel of life itself.

The Counterfeiters   André Gide

'It's only after our death that we shall really be able to hear.' From puberty through adolescence to death, *The Counterfeiters* is a rare encyclopedia of human disorder, weakness and despair.

A House for Mr Biswas   V. S. Naipaul

'*A House for Mr Biswas* can be seen as the struggle of a man not naturally rebellious, but in whom rebellion is inspired by the forces of ritual, myth and custom . . . It has the Dickensian largeness and luxuriance without any of the Dickensian sentimentality, apostrophizing or preaching' – Paul Theroux

Talkative Man   R. K. Narayan

Bizarre happenings at Malgudi are heralded by the arrival of a stranger on the Delhi train who takes up residence in the station waiting-room and, to the dismay of the station master, will not leave. 'His lean, matter-of-fact prose has lost none of its chuckling sparkle mixed with melancholy' – *Spectator*

BY THE SAME AUTHOR

'No critic worth his salt would deny that Evelyn Waugh was one of the finest satirists in modern English literature, an artist of ruthless integrity whose savage indignation was distilled into consummately civilized prose . . . He had the sharp eye of a Hogarth alternating with that of the Ancient Mariner' – Harold Acton

'The funniest English novelist of the century' – Philip Toynbee

Novels

Brideshead Revisited   **A Handful of Dust**
Decline and Fall   **Helena**
Scoop   **Put Out More Flags**
Black Mischief   **The Loved One**

A Handful of Dust *is also available as a Penguin Audiobook, read by Simon Callow*

and The Sword of Honour Trilogy

Men at Arms
Officers and Gentlemen
Unconditional Surrender

The Sword of Honour Trilogy *is also published in a single volume*

Stories

The Ordeal of Gilbert Pinfold
(*with* Tactical Exercise *and* Love Among the Ruins)
Work Suspended and Other Stories
(*with* Charles Ryder's Schooldays)

Autobiography

A Little Learning

Travel writing

Ninety-Two Days   **Lables**
Waugh in Abyssinia   **Remove People**
When the Going was Good